THE *Lotus* BLOSSOM

LILA LEE

WESTBOW
PRESS®
A DIVISION OF THOMAS NELSON
& ZONDERVAN

WestBow Press books may be ordered through booksellers or by contacting:

WestBow Press
A Division of Thomas Nelson & Zondervan
1663 Liberty Drive
Bloomington, IN 47403
www.westbowpress.com
1 (866) 928-1240

ISBN: 978-1-5127-7113-8 (sc)
ISBN: 978-1-5127-7114-5 (hc)
ISBN: 978-1-5127-7112-1 (e)

Library of Congress Control Number: 2017900231

Print information available on the last page.

WestBow Press rev. date: 02/21/2017

THE LOTUS BLOSSOM SYNOPSIS
By Lila Lee

*I*n spite of the fact that Kitty Farrell has everything a woman could want—a successful career as an attorney in New York City, a certain degree of sophistication, and Luke Filbey—an aching loneliness fills her when she reaches thirty. Was it because she had read an old French fable about two persons born to one soul which split apart in Heaven? When Luke Filbey walks out on her, she leaves her career behind to return to Kansas. After a violent thunderstorm along I-70, she goes missing. Her Mustang is ticketed, and her friend Olivia from New York City arrives when she is found.

She awakens in a hospital to what she believes to be the Muslim call to prayer. She has returned to India where she spent a year's time with her parents when she was sixteen, but this time it is 1856 during the days of the Raj when the English rule India.

Unlike the two lost souls in the fable who searched in vain for each other, Kitty and Christian Skye, who is a captain in Queen Victoria's service, find each other, but their marriage begins in strife and chaos. It is not until they are on a lake in Kashmir that they finally become one soul.

When the Indian Sepoys' revolt, yet another violent thunderstorm erupts and Kitty returns to Riley County Hospital in Kansas. Her search for Christian Skye begins. When she discovers the sash she gave to her husband is unfinished, and the watch she gave to "his son" Colin is lying in a dresser drawer with her mother's old costume jewelry, she begins to wonder if Olivia was right when she said, "You didn't go to India. Not in 1856."

It is true she had suffered severe trauma when both of her parents died within a few weeks's time, and then Luke walked out of her life. When The Big Red One returns to Kansas after the war in Kuwait, her eyes meet those of Alexander Collins. She becomes frightened and finally puts her life back in order again. What was she to do about Alex?

Olivia, an attorney herself in New York City, finally finds time to read the time travel novel Kitty's mother began and Kitty herself had tried to complete. Something was wrong. Olivia sends the manuscript to Dr. Goddard who understands at once. Kitty had never married Captain Christian Skye, except in the novel she tried to finish. Alexander, too, understands and explains it to Kitty when he tells her that many young men are suffering from PTSD after their tours in the Middle East. It has become quite normal after suffering severe trauma.

PROLOGUE

*L*ouise Farrell was homesick. She had seen hundreds of examples of ancient architecture, mosques, and Hindu shrines. She was bone tired and irritable, tired of the culture, the filth and poverty, the red dirt piled about everywhere, the crowds of humanity, and the odor of chapattis being baked over cow dung fires. Truth be said, she was eager to return to the clean, wide-open spaces of the Flint Hills of Kansas.

Although her husband Richard had been told that no one could capture the essence of India in the written word, he had notebooks filled with his impressions of the history, the Vedic literature, the agriculture, the hundreds of dialects of the Hindi language, the political turmoil, and the warring religions of the country. Louise had a story of her own in mind.

How did it happen that a basketball coach and mediocre teacher of history from the Midwest wound up in India after one of the countless famines which had struck the country, this one more severe than others because of the rice crop which failed in Bengal after independence and partition? The United States sent aid to this fledgling democracy, of course. Problem was this: India could not repay her debts except in rupees. What was the United States to do with hundreds of millions of rupees which could only be spent in India, one of the poorest countries on the face of the earth? Senator Fulbright came up with the solution. The United States would send teachers to India to study and spend those rupees there. And so it was that Richard and Louise Farrell and their daughter Kitty went to India to study and to travel in order to learn about one of the oldest cultures on earth.

Richard Farrell's sabbatical was ending. His family had lived throughout India for almost a full year. He and Louise had studied throughout the country under the most important teachers, heard the great political leaders speak, and met artists and theologians of all of the major religions in the country. The last weeks of his fellowship were to be spent in a whirlwind of travel--to Madras beside the sea, to Calcutta where the fallout of India's population explosion literally covered the streets and where they were to meet Mother Theresa herself, to Varanase where the ashes of the dead were scattered on the holy Ganges, and then on to Agra to visit yet another treasure, the Taj Mahal. Was it just another treasure to be chalked off the list of "must sees" before they returned to their home in Kansas where Richard would resume his teaching?

At first Louise Farrell had been impressed with India's treasures, the palace in New Delhi, the Red Fort, Fatapher Sikri, and Mahabalipuram, but after a year of becoming saturated with India's many monuments and shrines, she was eager to settle back in her old, worn Lazy Boy or wander through the Flint Hills and let the wind have its way with her hair without another living soul in sight. She was exhausted by India's extensive culture and the ever-present crowds of humanity.

The small two-engine plane circled over the town of Agra beside the Jumna River. Louise was eager to chalk off this last treasure on their list. It didn't matter that the Taj Mahal was said to be the most beautiful structure in the world. She had read the handouts. It was simply a mausoleum, a tomb for Shah Johan's favorite wife and constant companion for nineteen years.

She had read extensive accounts about Shah Johan, the Mogul ruler who had a passion for architecture. He had erected a completely new capital city at Shahjohanabad and had enriched India by constructing many beautiful buildings throughout India. The Taj Mahal built of white marble as an eternal statement of his love was just one of his many accomplishments. His own identical tomb to be built of black marble was to stand nearby, but with the country on the verge of bankruptcy in 1658, Shah Johan had been imprisoned by his son who seized the imperial title. His tomb was never built. Louise knew the story just as she knew the history of Akbar, the greatest of the Mogul rulers. She knew about the Hindu-Moslem clashes in the forties. She had visited the simple, small space Gandhi occupied as well as the palaces of the rulers of India.

The man sitting beside her on the plane spoke softly, "If you look down beside me, you can see the Taj."

Louise glanced down and then gasped.

There it sat below, a jewel shimmering in an exquisite setting, the expression of joy and happiness, of grief and sorrow, of a man's great love for his beloved.

Had someone hit her in the pit of her stomach? She forgot her longing to return home. She forgot her weariness. She forgot her irritability. Below her sat unadulterated love, love in all its simple glory, the most beautiful expression of love she had ever witnessed.

She and Richard would visit the Taj often in the hours that followed, the hours that became their last in India. They never tired of its beauty. When the sun shone on its shimmering dome of semiprecious stones, it spoke to them of laughter, of dancing, and of romance. When a rain shower fell, they knew the tears of sadness that Shah Johan had spent when he watched from his jail cell across the Jumna long ago.

When the moon came up and the Taj once again spoke to them, Richard put his arm around his wife and said, "We have experienced it all now. Are you ready to go home?"

CHAPTER ONE

*K*itty Farrell stepped from her shower, put on her long terrycloth robe, wrapped her blond hair in a towel, and went to the kitchen for coffee.

"Good morning. Coffee ready?" she asked Luke Filbey.

Luke folded his morning paper and pushed his coffee cup aside. "I'm moving out, Kitty."

"You're what?" She heard his words, but she couldn't believe what he was saying.

"I'm moving out. I've been trying to tell you, but. . ." his voice faltered. "The apartment, the furniture, and the Mustang are yours. I've signed them over to you. I'll take the cabin, the Vette, and the boat. There'll be no need to settle out of court."

She smelled the toast he had burned...heard the metallic tone in his voice...saw the hardness around the corners of his eyes.

"No need to do what?" Kitty had the distinct feeling she sounded like a parrot and hated herself for it.

"Surely you knew. Something has been happening to our relationship."

She heard the tone he used in court when he meant to appear to have all the winning cards in his hand. It must have been someone else. She tried not to believe that had happened, yet she knew it could be true.

"Get out! Get out!" she cried, and her voice caught in her throat. Her head spun, her insides heaved.

He put his jacket over his arm, calmly picked up his paper, and walked to the door. She heard the door close and sank into a chair at the kitchen table.

"What a fool I've been! I should've known. I should've known a man who walked out on a wife and three kids would do it again. I was a fool

1

to think he'd actually marry me one day." She shut her eyes and struggled against a deep sob. Anger welled up within her. She threw the wet towel to the floor and knocked his coffee cup off the table. She paced the kitchen floor, kicking at the chair where he had sat earlier. The burned toast was still in the toaster, and she slammed toaster and all to the floor.

She didn't know where to direct her anger next, so she went to the bedroom and began to go through his closet. She took his fine suits and shirts from their hangers, shoved out the screen, and threw them to the ground below. Then she went through his dresser drawers and pitched his socks down to the sidewalk below. When she had emptied the tie rack and had thrown his shoes below, she fell across the bed and sobbed.

An hour later her telephone rang, and she raced to answer it. Luke was playing a joke on her. He was not leaving her after all.

"Hello, Kitty Farrell speaking," she answered. Her voice was metallic and strained.

"Kitty, are you all right? Why haven't you come in? You're due in court in less than an hour." Olivia Stewart's voice rang with concern.

"Take over for me, Livy. I won't be in today." A sob escaped her.

"Kitty, what is it? What's wrong?"

"Luke just walked out on me."

"He did what?"

"He walked out on me. It must be another woman like always."

"Oh, no! I don't think so, Kitty."

"I'll be fine, but I'm leaving Butler, Cameron, and Filbey, as of this moment. If you move quickly before Ted Butler remembers you're a woman, my position as junior partner is yours. I never want to see Luke Filbey again for as long as I live."

"I know how you feel, but you just can't give up everything you've worked so hard for. What about the Carmichael case you've been working on?"

"It's yours, Olivia. Like I said, I'm finished."

"You haven't given yourself enough time to go through all the grief processes since your parents died. . . . Now this. Think it over. Take some time off."

Kitty winced. Her father's death, it was true, had caught her off guard. Luke's announcement was the last straw.

"Perhaps you're right, but I'm through."

"Luke Filbey! He ought to be kicked for springing this on you now. Can't believe ...why? What'll you do for money?"

"My parents left me the land and a house in the Flint Hills of Kansas and some money. I'll give up the apartment here and hire the Marlow sisters to sell the furniture...everything but the clothes I wear."

"You're going into this too fast, Kitty. You mustn't part with your lovely furniture...your antiques you've taken years to acquire."

Kitty heard the disbelief in Olivia's voice, but it didn't matter.

"Where will you live? What will you do?" she asked. "Apartments are out of sight in New York City."

"I'm going back home ...home to my roots...try to get my bearings... see what I can salvage of my life." She tried to keep the desperation out of her voice.

"To the Flint Hills?"

"It's a lovely stretch of land in Kansas ...not very wide that spills into the most beautiful Bluestem prairie in the entire world."

"But Kansas?" Olivia's voice told her she thought it was the end of the earth. "Take some time off before you do anything rash. Let's talk it over."

"No, Livy. I'm going to find something very dear that has been missing from my life. I don't know what it is, but I'm beginning to see it all now. Luke Filbey and I were not meant for each other. I've been hanging on too long. Luke is forty-six years old. His hairline is slipping, and his male ego has been challenged by time. He's in a mid-life crisis, trying to recapture his youth. I should've seen it coming. Should have known better. I'm going to search for something I've lost, a part of me for which I've been searching."

"What you need to do is meet someone new. Come to Lucia's cocktail party with me at three. I'll introduce you to Harry West. You were meant for each other. He's amusing and fun. You're just tired. You need to take some time off, relax, and meet new people. I've been telling you that for months."

"No, Olivia."

"Harry West is different."

"I'll just bet he is! There's no use talking about it. I'm selling out just as quickly as I can. I'll toss my clothes, my silver and Lenox in my Mustang and head out for Kansas." Suddenly, she was free...free from answering to Luke Filbey ...free from her clients demands ...free from the courtroom and the endless round of cases. The new job with the Justice Department in Washington could have been a plum assignment, but she no longer cared.

"You're giving up. Just like that. Bingo! And Kitty Farrell simply fades away into the sunset." Olivia's voice registered disgust.

"You're probably right. I've given up. I'm scared. Scared half to death, knowing there's not a chance in the world I'll ever meet anyone I want to spend the rest of my life with." Her hands shook. She was thirty years old; her biological clock was ticking away.

"But why? Filbey is not the last man on earth. Besides you're the best attorney Filbey has. Why are you giving up without a struggle?"

"It's something pulling at me ...something I can't explain. Besides there's another plan afloat I can't tell you about now."

"Maybe it has something to do with your experience in India. It's been in your blood for years, you know, and what is it you're not telling me?"

Olivia's suggestion offered little comfort, but her words struck a cord in her. India...the poverty and the wealth...the filth and the sanitary habits as prescribed by the Hindu and Moslem religions...the crumbling monuments amid piles of red dirt and the Taj Mahal, a shimmering jewel of incredible beauty.

"Sure, Olivia, but it is something big I can't mention."

Olivia could never understand how it had been when she and her parents had spent that year in India, nor could she tell anyone about her upcoming appointment with the Justice Department.

"I'm going to miss you. You're the best attorney at Butler, Cameron, and Filbey."

"And you're stepping into my shoes. I'll see you before I leave."

A month later she watched thunderheads building in the West while she gulped down a Reuben on toasted rye, and drank three cups of coffee to keep herself awake at a truck stop on I-70. In less than two hours she would be home.

Daylight quickly slipped into darkness. When she neared the first Fort Riley exit, wind and rain beat against her Mustang, but she was in Kansas where the relentless wind blew constantly, where the heat of summer scorched the earth and whipped up thunderstorms quickly. In winter the wind roared across the plains like a banshee. The rolling hills with outcroppings of limestone tumbled into valleys where cottonwoods reached tall for the sky. In summer the prairie spread a riotous carpet of flowers on her floor, Kitty's favorite the wild larkspur.

"Home...at last," she sighed. "Now I can straighten it all out."

The rain pounded against her windshield while she strained, watching for the Fort Riley exit.

"I've missed it! Where is that road? I should pull over until the worst is over. Why didn't I stop earlier? Now I've missed my exit, and I'll have to drive miles before I can turn back. It'll be midnight before I find a motel."

She was driving slowly, searching for a sign or anything that would give her a clue to her whereabouts. She pulled off the road and turned off the motor.

Lightning crashed and a flaming sensation shot through her.

"What's happening? Why do I feel so strange? Help me! Help me, God. I'm slipping over the edge." She grabbed her purse with the cash from the sale of the last of her household furnishings.

Suddenly she was being sucked away by a strange force. "Is this what it's like to die?" she asked aloud and was shocked at the sound. She saw lights flashing and imagined she saw others running through a maze of red and yellow. A series of disconnected thoughts flashed through her head before she blacked out.

The next morning a highway patrolman posted a red sticker on her Mustang and took down her license number. Two days later someone found her sitting alongside a lonely country road.

Kitty awakened. Then she drifted off again into that half-sleep, half-awake awareness of one regaining consciousness in a recovery room following surgery. Time passed. How long she could not know. When she opened her eyes again, strange sensations and a numbness shot through her.

She tried to move, but her body felt heavy and limp, so she gave in to it and shut her eyes again. She half remembered leaving Olivia's house and driving across Ohio, Illinois, Missouri, and then into Kansas along Interstate 70. In that world of half-reality, half-dream, she drifted away again.

The next time she awoke, she became aware of an odor she once knew, and then she thought she heard the Muslim call to prayer. A sound outside her window and the call to prayer floated through her subconscious state. She shut her eyes, rolled over, and lay still while the mixture of sensations reached into her. At last she became alert to the sounds around her and slipped from the bed. When she groped her way to the window, three monkeys or perhaps they were squirrels on the roof of the porch below her, scampered into the trees. Her strength suddenly drained away, and she sank into a chair.

She had often dreamed of returning to India after her father had been awarded a Fulbright Fellowship to study Asian literature and history in India. He and her mother had shared their journals with Kitty...impressions about India, but she had found it impossible to know everything about India where Hinduism alone with its 330 million gods and goddesses was confusing, even to Hindus.

Her parents had jotted down bits and pieces of what they had experienced and impressions they had formed about the country, nothing more. Her mother had been writing a time-travel novel about India for years. Before she died, Kitty promised to finish her story.

The sound of a bell ringing and people in white moving about constantly were familiar but strange. Was she actually in India? " When?" " How?"

"There you are, Miss Farrell!" A gentle voice called behind her.

Kitty turned and saw a tall, thin woman wearing a white dress gliding effortlessly toward her. She smiled, and Kitty returned her greeting.

"And how did you sleep, Kathleen?"

"Fine. Just fine." She was surprised to hear her name from the lips of a stranger.

"I see you're an early riser like myself." The woman's speech was soft and reassuring.

"It's a habit formed from years of frantic activity as an attorney. Rather difficult to break, I'm afraid."

Kitty couldn't remember having seen the woman before, but her voice was familiar. She had a pleasant, open face and wore her light brown hair pulled back under a white cap. She put a thermometer into Kitty's mouth, hesitated a moment or two and then shook it down. Other people dressed in white moved about in the hall outside her room.

This, too, like the people in white, was India, the India she once knew.

"Where is my mother's manuscript?" she asked the woman in white "I have been editing it and adding . . ." her voice broke then.

"I'm sorry. I haven't seen a book since you arrived."

"I do hope I haven't lost it. I had almost finished it. Just needed to find out what happened to Colin."

"Your mother was a writer?"

"Her book wasn't finished. I was working on it. . . promised..."

"Your friend Olivia must be keeping it for you. She has your things."

"Thank goodness. I was afraid it might be lost."

"Here's your medication, my dear."

A young girl no more than twenty appeared with a small white cup with two small white pills in it. "How are you feeling today, Miss Farrell?"

"Where am I?"

"You're at Riley County Hospital. Did the pills go down?"

CHAPTER TWO

"Now, Kathleen," a woman wearing a long, lavender dress sighed and indicated that Kitty was to sit at the large table in the formal dining room. "Tell me how it was that you found us here in Lucknow."

Kitty looked at the woman closely. She was expecting an answer.

"I don't seem to remember how I arrived here. Am I truly in India?"

"Of course, you don't remember. You had a terrible shock. And such a long trip."

"Yes, I'm suddenly very, very tired." She told the truth. Her head ached and her knees trembled under the table.

"You're among friends here. We'll do everything we can to help you." Her voice rose and fell like soft music. We met last night. My name is Maria Oliver."

"Thank you. It seems that I felt a necessity to mourn for the death of my parents...had no time before. The grief had a way of just building and building until finally. . ." Her voice caught in her throat in a tight little ball of pain. She didn't like being out of control and sharing so intimate a need. It must not happen again.

"I understand, my dear."

A boy Maria called Kadir brought a tea tray to the table and placed it before the stranger who had called her "Kathleen." He placed his hands together and bowed towards Kitty. She remembered in a rush that Indians do not shake hands; they smile quietly and bow. She smiled to acknowledge the boy's presence, placed her hands together, and then nodded.

"Sugar?" Maria's brows lifted in question.

"One lump, please, and a small amount of cream."

"You may want to be alone. There are books in the library. The garden is quiet and secluded. Dinner is served at one…tea at four…supper at eight. The other young ladies will join us soon for breakfast. I think you will like them. We dress for tea and again for supper, of course. Afterwards we shall retire for an evening of music."

"Thank you." She took a deep breath and tried to get her confusing thoughts under control.

"Now, just relax and make yourself comfortable, Kathleen, while I see if Myla is preparing breakfast." She set her cup and saucer on the tea tray.

Kitty smiled her appreciation. but talking about her parents had brought something into the open, something she had tried to pretend hadn't happened. She had pushed their deaths into a corner of her busy life she didn't have to touch. But for Luke's announcement, she would have gone on and on, not facing the inevitable truth of her father's death. A sudden rush of guilt because she had left him to deal with his grief alone after her mother died fell over her. She shook her head, drank the last of her tea, and then wandered to the library where fine, leather-bound editions of old classics hid behind glass doors.

She heard a cough behind her and looked up. A thin, young woman stood in the doorway.

"Good morning," Kitty said.

"Excuse me. I didn't mean to intrude."

The look of impending death in the young woman's eyes disturbed Kitty.

"It's quite alright. I'm Kitty Farrell."

"I know. We met last night. Perhaps you have forgotten; my name is Edith Skye. May I sit down?" Edith's face had changed to the color of chalk and the veins at her temples stood out blue and wax-like.

"Of course." Kitty pulled out a chair for her and noticed that the young woman's hands trembled.

"Are you ill?"

"It's the weather. One never quite becomes accustomed to it here"

Then she remembered Olivia Stewart and asked, "Is there somewhere I can make a call?"

"Call? Send a message?"

Edith's eyes appeared dull.

"You know...a fax machine, a computer, or perhaps a long distance telephone. I must get word to my friend in New York City."

"I'm sorry, someone else will have to help you. I don't know what you're talking about."

Edith began coughing again and raised her handkerchief to her mouth. When she took it away, Kitty knew how ill she was.

"I'm not feeling well...couldn't sleep. Now, I'm dreadfully tired. You'll excuse me, please."

"Certainly, Edith. Are you taking something for your cough?"

"I rest a great deal."

"Is there anything I can do for you?"

"I'm afraid not, truly."

Kitty watched the young woman melt away, and then reached for a book in the closed case. On the front end sheet she read, "Maria Oliver. Lucknow, 1853. The pages felt crisp and new, and she wondered if she should have dared to touch an old first edition in the glass case. She put it back and reached for a well-worn book and sank into a chair, but her thoughts kept returning to Edith Skye.

A short time later she heard laughter and the sounds of voices coming from the dining room. For some reason, the sounds disturbed her.

Kadir appeared and bowed. "Madame Oliver kindly requests that you join the others for breakfast."

"Madame Oliver?"

Kadir looked at her with a mysterious smile. This, too, was India. The India she had known when she was in her teens.

"Breakfast is served in the dining room."

"Thank you, Kadir." The heat of an Indian summer rushed up to meet her.

Kadir waited until Kitty followed him to the dining room where four, fair-skinned young women giggled nervously at the table.

"Oh, here you are, Kathleen. Quiet, ladies. Must you chatter like magpies? Some of you haven't met Kathleen Farrell. You must introduce yourselves and get to know one another. She'll be with us for awhile."

Four pairs of eyes turned upon Kitty, so she smiled and slid into an empty chair.

remember, not knowing how or when she had reached India. Sweat trickled down her forehead, and she swallowed over the lump in her throat.

The carriage stopped and a small, dark Indian boy wearing a spotless uniform hopped off the seat in front to assist the ladies as they stepped down from the carriage. The driver remained seated, silent and unmoving. The boy then dashed to open the door of the bookstore for Caroline and her friends. Kitty did not move. She watched the masses moving as one in the brilliant sun. This was the India she remembered, the India of her youth she hoped to recapture.

"May I assist you?"

She looked down into light, brown eyes with flecks of gold dancing in them. A small, dirty beggar child came to the carriage and held out her hand. A leper on the street reached out with blunt fingers. The man with flecks of gold in his eyes held out his hand to her and she reached for it. When she stepped down, she realized he towered above her and wore a splendid uniform she didn't recognize.

"Didn't we meet last night?" he asked.

Kitty laughed, "Oh, I think not." . She added, "My name is Kitty Farrell."

"Ah, yes, Miss Farrell. Captain Skye. Captain Christian Skye, at your service, Miss Farrell. It is Miss Farrell, is it not?"

Perhaps his voice did sound familiar. Or she may have had a mystical experience, a thing that happened often in India. He held the door open for her and followed her into the book store, one of the few which did not open onto the street.

"There's a fine selection of books here, both English and Indian." His voice rolled out of his throat like deep, rumbling thunder from inside himself.

At once she knew she had heard it before. "Have you ever been to America?" she asked him.

"Well, no lassie. No further from England than India, I'm afraid."

"I do know your voice."

He looked confused for a moment. "What would you like to read? I come here often and can recommend the selections Mr. Nehru offers."

"Something purely Indian, I believe. Are you familiar with Indian literature?"

"The Gita perhaps or. . ."

"Nothing profound. Something light."

"Poetry?"

"Everything Indians write is poetic."

"You are quite right." He looked about and said, "I was about to recommend our regimental history, but I can see that you wouldn't be entertained by that bit of dull writing." He grinned and tried to overcome the awkward situation in which he had found himself. "I'm afraid I am out of touch and cannot help you, but it has been my pleasure to meet you again, Miss Farrell."

"Thank you, Captain Skye." She smiled and wondered why he had appeared at her side from out of nowhere and was disappearing just as quickly. Had he actually said they had met before?

The other young women paid for their purchases, so she quickly chose a small book of poetry and stepped to the counter where a tall, dark Indian wearing the turban of a warrior Sikh took her rupees.

She joined Caroline while they walked through the crowded bazaar filled with the sleazy specialties of each Indian. Then she realized that the uniform Captain Skye wore had been resplendent with gold braid. He even wore side arms and a brilliant sash.

Before she could think further about it, Caroline said, "I see you have our Captain Skye in the palm of your hand."

"You know him?"

"Oh, indeed we do. If I'm not mistaken, you may have met last night."

The warmth of the morning bore down on her, and she saw the carriage pull alongside and the other young women climb aboard. Kitty, climbed up, seated herself, and raised the umbrella Caroline told her she would need. Her head was splitting and her body ached all over. She had not responded to Caroline's, "You have him in the palm of your hand." She tried to remember that she had met him the evening before she awakened to the Muslim call to prayer in a room somewhere in India.

"Kathleen, black is quite becoming on you, but wouldn't you like to have some nice dresses and undergarments made up in some light fabric before it gets too hot?" Carolina asked.

"My own clothes? Where are they? I left New York City with a suitcase."

Caroline ignored her question. "I'll send for Madame Raschambra to come to take your measurements this afternoon. She has samples of fabrics and will have them made up for you within the week. Do you mind that it will take a day or two for them to do their sewing?"

She leaned forward and gave instructions to the Indian dressed in the soldier's uniform without waiting for Kitty's response. He nodded and smiled. Kitty didn't understand fully the dialect in which Caroline spoke, but she gathered from what was said and the way the man smiled and nodded that it was decided.

"'Tis done. We'll bathe and change into something comfortable. Madame Raschambra will bring samples of fabrics and take your measurements this afternoon. No need to dress until tea time. Oh, dear me, are you ill?"

"It's nothing," Kitty told her and wondered how she had reached India.

"You must have a special dress made for the Saturday night ball. It is to be the most important event of the season. And you will need clothes for the cooler weather in the mountains. We'll be leaving soon."

"Will you play whist with us this afternoon?" Mary Doolittle asked.

"I have her this afternoon. She's to be measured and will chose fabrics for her new wardrobe this afternoon.

Kitty felt herself drowning. In fact she was drowning in the heat of the day. Drowning without the slightest knowledge of how she managed to reach India, drowning without a hint of an idea of how it came about

CHAPTER THREE

*T*he afternoon passed quickly. She was measured and Caroline chose fabrics from the many samples Madame Raschambra brought with her, silks and batiste, and linen which Kitty insisted must be made up simply. Caroline also selected the undergarments she would wear, and she made certain Kitty ordered warmer clothing made up for the trip to the hill station at Simla.

In spite of the fact that all of the arrangements had been made for her new wardrobe, Kitty attempted to remember the time she had lost. She retraced her actions in her mind, trying to reconstruct her trip to India, but the more she worked the matter over in her mind, the more confused she became.

"You are far away, Kathleen."

"I am sorry. I am just trying to remember."

"Maria explained that severe trauma often brings on...."

"Strange, unexplained behavior."

"I'm truly sorry, Kathleen."

"That's quite all right. I will be fine in a few days and we shall have a good time at the expense of..."

"Yes?"

She did not respond, but she remembered that her decision to return to Kansas had come to her as a result of trauma. Her parents had both died within the week and then Luke told her he was leaving. Kitty's ordered life had fallen apart. She was no longer in control.

Madame Raschambra waited.

Caroline clapped her hands and said, "I knew I was right to insist that you have proper gowns to wear! I told Maria it was absolutely disgraceful to let you go out in those drab rags."

"Maria?" There was once again the name Maria. She tried to remember where she had heard it before.

"Madame Oliver."

"Maria Oliver," she repeated. It was the name in the first edition in the cabinet in the library.

"My women will have your ball gown ready for you to try on Saturday morning." Madame Raschambra gathered up her samples.

Kitty longed to lie down, but she asked, "So soon?" Her head was spinning.

"My women are expert seamstresses in the English style."

"See? I told you, Kathleen," Caroline crowed. "Soon you'll have all of us in Lucknow having new gowns made up in the latest fashion, thanks to you."

"What am I to do about these shoes I kicked off?"

Caroline laughed and Madame Raschambra fell to the floor on her knees and began tracing around her bare feet.

"There will be new shoes for each of your new gowns."

"Have we forgotten anything else? Oh, I'm certain Madame Raschambra will provide it if we have. And now, my dear, we have exhausted you. Rest now until I call for you at tea time."

"Must I?"

"'Tis not important, but you must dress for the supper hour."

"And what am I to wear tonight? Maria Oliver said to dress for supper."

"Let's see what you have in your chifferobe. There's bound to be something special there."

Caroline swung the door open and sighed when she saw the sorry array of black dresses. One by one she took them down and held them up, then she let out a cry, "Here it is! The dress to wear tonight. Maria will be pleased."

Kitty saw a black dress that could be worn for dinner anywhere. It was cut low with small jet-black beading around the neckline and down the front. The skirt appeared to be very full. Her arms would be bared completely. Only the huge bow cascading down the back of the dress troubled her. It could be removed.

"Rest now, Kathleen. I'll help you dress for supper."

She took off the wilted cotton dress she was wearing and lay across the bed, remembering Christian Skye. His deep voice had rumbled in an old, familiar way. He had told her he had never been to America, yet, she'd known him from somewhere. Had they met on the ski slopes in Switzerland or in France during the vacation she and Luke Filbey had spent on the Riviera. At the thought of Luke Filbey her stomach tightened into a tight knot, and when she tried to remember his face and the sound of his voice. There was nothing.

She awoke to Caroline's knock at the door. "Kathleen, may I come in?"

"Caroline?"

"I was afraid you would sleep through the supper hour. Maria would have never forgiven me."

"Would that be totally inexcusable? Surely I would not be missed."

"Oh, but your presence has been requested by none other than Colonel Oliver himself. One does not ignore such a summons. Come, now, do be a good, dear girl." She poured water from the pitcher into the wash bowl. "Now freshen up a bit and I'll be back shortly to help you dress. And..." she paused to draw a breath. "I found a pair of shoes you might find a bit more comfortable. They're rather shabby, I'm afraid, but they will have to do for the time being."

Kitty sat up and shook her head. She tried to imagine why it was so important for her to make an appearance at the supper hour when she still ached all over.

"I must be getting the flu," she told Caroline.

"Oh, no. You must not be getting the flux so soon!"

"Maybe it is just jet lag. If you insist, I shall dress for supper."

"That's a good girl now. You'll feel better when you look beautiful."

"Afraid that's impossible."

"I do insist."

"So be it then. Maybe I can make an appearance and then just slip away unnoticed?"

"Afraid not. Now do hurry. I let you sleep a bit too long as it is...tit for tat, you see."

Kitty wished for a shower while she bathed in the bowl of tepid water. She stood before the door of the wardrobe in a thin black wrapper when Caroline knocked.

"Caroline? Come in."

"I'll lay out your underclothing. Now do be a dear girl and slip into these."

Kitty looked helpless and Caroline let out a cry, "Let me help you!"

So Kitty let herself be dressed. Strange undergarments...old, worn shoes that were too large for her feet...black, cotton stockings held up by round rubber rings. "Couldn't I just have a tray in my room. I am not at all hungry."

"That is not the point, Kathleen."

"Call me 'Kitty.' No one calls me 'Kathleen' these days."

"The point is, Kitty, that everyone who is anyone will be at Maria's supper party. If you are to make your mark, you must attend. We'll be dropping cards soon. Now step into the crinoline like a good girl before we put on the dress."

"I can't even move in all of these clothes now. Is the crinoline mandatory?. And why is it important to drop cards?"

"I'll have to agree the Empire of the French style was so much simpler, but not nearly as stylish you must agree .The cards are a must, you know."

Caroline tied the crinoline in the front and then helped Kitty slip on the heavily beaded dress.

Kitty took one step. "Good grief! I'm a kite about to take off in a strong wind." The crinoline swayed from side to side, and the bare-shouldered dress slipped downward.

"Come, Kathleen...Kitty. The gentlemen are waiting for us."

"Gentlemen?"

"Of course."

She watched Edith Skye slide gracefully down the stairs ahead of her, and in the next glance saw Captain Skye go directly to her and kiss her forehead. He then put his side-arms in a case and held out his arm to her.

A young man dressed in a crisp, white uniform held out his arm to Kitty, and she took it gratefully. Her stockings slid down her slim legs to the top of her shoes. Would the stockings or the crinoline throw her to the floor first?

"Miss Farrell," the young man in the white uniform spoke at her side. "It is my distinct pleasure to escort you to supper. I am Lieutenant Jacobsen."

"Thank you."

He guided her to the formal dining room where exquisite crystal gleamed in the light of hundreds of candles in chandeliers. She marveled at the delicate china and polished silver. The table appeared to be set for a banquet of importance. She watched to see what was expected of her next. Lt. Jacobsen smiled and held her chair out for her. The other ladies were being seated, so she gathered her voluminous skirts together and sat down. When the crinoline flew up in front and startled her, she jumped inwardly and recovered it quickly. A frozen smile found its way to her face. She started to lean back in her chair, but the enormous bow she hadn't removed did not permit her to sit back comfortably. At this point Kitty noticed that all of the ladies sat on the edges of their chairs with their backs straight.

After all the couples had seated themselves at the formal dining room table which had been extended to seat all of the women and their "gentlemen," Kitty noted that the men wore freshly-ironed white uniforms which smelled faintly of starch.

"Good evening, Miss Farrell." It was the older man whom Kitty identified quickly as the husband of Maria Oliver when he held Maria's chair for her. His eyes were cold and his smile forced.

Edith sat next to Kitty on her left and appeared to be in fine spirits. She wore a gown of light fabric with silk butterflies embroidered on the voluminous skirt. Only the two round spots of rouge on her cheeks betrayed her illness.

"Kitty, I hear you met Christian again."

"Just barely," Kitty told her.

"We met at the bookstore this morning. And did you find a book to your liking?" he asked.

"I chose a small book for its cover...a lotus blossom, all embossed in gold?"

"You have a lovely name. It suits you," Edith told her.

"Miss Farrell," Lt. Jacobson spoke on her right, "they tell me you are from America. Stunning!"

Kitty picked at her food and felt all eyes upon her at some time or another. Edith Skye was pleasant and smiled at everything anyone said. The courses followed one after another until at last the cheeses were brought to the table. She had no idea what to expect next. When the last course was over, she emptied her glass and rose to follow the couples as they wandered off toward the music room for the concert.

Maria Oliver stepped to her side and spoke in a low voice, "Miss Farrell, my husband wishes to see you in his study. Kadir will show you the way."

Lt. Jacobsen stood stiffly while Kadir led her away.

Maria's face showed no hint of what Kitty should expect. She smiled a frozen smile, turned, and followed the others to the music room where the players were tuning up their instruments.

Kitty felt the heavy onyx beads on her dress clinking against one another while she followed Kadir to a room filled with dark furniture, dark walnut walls, and the air heavy with the odor of an unusual smoke.

"Please be seated, Miss Farrell." Colonel Oliver nodded toward the leather chair opposite his desk.

She sat on the edge of the chair while the officer seated himself at his desk facing her and opened a drawer.

She gasped when he reached inside and pulled out her white shorts, her T shirt, bra, panties, and sandals. He placed them on the desk in front of her as though they were contaminated.

"I see you recognize these." He lit his pipe and drew in a long breath while he studied her face.

"My clothes!"

"Can you explain why you entered my house at the supper hour wearing nothing but these disgraceful things?"

"I don't remember."

He next produced her purse. "And can you explain how you arrived in this country with these counterfeit bills?" He shoved them toward her.

"Counterfeit?" She felt her temper rising. "Sir, those bills are legitimate... the result of the sale of my household furnishings. I meant to deposit the money as soon as I reached Kansas."

"Do go on." Disbelief was written on his face. He waited for her to continue.

"I was driving along Interstate 70 near Junction City and drove into a blinding thunderstorm. I can't seem to remember what happened after the flash of lightning. I must have flown out of Topeka, or I could have driven on to Denver and flown out of that airport."

"You flew? Airport? And you have spoken about sending a message to a friend in New York City. Please explain if you can."

Before she could answer, he slid her driver's license, her ID cards, her charge cards, and pictures across his desk. "And what may I ask are these? How were they made? For what purpose?"

"Have you never seen plastic?" Kitty drew herself up and said, "Sir, I'm an attorney. You have no right to question me like this. If you don't mind, I'll take my things and go."

"Just a minute, young woman. We have serious charges against you."

"Charges? Charges against me? For what, may I ask? I'll not have you treating me like a common felon. I know my rights."

"Madame, I'm quite willing to permit you to stay on here a few days until we decide what is to be done with you. In the meantime, bear in mind that you are to keep your clothes on. I'll not have a woman like you running around half-naked. I have nothing more to say. Please sign and date on the dotted line. Then you may take your things to your room and return to the concert, but we don't want to see you in these things again."

He shoved a paper across his desk. She read it, then signed her full name and the date, March 6, 1987, and returned it to him.

"Now see here, Miss Farrell. I don't know what kind of game you're playing, but this is a military establishment. I won't put up with your insubordination any longer. If you don't sign properly with the correct date, I'll have no other recourse than to incarcerate you at once."

"On what charges?" Her temper flared and she rose from her chair, no longer intimidated by the man.

"Indecent exposure, impersonation, fraud, lying to an official, witchcraft, counterfeiting, refusing to obey an order." He stood facing her, his eyes blazing.

"Refusing to obey an order, sir! I heard no order."

"I asked you to sign and date the form for the requisition of your personal effects."

"I did so." She looked into his eyes defiantly. "My complete name! Today's date! Or is it the seventh?" She looked into his eyes defiantly.

"You ridicule my order, Miss Farrell." He slammed his fist upon his desk. His eyes blazed.

"Tell me what you want me to write, and I'll do it. I'll take my clothes and leave."

"Lady, just write the date. March 6, 1856."

Kitty's hands trembled while she wrote what the man who called himself "Colonel Oliver" told her to write.

"One more thing, Miss Farrell. You must remain on the post. You are under house arrest This is a highly irregular case. It is clear to me that your morals leave much to be desired...you arrived here in a state of...er... undress, but you will dress properly at all times, speak in a low tone of voice without screeching vulgarities, and under no circumstances are you to fraternize with the men under my command. Do I make myself clear?"

"Quite."

"You may come and go on the premises as you wish, but you are not to discuss this matter with anyone. Do you understand?"

"Yes, sir."

"You are to remain on the grounds of Oliver Place. That is the garden, on the porches, or when you are in company of the other ladies who live on the grounds."

"And how long is my term of imprisonment?"

"A year. Then we shall see."

"And if I should wish to go home."

"Home?"

"Kansas. Near Junction City, Kansas."

"Kansas? You jest! I read the American newspapers. Do you take me for a fool? Kansas Territory has barely opened for settlement."

"Of course, how stupid of me not to have guessed." She raised her eyebrows and almost laughed aloud.

"Is there anyone in India we should contact about your whereabouts?" His tone had suddenly softened.

"If you'll just telephone my friend Olivia Stewart in New York City... tell her not to worry. Her number is..."

"What in the world are you talking about now?"

"Where am I?"

"You are at the military cantonment of Lucknow. I'm in command of the regiment here. If you have any further questions, please direct them to Madame Oliver. Perhaps in a day or so you'll speak more rationally."

Then she remembered the appointment with the Justice Department. It occurred to her that the department had prepared an elaborate charade to determine how she would handle a difficult situation.

"We can quit playing games now Colonel Oliver. I don't know how you managed to bring me to India without my knowing about it, sir, but if this is some sort of complicated scheme to prove myself to the department, it is in poor taste. But why?" She began to pace the floor. "I see no reason to subject me to any further study. Although the government sometimes goes to every expense to experiment with the minds of those who apply for certain positions, I withdraw my application, so you can just pack up this entire farce and let me go home now. I'm no longer interested in. . ."

"You are stark, raving mad, woman."

"No Colonel, or whatever name you go by, I am just onto your game, and there is no reason to subject me to it any further. You need not pursue whatever it is you are doing here to confuse me."

Colonel Oliver choked and his face grew livid. "Enough. . ."

"I am an attorney. Even here, I know my rights. I have a right to know."

"Get out! Get out of here before I. . ." His hands were shaking and he grasped a brass candlestick.

Kitty saw the look of fury on his face. Frightened, she turned and rushed from the room. Her hands shook and her knees buckled. Something rose in her throat. She untied the crinoline, stepped out of it, clutched it under her arm and raced up the stairs. Her heart pounded when she opened the door to her room. She kicked off the shabby shoes and put on her sandals before she quickly wrapped her clothes in a shawl and put her credit cards and American bills in her own purse.

As an afterthought, she put the rupees in her purse as well and slipped down the stairs. She could hear the chamber music floating down from upstairs. Outside the darkness of night was total except for a ribbon of light on the road which stretched before her in the light of the moon. She stepped off the porch and into the street.

Almost at once she felt a presence beside her and turned.

"Miss Farrell, I have to ask you to return to your quarters."

"Lieutenant Jacobson!" She was stunned by the harsh tone of his voice.

"I believe you have been placed under house arrest. Please don't force me to take drastic measures."

"What in the world is going on here?"

"I'm not permitted to speak of it. You must return to your room."

"All right. You win. I lose."

"I have my orders. Please, Miss Farrell, do be careful."

"Very well, but answer this one question, Lieutenant. What is the day, the month, and the year?"

"The sixth day of March 1856. Why do you ask?"

"And what is the name of this city?"

"Why it is Lucknow. Didn't you know?"

"Maria Oliver. Lucknow. 1853." It was the name and the date in the set of books in the library.

She turned without a word and retraced her steps to her room. She heard the instruments playing an unfamiliar refrain which drifted down from above, and when the music ended the clapping began.

They are playing games with my mind.

A lamp on the table beside her bed sputtered.

Suddenly a heavy sensation overcame her, and she removed the long, black dress. The heavy beading around the neck and down the front made a clanking sound on the floor when it fell, and she knew she had been drugged.

Something in the after-dinner glass...should not have even tasted it... so...so sleepy.

CHAPTER FOUR

She awakened to the sound of children's voices in the street outside her window, but she had no inclination to leave her bed. Other voices joined those of the children, and she heard them gradually dying away while the carriages rolled on. After the morning grew quiet, she shut her eyes and went back to sleep.

When she finally awoke, she splashed water on her face and arms, and searched through the wardrobe for a dress in a lightweight fabric. She found a faded black, muslin dress in a plain style and flung it on the bed. From the bundle of clothing, she took out her underclothes and put them on. The dress was old and ugly, but she didn't mind. It reached her feet and covered her thoroughly, so she pulled it over her head.

She had no idea what she was going to do after she left the room, but she slipped on her sandals and opened her door.

The house was quiet. House arrest...1856...

"Oh, God, please help me," she prayed!

Kadir appeared on the stairs with a tray of food for Edith Skye.

"Kadir," she called. "Is there a newspaper?"

"Yes, Miss Farrell. You'll find *The Daily Mirror* in the library."

"Thank you." She raced down the stairs and into the stillness of the cool, book-lined room. The newspapers hung on racks along one wall. With trembling hands, she reached for *The Mirror*, and the date leaped out at her. "January 30,1856." From the headlines she saw one word "Victoria" and groaned.

The Justice Department was playing a game with her mind. She became convinced of it. She had read how they sometimes set up elaborate schemes to test their prospective people to see if they could stand up to unusual circumstances.

She retraced her steps to the door where Kadir had stopped with the tray. She knocked lightly.

Edith's voice came to her. "Come in, Kathleen."

"Please call me, Kitty, but how did you know?"

"The others have taken their children on an outing today. You were sleeping when I knocked on your door."

"And you have no children."

"Oh, goodness, no." Edith's pale hair appeared tangled and matted, and her light, blue eyes watered.

"Let me take the tray if you have finished."

"Thank you. Kadir will come for it soon." She leaned back wearily. "I can't eat another bite."

"Would you like for me to brush your hair?"

"Oh, yes, that would be very nice," she sighed and made a motion toward her dressing table.

Kitty was reminded of her mother...ill...pale and thin with the ravages of cancer taking her life. She had enjoyed having what was left of her hair brushed until the end.

Edith's face felt hot to Kitty's touch, and when she began brushing, Edith said, "Tell me about America."

Kitty paused and finally asked, "The America I know or the America I never knew?"

"Your America. I want to know everything."

Edith Skye shut her eyes and Kitty brushed slowly and began, "I was born in the Flint Hills of Kansas. My parents were high school teachers and drove an old blue Dodge until it fell apart. In the seventies we flew to India. Daddy had been awarded a Fulbright Fellowship to study for a year. We had a layover in England for thirty-six hours."

"I was born in England actually close to Scotland...up near the border." A smile lingered briefly on her pale face.

"When? What year, Edith?"

"In 1826? The twenty-first day of November to be exact. Over thirty years ago.

"Do go on."

Edith had no way of knowing that she had unlocked the door with the proof for which Kitty searched.

She tried to get her emotions under control before she spoke calmly.

"We flew on to Iran where the 747 refueled. We didn't have a layover there, for the airport was guarded by soldiers carrying machine guns...really rather frightening now that I remember it. In less than a day's time we reached the New Delhi airport in the dead of night. It was hot, and I don't think I ever remember seeing a place so dirty. When we returned to leave for America a year later, we didn't notice the rugs rolled up in the lobby of the airport, the piles of luggage tossed about collecting dust, or the stench that was India...not until we reached the United States and walked into Kennedy and saw polished marble and spotless floors, everything glistening and clean. We spent a full week wandering through the supermarkets and shops, marveling that there was no red dust anywhere."

"Yes, I know. It was the same for me when I first came out to India, but I want to hear about America. What was your life like in America?"

"I was an attorney," she began. "My office was on the 32nd floor of a high-rise office building in New York City where every type of business machine was at my disposal. I could fax messages from one place to another in a matter of seconds...or use the telephone to talk to my clients and friends."

"The fax machine...the telephone. How wonderful!"

Kitty could see that Edith was tiring. "Please don't mention anything I've told you. No one would understand." She put the brush on Edith's dressing table.

"It's our secret...yours and mine. You must tell me more later. I want to know about the 747 that could whisk you from one place to another so quickly. The ship on which I came to India took months to reach Bombay."

"You do believe me, don't you?"

"Of course. That's why I will tell no one." She closed her eyes and added, "Not even Christian."

"Christian?"

"Yes, not even my brother Christian."

"Christian Skye is your brother?"

"Yes, I thought I told you so." She shut her eyes and in a matter of seconds, she was asleep.

Kitty tip-toed from the room taking the tray with her as she went.

She shook her head to clear it. Christian Skye had orders. He was not to fraternize with the prisoner. She was to have no contact with Colonel Oliver's men. It was made clear to them, or so it had been said. Kitty could see the plot developing. She had been brought to India under sedation. An elaborate scheme to break her had been set up, even Christian Skye, obviously a gifted actor, had been hired for the occasion.

Kitty returned the tray to the kitchen, and Kadir's face registered shock and fear. Suddenly, she knew she was performing the work of a servant, something unheard of, putting her even lower than she had been before in India's complicated caste system.

"I was coming this way, Kadir, after visiting with Edith. Are you boiling Edith's dishes and silver?" She addressed Myla and the kitchen servants. They gave her a stunned look and she continued, "Edith is quite ill, you know. The tuberculosis is spread easily unless precautions are taken. You must boil everything she uses."

She heard a movement behind her and knew at once why the kitchen servants had not answered. Maria Oliver had overheard her instructions.

"You are an authority on the spread of the lung fever?" Her voice was low and controlled.

"I know a great deal about the spread of disease, yes. I'm sorry I interfered. I had no right to speak to your servants. It seemed important. Forgive me."

Maria smiled and spoke to Myla, "Boil all the utensils and dishes Edith eats from. The lung disease must not spread." She turned to Kitty with a smile, "Have you had anything to eat?"

"Do you have coffee?"

"Coffee?"

"It's an old American custom. Tea will do just fine."

"Kadir, bring tea and biscuits to the dining room for Kathleen."

"Please call me 'Kitty'."

Maria smiled. "And did you sleep well, Kitty?"

"Yes, indeed. Am I to call you, Maria?"

"Yes, by all means."

"I understand I have been placed under house arrest. Will you please explain why?"

"We are not permitted to speak of it'

"I see."

Kadir brought a steaming teapot and biscuits.

"I'm sorry." Her words apparently came from her automatically from long years of practice.

The sounds of children's voices in the foyer ended her conversation with Maria. The ladies of Oliver House and their children had arrived for tea. It was the middle of the afternoon. Maria rose and swept away to the kitchen to give instructions to the servants.

"Kathleen, you missed our sight-seeing expedition. What a day! Benny...Lucy...this is Kathleen, our new resident."

"Please call me Kitty," she said and looked into Lucy's warm, brown eyes.

The other ladies and their children appeared hot and tired.

"What did you see today, Lucy?" Kitty asked.

"Ruins and ruins and more ruins." Lucy sighed.

Kitty laughed. Her father had written in his journal, "Hindu ruins upon Hindu ruins. Muslin ruins upon Muslim ruins. Hindu ruins upon Muslim ruins..."

Kadir brought cups and Kitty relinquished her place at the table. Maria entered, and the children sat up straight and folded their hands for the prayer.

Kitty excused herself and went upstairs. At Edith's door she paused and knocked lightly.

"Come in, Kitty."

"You're reading. I won't interrupt."

"Please stay. I can always read." Edith laid her book aside. Her face showed no color. Her eyes appeared tired.

"Are you feeling any better?" Kitty's voice, too, sounded tired.

"I live for the supper hour. The days just drag on and on."

"Of course.'

"Sit down, Kitty. You're upset."

"Yes, I suppose I am upset, and there's nothing I can do about it. I'd like a bath and don't know who to ask. There's been an awful misunderstanding which can't be turned around. Must I dress and go to supper? Am I expected at the social hour following?"

Edith laughed. "Well, if you don't want everyone in Lucknow to buzz about it, I think you should go down to supper and listen to the terrible entertainment afterwards."

For one brief moment, Kitty found herself being caught up in the charade. "Do you suppose I could just get out of this right here and now, Edith? My application with the Justice Department no longer interests me. I just want to go home."

"That's impossible, isn't it?"

"How can I explain?"

"You have no memory of it?"

"None whatsoever.:

"Oh, my! You asked about a bath. I'll ring for the house boy to prepare your bath. He'll bring the tub, warm water, towels, and soap. And you must appear at the supper table tonight. People will talk if you hide away in your room."

Edith reached for a small bell and a young Indian boy appeared, placed his hands together, and bowed.

"Miss Farrell would like a bath prepared, and when she is finished, you may prepare my tub for me."

"Yes, Miss Skye. Is there anything else?"

"Don't forget the towels and the sweet-smelling soap."

The Indian boy backed out of the room, bowed again and disappeared as suddenly as he had appeared.

"And the entertainment tonight?"

"Let's see. It's Wednesday. That means everyone who has talent will perform. Ghastly boring, but then most of Maria's evenings of entertainment are dull affairs. Things do run on a prescribed schedule here."

Kitty laughed. Edith Skye had spirit...perhaps more than any of the ladies she had met.

"Tell me about England," Kitty said.

Edith sighed. "It's a beautiful country, spotted about with lovely old villages, ancient hedges, and church yards. It's a place one longs for when one comes to India. They try to reproduce it, but the climate isn't right... the flowers don't bloom the same. Only the lotus blossoms are as lovely... pink and delicate...larger than any of our roses."

"Appearing suddenly to delight the soul."

Kitty sat quietly, reflecting on the thoughts of home. It made no difference whether one longed for hedges and villages or the grand sweep of hills and Bluestem prairies.

The house boy knocked and opened the door. "Your bath is ready, Miss Farrell."

"Thank you. I'll come to fix your hair before supper, Edith."

"I'm so glad you're here. You must not go home."

Christian Skye leaped to his feet when Kitty and Edith entered the parlor. He kissed Edith's forehead.

"You look lovely this evening," he told Edith, but he looked over her head at Kitty when he spoke.

"Thank you, Christian."

"And Miss Farrell is joining us, I see." He looked amused.

Kitty smiled...a frozen smile that made her feel foolish. Then she remembered her orders, "You are not to fraternize with my men!"

It was obvious that Captain Skye knew of those orders, and it appeared that he was deliberately setting her up for a fall. He reached for Edith's hand and they marched ahead of Kitty.

The meal progressed slowly. Caroline Bradley appeared animated while she told her husband about the outing with the children. She spoke too loudly. Mary Doolittle sat on her right. She could think of nothing to say. Poor little Maggie Milford, sitting across the table from Kitty barely raised her eyes. Edith saw and reached for Kitty's hand and gave it a reassuring squeeze beneath the tablecloth.

When the evening of entertainment began, Maria sang English lyrics. The gentlemen's choir sang several raucous numbers, and Maggie played her sitar and sang Indian melodies. Kitty yawned. Edith was right. The talent was missing.

When she and Edith returned to their adjoining rooms after the mediocre performances were over, Edith whispered to her, "Christian has asked to see you in the garden."

Kitty's first thought was to fly through the darkened hallways, stumble over sleeping houseboys in order to seek out the garden she had viewed through the double doors of the library.

With her senses running rampant, she turned the wick on the lamp down low. She wondered how she knew that the wick had to be turned down low before she blew out the light.

"Follow me." Edith's face glowed in an eerie incandescence of the candle she held.

Kitty followed. A houseboy slept on the floor outside someone's door.

Suddenly Kitty realized the perilous position in which Christian Skye had placed her.

"Do you have paper and a pen?" She hoped her voice sounded calm, but with the rush of emotions that surged through her, she doubted seriously that her voice was under control.

"Paper?"

"I will not go to Christian tonight. I'll send my apologies all the same."

"I told him you shouldn't be out alone at this hour. Men! They don't think about how it would look to others. I'm relieved to know that you, at least, are being sensible about this silly summons." Edith opened her door and put the candle on her writing desk. "I rarely write. I think everything you need is there. Can you see well enough? Should I light the gas lights?"

"It won't take long for me to write what I have to say."

She picked up the pen and jabbed it into the ink and wrote, "How dare you compromise my integrity." Then she scrawled her name in large letters across the bottom..

"Go to sleep, Edith. I'll wake the boy and tell him to deliver my message to Christian."

"Ali doesn't know you well. I'll wake him and explain that he's to take your message to Christian. You did the right thing in not going. 'Twill do him no harm to wait." She laughed a short, little laugh and said, "Waiting never did any harm."

Edith held the candle high above her head while Kitty returned to her room. Filled with anger, she undressed in the dark and fell into bed.

She reminded herself that she was no lovesick girl, eager to rush into the arms of a stranger. Besides, he was nothing but an actor, hired to lead her on. A captain in her majesty's service at Lucknow. Lucknow? Lucknow? Something dreadful happened once at Lucknow? What was it? She couldn't remember.

She tossed and turned all night, thinking about Christian Skye waiting for her in the garden. She dreamed about Lucknow and Edith.

She awoke early, bathed in the washbowl with tepid water, slipped on the old, faded muslin, and ran the bush through her hair. She went to the kitchen where the servants were preparing breakfast.

"Just a cup of coffee," she said when they looked up at her.

When no one brought her coffee, she realized that once again she had blundered. A strict division of labor existed in India as nowhere else on earth. Each caste had its own labor to perform, even in the kitchen. She must have spoken to the woman who swept the floor or the one who washed the dishes . . positions far below those who prepared the food or those who served it.

She felt more like herself, full of vitality and ready for the day, and decided to forget about the coffee. It would be no problem to leave Lucknow, after all. She'd seek out the nearest consulate and do something about a new passport. Her mind was in a whirl of activity while she wandered out to the front porch and saw men on horseback, parade down the street, sitting erect in their saddles, boots shined, colors flying, swords swinging. Behind them the masses of India filled the street, white forms bobbing along, the people she remembered, not the pretense of Oliver House and its occupants, not the soldiers riding down the street on their mounts. That part of England left long ago.

She was reminded of something her father had written when they had been in India in the 70's, and a lump formed in her throat. The masses of poor and the villages are the true India. How he had loved this country... the poverty, the palaces falling into disrepair, the complexity of the system, the villages! Above all he had loved the lotus blossom, so fragile and waxy, appearing as though it could melt in the sun, yet strong and enduring, a symbol of India.

It was still early in the day. The women at Oliver House wouldn't rise for another hour at least. She returned to the foyer and entered the library where she planned to make her next move. Reading had been her salvation as an only child. Her parents had each other. She had had no one except the companions she met between the covers of her books. The thoughts of her mother and father reached into her, and the gut-wrenching returned, but she had made up her mind to leave the city, to return to Kansas. The position with Justice no longer held her.

It was her mother and father who made India real to her, but she had no time for them after she left home. It was off to college and then grad school to get her law degree. When she went to work for the law firm in New York City, she met Luke and she seldom retuned to her parent's home. It was vacations in Europe or skiing in Colorado or antiquing in New England. She called occasionally, but she had no time for them. Now they were both gone, cut out of her life--her lifeline severed. Adrift in a sea of guilt, tears stung her eyes.

She took a paper from the rack. The news was stale. An article about the Crimean War and Florence Nightingale attracted her attention. She couldn't remember the details of that war, but while she read, Tennyson's *Charge of the Light Brigade* sprang into her mind.

Kadir spoke at her side. "Miss Farrell." He appeared cautious about disturbing her. "You are to go with Corporal Whiting."

"Corporal Whiting?"

"Yes. He waits on the porch."

"Do I have time to change?" She thought of Colonel Oliver wearing his spotless uniform, starched and ironed to perfection, but she was ready for him. She drew herself up and stood as tall as she could.

"No, the corporal is waiting."

She had neglected to wear the crinoline bird cage to hold her skirt out like a bell, but with her head clear she had nothing to fear. Oliver was a narrow-minded man hired by the Justice Department in Washington. She no longer wanted the position there. She would be home tomorrow.

A young soldier, she guessed to be Corporal Whiting, waited on the porch. "Please follow me," he told her.

Corporal Whiting marched away and Kitty followed. The heat of the sun beat down on her head unmercifully, and the fine, red dust of the street filled her sandals, but it didn't matter. It was useless to ask Corporal Whiting where he was taking her. For a moment, she thought of bolting away in a vain attempt to disappear into the Indian countryside, but that thought left her quickly when she remembered that Oliver House was simply one of many buildings inside a well-fortified complex. No one could enter or leave without permission. Here was order on a scale she had never dreamed possible.

She fell back deliberately and Corporal Whiting proceeded until he realized she was no longer behind him. He stopped and stood straight until she drew near, then he marched on again.

He opened the door of a long, white building, stood silently then indicated that she was to enter.

He followed upon her heels, drew up sharply and saluted the officer bent over his papers at his desk.

"Corporal Whiting, reporting sir." He clicked his heels together and saluted stiffly.

Captain Skye stood and saluted. "At ease. You may go Corporal Whiting. Wait outside."

Kitty stood with her arms at her sides. She did not look at him. Anger possessed her. He did not look up but kept her standing in the heat with sweat trickling down her back inside her thin, black dress.

They were alone, but neither spoke. Finally, he rose and walked around her, looking her up and down.

"Where in the world did you find that dress?" he asked at last.

The thin, muslin dress clung to her, and she became aware he could see through it with the sunlight behind her.

"Surely you didn't have me brought here to discuss my wardrobe, or the lack of it." Her voice was defiant, but she was long past caring.

"And why are you wearing a lady's garter in your hair?"

His voice dropped into that low, rumbling, musical sound she seemed to know from somewhere she could not recall. She refused to meet his eyes and fixed them upon a large, brown cockroach crawling across the wall behind his desk. She wondered silently how he knew she had tied her pony tail back with a lady's garter.

"I'm glad you refused to meet me in the garden at such a late hour. I should not have asked it of you. I want to apologize."

"Apology accepted."

Surely he did not expect her to stand there with her sandals filled with sand and say more. She longed for a shower and the cockroach still crawled on the wall behind his desk.

"What, exactly, are you doing here in Lucknow, besides driving me crazy, Miss Farrell?"

"I wish you hadn't asked what I'm doing here. You know perfectly well why I'm here."

"I'm positive I know you from somewhere," he thundered from deep inside himself, and he came forth with a gruff growl. "There's something about you. Have you ever been to England?"

"Yes, but we have never met."

"Or it may have been in Calcutta." He was musing over this fact and added, "Or was it Delhi, the Red Fort perhaps."

"I assure you, Captain Skye. We have never met."

"You came here from America?"

"I did."

"Sit down, Miss Farrell."

She sat stiffly in the chair he indicated before his desk, and he sank into his own. He picked up a pen and tried to write. His hand shook, and he laid the pen down even before he dipped it into the ink.

"You're making this interview extremely difficult," he told her.

"I assure you I didn't ask for an interview, and it is quite unnecessary. As for last night's summons. You had no right to expect me to come sneaking down to the garden in the dead of night to meet you in a clandestine affair. In spite of what the gossip of Lucknow is saying, I'm deeply insulted. Your indecent proposal was the last straw. Surely you didn't think. . ." She stood then, her eyes blazing into his.

He began laughing at her outburst, and she felt herself careening over the edge into a place of oblivion.

"I'm quite aware of that fact, Kitty Farrell. My proposal...what the ...I did hope you'd come to me."

"For what possible reason? Just to get acquainted?" She laughed.

His confusion touched her. He looked vulnerable for a moment. A frown appeared between his eyes, then he looked at her helplessly and held out both hands.

Why did she want to reach out to touch him, and what force was at work within her that drew her to him.

"The money?" he began and tried to gain control over his voice. .

"Ah, yes. The money. It is always the money men ask about first. I'm shocked at Colonel Oliver's ignorance, sir."

"Far too much money for anyone to be carrying around in a handbag, and you spoke of things that are impossible."

"Such as."

"Flying out of Denver...driving across Kansas."

"You have to be kidding."

"Impossible."

"Not at all. In fact, I drove from New York across the country to Kansas. I was almost home."

"All right. I agree, but you appeared in your underclothes. And look at you now."

"I'd have dressed suitably for this occasion had I known. Would have even worn one of those ridiculous crinolines in which one can do nothing but stand, and I do take offense at the charge of appearing undressed when I appeared here. You've been in India too long, Captain Skye."

Tears stung her eyes, and she rose to leave. .

Captain Skye rose slowly, stepped around his desk, and came to her side. He turned her to look into his eyes. Then he did a strange thing. He took her in his arms.

She knew how his arms would feel, strong, protective, sending quick little tremors surging through her. She had never meant to let him affect her like this. Her heart raced. His lips came down upon hers, and she clung to him, returning his kiss.

He regained control first and backed away, his face registering disbelief.

"I'm sorry, Miss Farrell. I don't know what came over me. I don't know who you are or how you came to be here, but I know something is happening over which I have no control. Oliver charged you with witchcraft. Have you cast a spell over me, my sweet witch?"

"The charges against me were made by a fool. If there's witchcraft involved, I'm the victim not the perpetrator of the deed."

"I'm undone. You'd better go. I'll call for your escort."

He hesitated, and she lifted her eyes to Christian's and what she saw there frightened her.

"Christian...Captain Skye, I have not obeyed Colonel Oliver's orders. I was not to fraternize with his officers or men."

"I, too, had those orders, Kitty Farrell."

"I don't know what to say, ...I...that is. . ."

"Much more than kissing passed between us, Kitty. Tell me you know it, too. My life passed before me...as though I were dying. I know you as well as I know myself. What is happening between us?"

Christian Skye was visibly shaken.

"Please, may I be excused?" Her voice sounded strained. She couldn't understand her emotions. Days ago, she had never laid eyes upon Christian Skye, and now she was struggling to gain control of her emotions, she an attorney who could always speak when the occasion arose. Suddenly she could think of nothing to say.

Christian's face was still flushed. He broke into a deep, rumbling roar, as though he could no longer bear to have her in his presence. "Corporal Whiting!" he roared.

"Yes, sir." Corporal Whiting appeared and saluted.

"See that Miss Farrell returns safely to her quarters." He barked out the command.

"Yes, sir!"

From a minaret somewhere in the town came the call of Muslims to prayer. A pair of oxen with horns painted blue and gold pulled a cart down the street. The heat of the morning sun blazed upon her bare head and radiated off the buildings in the complex. She no longer wanted to remain in India. Nothing was the same as it had been when she had been there when she was sixteen.

"I must go home."

CHAPTER FIVE

She heard the voices of the ladies of Oliver House at dinner in the dining room, but although she hadn't eaten, she felt no hunger. She dashed to her room, splashed water on her face and arms. She washed her feet, and then lay upon her bed until she felt she could face the occupants of the house. Not desiring to face the others who must have known about her interview, she slid down the stairs and crossed over into the library where she opened a book lying on the table. It fell open to an account about the Black Hole of India. It was impossible for her to read.

She had never felt like this before. It wasn't as though she had never been kissed and held in a man's arms. Much more passed between the two of them, something neither of them understood. Yet it was there, strong, demanding.

Her eyes fell upon the page describing events in Calcutta when the French ruled India. She forced herself to concentrate on the words in order to take her mind off what had happened.

"Young Robert Clive had been a desk clerk employed by the East India Company when he persuaded the officials to let him try to repulse the French and their native allies. His success had been astounding and after that time the British alone traded in India."

She had never before been kissed like that by a stranger.

"Clive returned to England and while he was there the Prince of Bengal attacked Calcutta, captured the fort and drove over seventy Englishmen into one small room without a hint of ventilation."

It had been real.

"The next morning, only twenty-three men were still alive. The prison of death became known as 'The Black Hole of Calcutta'."

She tried to concentrate on the history she was reading. The word

40

Lucknow came to her mind, and she realized that something important happened at Lucknow, here at this post called "Lucknow."

She tried to concentrate on the history of India and flipped further in the book to learn what happened at Lucknow...Lahore...Delhi...Meerut...Cawnpore and the other posts up and down the Grand Trunk Line, but no records appeared in the history, so she returned to the earlier history. Her mind kept returning to Captain Skye.

"When Clive returned to India he called a council of war, but the commander of the station was convinced that victory was impossible. After an hour's thought, the commander reversed his decision and gave orders for an attack the following day. The English won a hard-fought victory and maintained the Company's exclusive right to trade."

She turned the pages in the history again, searching for Lucknow...Lahore...Delhi . . Meerut, and tried to remember what happened at those places.

"I hope I'm not disturbing you, Kitty. We missed you at dinner." Caroline Bradley joined her at the table. Her crinoline tossed her skirt up, exposing her legs when she flopped comfortably into the chair opposite Kitty's. She made no effort to cover her legs.

"Not at all. I was searching for an event that happened here at Lucknow. I know I studied about it when I was here before. Do you know what it was?"

"You have been here before? Perhaps it was the date the fort was built. Goodness, I don't know when that was myself. I was never good at history."

"Never mind. I'll remember...sooner or later."

"Kitty, I hope you don't mind. I went to see Colonel Oliver this morning. I know there's no truth in what they're saying."

"Thank you, but it is not important. I will be leaving soon."

"I want to help you." Her eyes pleaded with Kitty to tell her something that would prove her innocence.

"Colonel Oliver wouldn't listen to a word I said. I had no lawyer to speak for me, couldn't even defend myself. It's clear the law does not exist here in Lucknow"

"He was quite morose. I've spoken to Maria. She refuses to listen."

"I suspected as much." Kitty shrugged. "So we're back to square one, but it doesn't matter."

"I've asked Charles to plead your case with Colonel Oliver. He's reluctant to speak out." Caroline toyed with the book on the table, but she didn't open it.

"Then the case is closed. The defendant is guilty as charged."

"Were you questioned by Captain Skye this morning?"

"I was escorted to his office, questioned, and released." She dared not tell her more.

"I'd hoped he would be sympathetic. He did speak kindly of you and I thought...Oh, well. Men are men the world over. They live in their own world...the mess, polo, parading about all the time, galloping off into the Northwest Frontier stations...enough to drive a sane woman mad."

"Thank you for trying to save my cause." Kitty's voice was unyielding.

"I almost forgot. Madame Raschambra has your dresses finished. She'll be here for you to try them on after tea today."

Kitty glanced at her watch.

"Where has the day gone? Tea will be served in five minutes."

"Your watch...your sandals...the clothes you wore that night? Who are you Kitty? Where did you come from?" Caroline's eyes begged for an explanation.

"I am the daughter of a man who came to India long ago."

"You're not what they say you are. I'm certain of that fact, my dear girl, but who you really are has me baffled beyond belief. You must not leave us, not until..."

"Until when, Caroline?" Her voice dropped off, she closed the book she had been reading, and rose to leave.

"The bell is ringing. Come join us for tea."

"I'm dirty and hot and unsuitably dressed. Besides I want to see the garden."

Caroline smiled and patted her hand before she rose to join the others for tea. For an instant Kitty wondered what she would tell the young women about their conversation.

While Kitty strolled through the garden that opened off the library on the main floor, she knew Edith had been right. The climate was wrong for English roses and delphiniums. The red dust of India covered the shrubbery and a few zinnias trying bravely to bloom. The pathways were brick-lined and warm beneath the thin soles of her sandals. Soon the full heat of summer would arrive and then the rains would begin...six months of intense heat and humidity, and after that the splendid days of winter. Then, for a short season, the flowers would bloom.

She retraced her steps and returned to her room where she washed her face and hands. Edith Skye had not answered her knock earlier, so she went to her door and tapped lightly.

"Come in, Kitty," she called.

Edith appeared to be wasting away. She lay exhausted on her bed.

"Have you had tea?" Kitty realized she was making light conversation.

"It is of no consequence. I went to see Christian early this morning before the heat of the day began...gave him a piece of my mind...a sister's privilege, you know."

"He sent for me after breakfast. I think the matter is closed."

"Oh, no, it is only beginning, but he'll not make indecent advances toward you again. I've seen to that."

"Tell me about Christian...your lives in England."

"I'm the youngest of four children. My older brother Will is in the business...trading in wool. Our sister married well, and Christian being the younger son has made the army his career. When our parents died, I came out to India to be with Christian's wife."

"His wife?"

"She came out to India over ten years ago. She was a cousin...a delightful girl, so full of laughter and fun."

"I see." She managed a weak smile, but her insides were heaving.

"Their son is in boarding school in England, of course. His grandmother writes that he is a delightful child with his mother's sweet smile and gentle ways. We hated so to see him leave us."

"Of course."

"There was never a dull moment when Emma was here."

"And she is in England?"

"Oh, dear me no. Emma was quite ill before Colin was born. That's why I came out to India."

"A son...in boarding school in England."

"Of course, all children must be educated in England."

CHAPTER SIX

The gowns were lovely. Kitty had insisted on simplicity, but Madame Raschambra managed to add piping and insets of satin and other fabrics in all the right places. Overskirts and peplums and pleated additions to the skirts took the place of ruffles and lace. There were special dresses to wear in the morning, afternoon dresses, dresses for tea, and gowns to wear to the club at night. She provided gloves, shoes and stockings to match each costume, as well as umbrellas, and underclothes made in the finest cotton she had ever seen.

"Your ball gown will be finished tomorrow, and the clothes that you will need to wear to Simla are progressing nicely."

"Simla?"

Then she remembered. During the heat of summer the women and children were always dispatched to the hill stations in the mountains in order to avoid the severe Indian heat wave.

Madame Raschambra explained how and when she was to wear her gloves. "At all times except when you are eating."

"I'll fix your hair," Caroline said while Kitty let the little maid who had been assigned to her fasten the buttons on the back of her dress.

"There's not much you can do with it, I'm afraid."

"We'll curl the bangs and work jasmine into a braid for the back."

Kitty laughed. "All this dressing and undressing all day. A new set of clothes for every hour of the day!"

Her father had written that the English women had never integrated with India. They lived secluded lives. Servants attended to all their needs. Unless they dressed and undressed, visited over Whisk and games and socialized at tea time, they had very little to do during the day, as far as he could tell. At night they went to the club or dined with friends, but that had been during the old colonial days when England ruled half the world including India. Surely this was not a hangers on group of military officers and their ladies. Nothing about this special group of people made sense to her. And where was Lucknow?

Kitty and her parents had spent their year in India with Indian sponsors. They lived for a month in a village where she had learned to forage for wood and had carried big bundles of it on her head the way the Indian women did. She learned to cook chappattis over a dried cow dung brazier and had eaten rice and hot curried dishes.

Madame Raschambra bowed and said, "I'll leave you to rest. I know you must be tired. The heat is becoming unbearable at this time of year."

"And the cards?" Kitty asked Caroline when they were alone. "What are they for?"

"The dropping of cards will get you invitations. They're very important, for you'll never get invited to dinners and dances unless you drop a card."

"And you do this every time you go out?"

"By all means, and when we go to Simla, we will drop cards to tell people we're leaving, even though everyone else is leaving for the hill country, too. Now, of course, you're new to Lucknow and our ways, but you're not a stranger to those who live here. There is so little for us to talk about except to gossip about what everyone else is doing."

"And I'm certainly a controversial topic of conversation, to say the least."

"Everyone is dying to meet you. 'Twould be the worst of manners not to drop cards."

"Well, I mustn't disappoint them then."

Kitty and Caroline stopped at Edith's door before they went downstairs to go to the club in the carriage.

Edith appeared to be in good spirits, her eyes bright with anticipation.

"My! My! You are elegant. Forgive me for being too lazy to dress. I almost wish I were going with you, but I'm quite unwell this evening. Please forgive me."

"I have no idea what to do at this kind of affair...was always uncomfortable at cocktail parties...could never master small talk. Someone always managed to cut in with witty sayings and left me floundering like a fish out of water."

"I cannot believe that, but in case you find yourself floundering remember this. Just answer the person on your right at supper, then turn to the one on your left. It's the way things are done. Do you know polo or cricket?"

"Only baseball!"

"Baseball? It must be an American game. What a shame! Everyone talks sports into the ground, but it won't matter. Ask a question about polo, and that will be good for a long explanation. Caroline will guide you along the way."

Edith smiled, and for a moment Kitty felt a conspiracy had developed between the two of them. They had decided to take the American in hand, it seemed. For what reason she could not fathom. It had been years since she had felt out of control. Now, for some strange reason she was letting two women, one of them seriously ill and the other trying to guide her along the way, take control of her life.

After she told Edith good-night and followed Caroline downstairs, she tried desperately to manage the crinoline cage that held her skirt out like an inverted lamp shade. Her main concern was what she was going to do to keep the whole thing from turning up or doing something crazy when she sat down. She tried to keep from tripping while she negotiated the narrow hallway and the stairs.

At the bottom of the stairs she looked up and gasped. Lt. Charles Bradley and Captain Christian Skye waited for them in the foyer. They looked elegant in their freshly-starched, white uniforms with crimson sashes. Christian carried his cap under his arm, and Kitty noticed that his hair was still damp from his bath.

He looked amused when she struggled to control the cage beneath her skirts.

"Can't do anything with this thing!" Kitty said.

"You look lovely, Miss Farrell. May I have the honor of escorting you to the club tonight?"

"You mustn't do that!" she blurted out. "I'm not to fraternize. . ."

"I have the privilege of keeping the prisoner under my watchful eyes tonight." His eyes met hers playfully.

She was shocked at his statement, yet there he was looking freshly turned out in full dinner dress.

"And who is going to protect you, Captain Skye?" She felt her face growing hot and longed to take off the long gloves, but she took the arm he offered and held her head high.

"'Twill take some careful adjusting to the circumstances."

Caroline and Charles had gone on ahead and had seated themselves in the carriage. Christian turned to her and added, "You've bewitched me, Kitty. 'Tis true. You're a witch."

"And you, Captain Skye, have no conscience."

Kitty stepped up into the carriage with Christian's hand assisting her. She stood a moment, not quite knowing how to sit in the stiff crinoline. She hadn't watched Caroline make the transition, and Christian Skye laughed when he saw her pulling her gown lower in an effort to keep the crinoline from flying up. She quickly recovered.

"Captain Skye, we hear your team won this afternoon." Caroline dimpled sweetly.

"It's too hot for fast polo. Our ponies tire quickly. Major Clements played a couple of slow Chukkas, but he has to ride home tonight and back again in the morning." He turned to Kitty to explain. "Our ponies are our lives."

Kitty knew she would be lost if this kept up.

Charles entered the conversation, and Kitty remembered that her father had once told her, "When you're in the dugout, talk baseball." She knew nothing about cricket...polo...only ponies and sticks and a thing they knocked about on the ground. Listening closely for a clue about a question to ask, she became further and further isolated from the conversation. Fortunately, she heard laughter and knew they were drawing near to their destination.

The veranda of the clubhouse was already crowded with soldiers, some sitting at tables in pairs and threes and fours. At the other end couples laughed over drinks. Everyone she saw wore full evening dress. A strange odor of horse, jasmine, and the ever present cow dung fires burning filled the air. Candles had been lit and cast a flickering glow over tables and guests assembled there. .

"Find us a table, Chris, while I order. Miss Farrell?"

"Whatever Caroline is having and please call me Kitty."

While they followed Christian through the crowd, Caroline stopped to introduce her to officer's wives. They dropped cards until Christian found a table for four in a shaded area of the veranda.

Charles joined them with a bottle of Scotch and asked Kitty, "Two fingers or three?"

"Only water, please."

"So you're from New York City," he mused. Something in his manner asked much more. He was obviously interested in her.

"Quite different from England or India, I assure you." She longed to tell him about her position before she left New York and headed out for Kansas, but something in his manner told her to say nothing more.

"And do women practice law in America?"

"Charles, you promised!" Caroline scolded him.

"What did bring you to India, Kitty?" Christian looked at her with a raised eyebrow.

"I'm not quite certain, but I was searching for something...or someone."

"Searching, Kitty? Searching in India?" Caroline's voice registered surprise. "How very interesting!"

"Have you not heard the old French fable about two souls searching for perfect happiness...the one that tells of two people born to one soul which was split in heaven? One part went to the man and the other to the woman. When they did not find each other on earth, they wandered endlessly in order to assuage their feelings of being incomplete."

"And if they did find each other?"

"Their lives were fulfilled, Caroline. The aching loneliness was replaced by magic or perhaps God."

"What a lovely story!"

"And true, no doubt."

Christian downed his drink quickly.

Kitty heard a band playing. She had a glowing feeling in spite of the heat, and she knew she was no longer floundering.

She felt someone staring at her and looked up. Colonel Oliver, with Maria, magnificent in white which flowed with every step, on his arm, walked toward them. She smiled, but Colonel Oliver glared at her and walked on. She longed to say, "Foolish Man" but thought better of the idea. Charles raised an eyebrow after they passed by, and Caroline jabbed him with her elbow.

"Shall we go inside and play a round or two before supper?" Christian Skye asked.

"Yes. Let's. Do you play Whist, Kitty?"

"I learn board games quickly." She rose and the bell which held her skirt flew out Christian Skye's hand shot out and steadied her and guided her through the crowd. They found a table and a servant hurried up with cards.

From the veranda voices engaged in conversation drifted into the room. In a corner several men in crisply-ironed uniforms played serious games of chess.

Kitty managed to gather her voluminous skirt under her legs at the table and was surprised to find Christian's eyes upon hers when she settled herself opposite him, but when the rules of Whist were explained to her, she put down her first card and waited for Caroline to play the same suit or play the trump suit. Instead she discarded. When Charles had played, Christian took the trick because he had played the highest trump.

"Aha!" Kitty cried. This is like taking candy from a baby."

The rest of the evening passed quickly. She and Christian won three games. At eight-thirty they rose and followed the others upstairs with Colonel Oliver and Maria leading the way. The leaders of the post sat at tables near them in what she observed as a "pecking order" around the dining room... She found her seating card next to Christian Skye and a young officer by the name of Burke sat on her left. Conversation was impossible. The young man talked constantly. Christian said very little. Kitty tried to remember the rule Edith told her about speaking to the one on her right and then turning to the one of her left, but nothing worked. Young Burke kept talking on and on, often trying to engage her in conversation then continuing on with his own... Once he asked her about America's railway system, but continued without drawing a breath and proceeded to tell her about the grand new railway of the Grand Trunk system in India.

At the end of the meat course, she heard Maria scream. "Dr. Knight! Quickly! My husband...he's collapsed!"

Dr. Knight rushed to Colonel Oliver's side and lowered him to the floor. Everyone gathered around while the doctor took the officer's pulse. He rose with a look of dismay on his face and shook his head.

"He has died," Burk, full of self-importance, announced beside Kitty.

"Have they given up so quickly?" Kitty turned to Christian.

"Dr. Knight is shaking his head. It is over."

Caroline tried to lead Maria away, but she clung to her and would not move. Colonel Oliver's eyes had rolled back into his head. His face had turned dark. The doctor took off Oliver's boots and stuck a pin in his foot. Still no response. Again he shook his head. "Colonel Oliver has suffered a fatal heart attack," he announced solemnly.

Kitty quickly slid behind a potted palm and loosened the string that held her crinoline cage in place. She stepped out of it and went to the doctor bending over Colonel Oliver.

"I learned CPR in college, Doctor. May I try?"

"Upon my soul, young woman. He is gone."

"Of course, but one must act quickly. With your permission, doctor."

"The man has died."

Kitty fell upon her knees and began administering CPR. She loosened his shirt, tilted his head back to clear his breathing passage, and searched for an obstruction.

She heard a shrill cry.

"Take her away! What is she doing?" someone else cried out.

"Please stand back. Give us air!" Kitty cried.

The heat was suffocating and beads of sweat rolled off her face.

Captain Skye yelled in his booming voice, "Stand back, everyone . Stand back."

Kitty continued to work over Colonel Oliver while sweat dripped profusely from her face. She didn't know how long she had worked over him when she felt her strength giving out.

She was at the point of collapsing when Caroline said, "Come away, Kitty."

Christian bent and touched her shoulder. "There's nothing that can be done, Kitty."

"Wait!" she cried. "Just a bit longer."

She continued to press sharply on his chest. He was a heavy man. Her arms hurt. She cried out inwardly, "God, please help me."

She felt his response before he gasped for air.

"Stand back! He's coming around. Someone keep the fan moving!" Christian Skye yelled. "Can't you hear! Stand back! Get that fan moving. Bring water and a stretcher."

She heard his voice over the protestations of the crowd around them. Then she heard someone say, "He's beginning to breathe."

"Bring that stretcher here." Dr. Knight fell to his knees beside Kitty and took Colonel Oliver's pulse. "He's coming around."

"I wasn't sure...had to try." She rose and Christian caught her in his arms when she stumbled.

With his arm around her, he handed her a glass of water, and she downed it quickly.

"Well done, Kitty. Well done!" Christian told her.

She heard Dr. Knight telling Colonel Oliver to lie still. Pandemonium broke loose and everyone began to talk at once.

Charles joined Kitty and Christian. "How did you know to do that?" he asked.

"She's a witch," Christian laughed. "Didn't you know?"

"'Twas no witch who pulled old Oliver around. Where did you learn to do that? He was dead. We all saw it."

"I was taught CPR in college years ago...didn't even know if I remembered how to do it...never had a chance to try before."

"What is CPR? No one has ever done a thing like that. Is it something that is done in America?"

"I don't even remember what the letters stand for. All I know is that it sometimes works."

"I'll take Miss Farrell back to Oliver House and look in on Edith," Christian said.

The band had begun playing. Colonel Oliver had been taken to the infirmary. The moment had passed, except Kitty Farrell had begun to suspect that Justice had nothing to do with Dr. Knight's ignorance of CPR. No twentieth century doctor would have given up so quickly. Any one of them would have known what to do at once. Something began to materialize in her mind. There were too many incidents that just did not add up, even with the Department of Justice testing her. Colonel Oliver's apparent "death" was not part of the plan. Even the CIA with all their elaborate plans could not have foreseen and engineered a death, a doctor's inability to use CPR.

The thought had entered her head before, but she had discounted the idea as quickly as it had come. There was absolutely no way a small group could have stayed on in India entirely cut off and unaware of not only the first World War but World War II and the events that followed. It was impossible. The position with Justice out of the picture, and the possibility that the British complex into which she had found her way had survived even more remote, Kitty began to think logically. If not Justice or a small group headed by Oliver which lived on, what then did happen to explain the unexplainable. She still could not account for the way she arrived at Lucknow, except that she must have suffered a severe blow to her head when her Mustang left the road in the thunderstorm. That would account for the amnesia.

She was climbing into the carriage with Christian Skye's assistance when she remembered her crinoline behind the potted palm. Her gloves were on the table. \

Christian slipped his arm around her when they pulled away from the club.

"You saved a man's life, Kitty." His lips were close to her hair.

"It is what one does in situations like that."

"Now tell me. How did you know what to do?"

"Do you mean to tell me that no one actually knows about CPR?"

"You're a witch, Kitty. 'Tis certain, and Dr. Knight is a fool."

"You actually don't know about CPR? Everyone knows how it saves the lives of heart attack victims."

"Do you mean to tell me that CPR is a medical procedure that you learned in college?"

Suddenly she knew. Dr. Knight, Christian Skye, Charles Bradley... none of them knew about CPR.

"Quickly. Captain Skye. Tell where you were born and the year."

"What kind of a question is that?" He pulled away.

"I must know."

"Well, if you must know, I was born in Scotland in February of 1822."

"And what is the year as of this moment?"

"It is 1856 the last time I looked. Why is that important at a time like this?"

"Oh, dear! You are telling me the truth. Yet, it cannot be. There is no way I could have gone back in time...to India in the time of the Raj when England ruled India. . .. over one hundred years ago. It just couldn't have happened. I am not here. I assure you, I am not here beside you."

She shook her head to clear it, but nothing had changed. "This can't be happening. I'm sitting here beside you, Christian Skye, a married man born in the early part of the nineteenth century and you tell me the year is 1856. It is so real to me that I can actually reach out and touch you. What happened to me back there in Kansas on Interstate 70? I thought... thought you were a part of a scheme by Justice, but now I know you are not with the Department of Justice after all."

"Upon my word, Kitty, what are you saying?"

She had no idea how to explain to him what she believed had happened. Indeed, she could not believe it herself. Was it some kind of mystical experiment? How could she tell him that he was over one hundred years older than she?

Darkness swallowed the coach and Christian called to the driver, "Thrice around the polo field, driver."

He pulled her into his arms, and she felt herself reeling as his lips sought hers.

"Kitty! Kitty! Kitty! I know your kiss...your voice...your eyes. How do I know you so well? I have never believed in love at first sight. I am a practical man."

"Surely our souls were parted in Heaven."

"Have I searched for you all my life without knowing? Have we finally found each other on earth"

"Hold me, Christian. Never let me go. Just for this moment hold me. Let me forget everything else. If I'm dreaming, don't wake me up."

Christian took her in his arms, and Kitty knew it was no dream. This was India. Christian Skye was a captain in the queen's service. She was Kitty Farrell, a New York attorney who had somehow broken a time barrier and had gone back to the days of the Raj in India.

"This simply can't be happening." She pulled away from his embrace.

"What is it, Kitty?"

"Quickly, Christian. Who is the Queen of England?"

"Why Victoria herself is the queen. What is it, Kitty? Your hands have turned to ice."

"Not Elizabeth?"

"Elizabeth died in 1601. Didn't you ever study history?" He chuckled.

"Oh, I am not. . . It is true."

"Yes, and I'm an addled man...shaken completely out of my senses over you."

"No more than I," she put her head in her hands.

"What have you done to me? I've never wanted a woman the way I want you. My sweet witch, you've cast a spell over me."

"The spell has been placed over both of us, but Edith spoke of your wife Emma. Where is Emma?"

"Emma? Emma died...after Colin was born ten years ago."

He withdrew inside himself.

For the first time since Kitty found herself awakening to the Muslim call to prayer from the minaret in Lucknow, she trembled with fear that this moment could end as quickly as it had begun.

"I'm sorry."

"It happened long ago, so long ago, I no longer think of it."

She heard the clip-clop of the horses' hooves on the hard ground. Overhead the moon shone down on the polo field. Everything was in focus...the clubhouse, Oliver House and the other buildings in the complex. She heard the music from the ballroom floating over the field. Laughter filled the air. Christian Skye, filled with questions and overcome with the enormity of what was happening to them sat close to her, so close she could smell the sweet musk odor of him, could touch him. She knew him, had known him from the first moment they met.

"When was it Kitty...that we first loved? Was it at Madras beside the sea? Why did we part?"

"I'm trying to remember."

"Or was it in Agra along the Juma we first made love? Was it in the ancient city of Hyderabad? Or perhaps it was near the caves of Aurangabad. I seem to remember but not well."

"All of those places, my love."

"Aye, but all that matters is that we have found each other, at last."

His lips sought hers again.

A prairie wildfire raged. He had been with her in the bluestem she knew as a child, when the wildflowers bloomed in the spring. He had been with her when the wind roared across the prairies, and in those lonely years when she lived in a make-believe world known only to her. He had been with her in the spring times of her life when tulips and daffodils and cherry trees sent forth their fragrances and in the fall of the year when ducks and geese made their pilgrimages to the lands in the South.. He had been with her in the India she had dreamed about when she was young. He had been with her in ages long past and forgotten by others.

When he released her, he said, "We must marry at once! Is there someone I should ask?"

"It is impossible, but before we marry, there are things you must know."

CHAPTER SEVEN

She told him everything. When she had finished the carriage pulled up before the Oliver House. "And now you know."

"Driver!" Christian yelled. "Make three more rounds around the field, slowly."

He turned to Kitty and said, "If you hadn't saved Oliver, I'd not believe a word you've told me. If I hadn't known you the moment we met, I'd say it couldn't happen. If I had not recognized your voice, Kitty. I don't know what's happening. I've been as daft as a schoolboy since the day you arrived. Nothing like this ever happened to me. I was totally sane until you came here."

"Half-dressed...in my shorts and T shirt, quite acceptable for a twentieth century Kansas summer."

"A twentieth century woman. 'Twas your legs!" He laughed a deep, rumbling sound. "When I watched you working over old Oliver you nearly drove me wild. What have you done to me? I'm as weak as water."

"We're meant for this time and this place. I'm certain of it. Something lies between the two of us over which neither of us have control."

He drew her into his arms,. "Kitty, we've been like this before!"

The next morning she wore her thin, green, muslin morning dress trimmed with navy piping.

When she entered the dining room, Caroline greeted her, "Thrice around the field, and thrice again!"

Mary Doolittle giggled and Maggie Milford's eyes twinkled.

"Is it not the done thing to do?"

"But, of course, it is!" Edith Skye joined the ladies of Oliver House for breakfast and seated herself beside Kitty. Her eyes shone with an unexpected glow.

"Ladies!" Maria spoke sharply. "Let's not step over the line of propriety. Let us bow our heads and give thanks that Colonel Oliver lives."

Maria made no mention of the fact that Kitty had worked over her husband until she was exhausted. She never thanked Kitty Farrell for performing CPR, breathing life into her husband's lungs, pressing her mouth against his smelling of garlic. The American woman had done what she would never have thought to do in the company of those at dinner, even if she had known how to do it. Maria Oliver had been humiliated by the American woman who knew what to do while she had stood wringing her hands. Kitty Farrell had simply stepped out of her crinoline and had fallen upon her knees to work over her husband who had died. Now Oliver lived.

Kitty had finished eating a slice of sweet pineapple when Kadir came to her side and said in a low voice, "Miss Farrell, you are to accompany Private Fiske in the trap."

"Ah. . ah. . ah!" Caroline laughed. "Your summons from the captain arrive early."

Maria tapped the table to restore sanity when the giggling began.

Private Fiske paced in the foyer.

"Miss Farrell, please come with me," he told her.

.

For the first time since she arrived in Lucknow, she appreciated the fact that ladies wore bonnets and carried parasols. The white heat of the morning sun burned down upon her like a furnace. She thought about Simla and knew why the wives and children went to the hill station during the summer time. She and her parents had gone to Mussoorie and had lived in a small house there. Her father wrote and taught a part time course in American history while her mother went into the village to buy gifts to take home. She enjoyed meeting the other young people in the American School there, and it was then she made up her mind to return, if not to teach in the school, to spend some time there once again.

The trap drew up before a large building in the complex.

"Follow me, Miss Farrell."

"Where are you taking me?"

She expected no answer and was rewarded by the same.

The interior of the building provided a measure of relief from the sun, but apprehension overcame her. There was an unmistakable odor of the ill in the building. She heard the cries of those in pain. The halls were dark, but she glimpsed wards filled with men on small, unmade beds.

Private Fisk marched on. She followed him down a long corridor until he stopped before a closed door.

"Please step inside." Private Fiske opened the door for her and then closed it behind her.

When her eyes adjusted to the interior of the room, she saw Colonel Oliver lying on what she believed to be a hospital bed. His eyes were shut. They were alone.

"Colonel Oliver?" She spoke in a low voice.

She saw that the light streaming through the window hurt his eyes and pulled the blind.

"Thank you, Miss Farrell. Please be seated."

"How are you feeling today?"

"Tolerable. What the I feel awful."

"You had a heart attack."

"So I am told."

He closed his eyes, and Kitty waited for him to speak again.

When he spoke, at last, he said, "I saw what you did, Miss Farrell. I don't know how you knew what to do, but I thank you for it. I'm convinced you are no ordinary woman."

"I'm an American, sir, but how could you see?"

"An extra-ordinary American from another time. I was watching... watching, as it were, from the ceiling of the dining room where we were eating. I felt myself leave my body and then hover over the sight...saw Dr. Knight shake his head...knew I was dead...saw my body lying on the floor...saw him remove my boots, use the pin. I didn't feel a thing. Then you stepped out of your crinoline and fell to the floor and began working over me."

"Oh dear, I forgot to retrieve the crinoline."

"How did you know what to do?"

"You watched me step out of that bird cage?"

"Indeed I did, and then I knew you weren't of this time and place. I knew I had died...knew you saved my life."

"I had no way of knowing if it would work for you."

"My wife screamed for someone to pull you away from my body when you put your mouth upon mine and breathed into me. You worked over me until you were exhausted. Then I was back in my body again...hurting."

"Yes. Yes, and Christian took me away."

"Dr. Knight took over. Told me I'd had a close call...took credit for bringing me around."

"It doesn't matter, sir. What's important is that you're alive and will recover."

"I owe the rest of the days of my life on this earth to you, Miss Farrell."

She was surprised to see him blink back tears, so she put her hand over his and said, "I had to do what I knew. I'm glad you are still with us, sir. Our lives here on earth are precious gifts. God saved you, sir."

"My wife...er, Maria, doesn't know about this. I've told no one and would appreciate it greatly if you'd not say anything to anyone about what I have said. Somehow, I think you are the only one here at Lucknow who would understand and not think I'll gone off."

"Of course."

"It was a miracle you performed. I'm not sure I'll be much good for a long time. Dr. Knight is sending me to Simla to escape the heat. To tell the truth, I'm not certain I can trust him again."

"Let's give Dr. Knight the credit for saving your life, sir."

"Poor Leonard. In his own mind, he thinks he did. I know differently." He looked at her and a smile spread across his face. "Miss Farrell, was it six times around the field?"

She felt her face growing hot.

"Sir, may I ask you to give Captain Skye permission for us to marry? I have no one else."

"It would give me great pleasure, Miss Farrell. May I call you 'Kitty'?"

"Please do. And sir. . ."

"Yes?"

"If you have any reservations about my past, will you please forgive them."

"One of these days, I want to discuss...Oh what can I say? Private Fiske," Colonel Oliver roared.

Private Fiske opened the door, drew to attention, and saluted.

"See that Miss Farrell gets back to Oliver House safely."

"Yes sir."

"Thank you, Colonel Oliver."

"Six times is a record, I do believe."

Suddenly Kitty knew. A man and a woman...a carriage ride...it was the way things were done. The carriage creaked and the clip-clop of the horses' hooves could be heard from the veranda of the club where the members gathered before supper.

She removed her gloves, her bonnet, and her morning dress and rang for a maid to call a dhobi to take her dress to be washed and ironed. She understood why everyone kept dressing and undressing all day. The heat had become unbearable. She wished for her antiperspirant, but bathed again instead.

She lay on her bed in her chemise and petticoat.

"Tea will be served in the garden at four," Kadir called and then moved on to Edith's room.

Kitty laid aside her book and rang a small bell for her bath.

Edith joined her while the maid who had been assigned to help her dress stepped into the room quietly. The girl's shyness delighted Kitty, and she called her "Allie" to shorten her name.

"You'll need your crinoline," Edith told her. "It was delivered while you were gone. Caroline will bring it to you before we go down to tea."

"And now everyone knows I took it off and stood it behind the potted palm."

"And your gloves were found on the table. It's a delightful story. Nothing like this ever happened before you came to Lucknow, Kitty. Everyone pretending...no one stepping out of bounds. What a bore!"

"I seem to break all the rules of convention, but so help me, I'll get the knack of it yet...the clothes, the customs, and what is proper and what isn't. I never had to worry about many rules of conduct before, Edith. New York was never like this."

She was trying to keep her crinoline petticoat under control when she and Edith entered the garden. Edith gave her hand a little squeeze as Christian Skye stepped toward her and raised her hand to his lips. He kissed Edith's cheek.

Charles Bradley looked amused, but he had the good sense to keep his mouth closed.

"We are saving a place for you at our table." Caroline's eyes glowed with mischief.

The biscuit stuck to the roof of Kitty's mouth. She tried to wash it down with tea. She smiled bravely, and asked about the game of polo. When the guests rose to leave, Christian rose and tapped his glass with his spoon.

All eyes were upon him while he spoke. "I have an important announcement to make."

Charles said, "Here! Here!"

Christian pulled Kitty to her feet. "Miss Farrell has graciously consented to become my wife. We'll be married at the church on Sunday morning. Colonel Oliver has given me leave to take a wedding trip to Kashmir, and I'll be stationed near Simla until we return in the fall."

"Bravo!"

"Now, if you'll excuse us, I'd like to show Miss Farrell the garden."

"Speech, Kitty. Speech!"

Kitty looked into Christian's eyes and smiled back at the guests. "Once in a lifetime," she began, "if one is extremely fortunate, a woman in her search for happiness, finds the one man for whom she was destined in the beginning. My search for the one for whom I was created brought me here. God smiled on us."

Edith began to cry, and she held out her arms to Kitty.

Kitty gave her a squeeze and whispered, "Thank you."

Christian led her away, and when they had passed beyond the hearing of the others, he said, "Kitty. I don't know if I can keep my hands off you until Sunday."

"All Lucknow is watching."

He pulled her into the shrubbery. His mouth came down upon hers, and Kitty felt her heart racing until she regained her senses.

"We can't return with my hair and crinoline array, Christian."

"No one rides around the polo field six times, Kitty. We're already the talk of the cantonment...and with good reason. You are beautiful...your eyes. . .your hair."

She raced away through the garden where daisies lay wilted and gasping for life and roses had given up their early blooms. He caught her at the pool. "Look Christian! A lotus blossom!"

"It's a good omen, Kitty." He stood behind Kitty and put his arms around her. "There'll always be beauty in our union."

"A cloud hangs over us, Christian."

"No longer, Love. Old Oliver reversed his decision. You are no longer under house arrest."

"I had suspected as much. Someday I'll tell you all about it."

"Kitty, my darlin'."

"When did we first fall in love? How did this all begin?"

"Fate cast us together long, long ago. Of that I'm certain. I've always adhered to the Christian faith, but there are things which are happening no one can explain in a rational manner. When I saw you sitting alone in the carriage four days ago, I knew I'd have you as my wife...knew then how you'd feel in my arms. I once had a wife, but, Kitty, there was no love in that marriage."

"I was with Luke Filbey for three years and during that time there was no beauty...no sense that God had placed us together."

"'Twill be a beautiful marriage...the union of two souls as God intended."

He kissed her, and they strolled arm in arm back to the others.

Christian whispered hurriedly, "Tonight, sweet love. Six times around the field."

"We'll dance all night at the ball before our wedding."

"We'll circle the field six times."

"Others will know?"

"Certainly."

"And when we are wed?"

"Others will need the carriage."

They ate at the club that night, waltzed to the music of the regimental band, danced all the wild Scottish reels and highland dances, and rode six times around the field in the lumbering carriage.

They danced all night at the ball on Saturday night, and Kitty wore her elegant new ball gown of red satin embroidered with intricate patterns in gold. The silk in the overskirt, which made her think of a peplum, shimmered with lights.

When he drew her into his arms later, she sighed with contentment. Then a sudden chill fell over her and she asked, "Christian, what happened here at Lucknow?"

"Two people who were lost in time found each other."

"Christian, I'm afraid. There was more here. Hold me. Don't let me remember."

CHAPTER EIGHT

"What are you remembering, Kitty?"

"Something that happened here...something to do with the Sepoys, the Indians in the regiments. What do they mean to you?"

"Why do you ask?"

"Something I remember in part. It plagues my mind because I can't remember."

"The Indian soldiers serving here play an integral and important role in the East Indian Army. They fill our ranks with loyal men and make the transporting of many troops from England unnecessary"

"Why do the Sepoys fight alongside the English? I have the impression that there is resentment among them."

"'Tis easy to explain. John Company pays them well."

"I see, but haven't the natives been resentful of English intrusion in the country." She was trying to remember something about a mutiny.

"Go on."

"I don't remember, but something seems to hang over India like a dark cloud."

"The Indian princes became alarmed when Oudh and other independent territories were annexed. Our efforts at building railroads and telegraph lines, and even promoting Christianity, have been resisted. Everything western is the blight of a gnat on the Indian elephant."

"Missionaries were not permitted in India when my parents and I were here in '72. Less than two percent of the people were Christians."

"Why were they no longer allowed to serve here? Surely the English wouldn't endorse such a thing."

He questioned her, and she knew he could not imagine how it had been before England finally granted independence to India. She had told him about her life in America during the twentieth century, but there were many gaps she had left open.

"I forget that you don't know about the two great world wars during the twentieth century, two wars which were actually one that exploded and spread over the entire world."

"England? Did she win?" he asked anxiously.

"Yes, but at the end her empire was gone."

"Who ruled England then?"

"Victoria's grandchildren held power all over Europe...and a Prime Minister named Winston Churchill was actually the power behind the throne, in England."

"And India? What became of India?"

"India was granted independence after the war and became a democracy."

"Don't tell me more, Kitty. Our garrison here has suffered greatly since the Afghan War of '42. The best officers have been promoted to political positions and military discipline among the Sepoys has been weakened. Is this what you're remembering?"

"I don't know. I seem to know more about the things my father did in World War II when he fought against the Japanese in the Pacific." She paused thoughtfully, "I seem to remember an incident that involved the Sepoys here in India, but what girl of sixteen cares about history?"

"What girl? Were you searching for me then, my love?"

"I have no doubt about that. I used to go out into the villages, and the women and girls welcomed me as one of their own. I've almost forgotten the Urdu I spoke then except for a smattering of words. We all tried to imagine who and when we would marry. All girls dream. To be truthful, I suspect I'd be more at home with the wives of your Indians than Maria Oliver."

Christian threw back his head and laughed. "She's typical of English women...cold and domineering I hear."

"Is that what the men say of her?"

"Not in the hearing of old Oliver."

"I'm glad twentieth century women are more liberated."

"Can't say how I would feel about that." He bristled and his voice grew angry.

"We've gained our independence and lost something we have forgotten."

"'T'was a sad thing that had to happen. Was it the war?"

"Probably. Women who had never held down jobs before went to work in factories to produce war materials. They had to do the work of men who had gone off to war."

"In England, too?"

"Women wore uniforms. Children were sent off to America when bombs began falling in London. It had become a different world by then. The changes began in a small way in America during the First World War and when women began to vote. Women were released to become what they wished to be in the Twenties, preparing them for what would happen when the next big war began."

"Don't tell me more. Come here you sweet witch." He pulled her into his arms. "Driver! Three more rounds."

His strong hands caressed her tenderly. "Oh, my dearest Kitty. It has been so long. Help me!" His cry of anguish reached into her.

They were married at the church the next morning with only the company's clergyman and a civil clerk in attendance. Kitty signed her full name "Kathleen Louise Farrell." Christian signed his name above hers and said, "Good morning, Mrs. Skye."

When they left the club bound for the vale of Kashmir, Edith held Kitty in her arms, put on a brave smile, and cried. When the carriage pulled away, old shoes flew after them from all sides.

Laughing together, they settled down in the carriage and Christian asked, "Do you mind that we're not bringing Allie with us?"

"On our wedding trip? We don't need anyone else. She'll join us in Simla. That is soon enough."

"Do you mind that there will be no privacy until we reach Kashmir?"

"No privacy until we reach Kashmir?"

He squeezed her hand. "We'll make up for that bit of inconvenience when we step into our cottage on the lake, my sweet witch."

"I have always wanted to go to Kashmir. Have you ever been there,

Christian?" She looked up, and saw a shadow fall over his face before he answered.

"Emma hated it...frightened of the water...the Hindus and the Mohammedans. She never saw the beauty in the mountains."

She had all but forgotten he once had a wife and had gone to Kashmir on their wedding trip. Suddenly, she felt that she was trespassing on hallowed ground.

"Why did she die?" she asked and tried to get her voice under control.

"Why do they all die? It's the climate...the infernal diseases ...blinding headaches ...chills and fevers. She was not mentally prepared for India. The glare of the sun and the unbearable heat took her in the end. She longed for the gray of an English day from the moment she arrived. Are you prepared for India, Kitty?"

"I've dreamed of returning. The Kansas summers prepared me for coming to you, my darling, and my parents and I lived in an Indian village on the plains of the Ganges for a month in July. We slept outdoors on a charpoy...always under a mosquito netting with our shoes placed up high on a table beside us so they'd not be occupied by a snake or scorpion in the morning. I liked to lie awake and look up at the stars through the top of the netting. The nights were terribly hot and sometimes we heard jackals crying like babies in the night. Inside the small bungalow in which we lived the wallah hand-pulled the punkah to cool us during the daytime. In the evening a bheesti came around with his goatskin bag and sprinkled water to settle the dust. I can still smell the grass after the heat had gone off it when he came with the water."

"Some things never change. A soldier's life is hard in India, but I've grown accustomed to it and rather enjoy the seasons when they come and go. It has been a man's world, though, and sometimes I thought I'd never have a wife...tried to imagine how it would be to have someone I could talk to...someone who would understand."

"I used to close my eyes and remember a village in India...the smell of the smoke of dried cow dung and charcoal fires. In the evenings it drifted over everything in a soft, blue haze. My father wrote in his journals about the peppery smells of the shops in the bazaar and the relief from the heat when the monsoon came."

"I never minded the heat. Beginning in May the hot weather has always been a challenge to me. I like to exercise in the early morning and play two of three chukkas or practice a few rounds in the afternoon. Then I bathe and go to the club. I shut it out of my mind until a day in September when I look up and see the sky filled with wild geese and cranes. They're coming down from Siberia, and I know that kulang is coming swift behind them."

"Kulang...the cooling down season! Will you miss the six months of summer this year while we're in the mountains?"

"'Twill be a relief. Besides a newly married man who's in love with his wife shouldn't spend the season alone in the heat of summer while his pretty wife goes off to the mountains," he grinned.

They put their pukka luggage in the racks on the train that would carry them further into the northern frontier. The journey would last several days, and Kitty looked forward to being alone with him while they traveled.

"I've married myself a clever wife, Kitty...one I can talk with comfortably." Christian's deep voice registered approval. "This has been a burra day for me!"

"A good day for both of us, Captain Skye."

Then Christian's voice changed, and he turned to her and said, "Tell me about Luke Filbey."

"We slid into a relationship. I wasn't in love with him...often wondered why we lived together."

"Lived together...together as husband and wife without marriage?" She felt him bristle beside her.

"It's quite a common practice in America today, and it is considered proper...even among respectable people. We worked together as attorneys in the same law firm. It just happened, so I shouldn't have been surprised when he walked out on me. I had become preoccupied after my parents both died. He'd divorced a wife...had three children by her."

"Divorce? It is a common thing?" His voice registered shock at the casual way she spoke of divorce.

"Too common for words."

"Wouldn't like to live in the twentieth century," he growled.

"Nor did I. I hated myself for living with Luke, and when our relationship ended, I hated myself again for letting it happen in the beginning. Then something called to me from out of the past. It was India...and you, my dear Christian."

India on that day of Kitty's wedding was sweltering in the heat. Dirt and noise filled the air. The train was crowded and the seats were hard. By the time they reached the outpost where the train ended and another began, the sudden twilight had fallen behind the plains and darkness descended upon them sharply.

Covered with the red dust of an Indian summer which had filtered through the air of the open train, Christian called out to a driver of a tikka-ghari at the station. "To the polo club!"

His deep voice suddenly sounded harsh to her ears. He hadn't reached out to touch her.

They jolted through the empty streets, and in the moonlight Kitty saw the huddled forms of street sleepers. The heat rose around them. This then was the real India. Here marriages were arranged by the parents of the bride and groom. Often they did not see one another until after the ceremony had been performed.

When they reached the club, Christian made arrangements for their room. He took the key to their room and without a word to her, he marched stiffly ahead.

"There will be no bath tonight," he informed her. She sensed a tension within him and was disappointed that he showed so little enthusiasm for what lay ahead of them. She had wanted to relax in a tub to wash the dust and heat of the journey away. She longed to lie in his arms, but Christian had become a stranger, stiff and unbending.

Christian led her to the room he had secured and opened the door for her. He lit a gas light.

Kitty poured tepid water from a pitcher into a wash bowl. She found no linens, so splashed water on her face and bathed her arms. Before she had finished washing in the basin, she heard his footsteps going down the dark hall. From the clubroom she heard the voices of men at games.

She waited for him to return. When he finally came to their room the heat of summer permeated the room. He bent over her and asked, "How many others, Kitty? How many others besides Luke whatever his name was?" His words came from deep inside him like an animal snarling.

Kitty bolted upright, "So that's it? How dare you ask a question like that! How dare you speak to me in that tone of voice!"

"I have a right to know. How many others?" He paced the floor and did not come near her again.

"So that's what's eating at you." She drew the bottom sheet up to her chin and said, "What have you been drinking, Christian Skye?"

"You led me to believe...so pure and winsome...and I wed myself a a !"

"Get out! Get out!"

He stumbled out of the room. He fell into the wall and bellowed out for all to hear, "She lied to me!"

She got out of bed and paced the floor. She'd never be able to convince him that she hadn't been promiscuous throughout her life. He had never wanted to tell her about Emma, the girl he had married. She had to drag the little information she knew about her from him. Now he was making comparisons all of a sudden, and for some reason she did not measure up.

Although Kitty Farrell had gone to church when she was growing up in Kansas, and she knew all of the Bible stories she had been taught, she was a girl growing up with the "Me" generation of the sixties and seventies when the lifestyles for many of the young people changed drastically from the way she had been taught. She went off to college when dormitories were no longer segregated, but she abhorred the life style so many others adopted. Luke Filbey came into her life when she went to New York after she finished law school. He never mentioned marriage.

Toward morning she fell into a fitful sleep.

The heat of mid-morning awakened her, and she remembered. Then she realized she was alone on a frontier station in a time long before her own grandparents were born. She had married a man who despised her.

She dashed to the pitcher, but no one had bothered to replace the water she used for bathing the night before. She pulled on a cord and waited.

"Yes, memsahib?" A houseboy appeared and she realized, too late, that she wore nothing but her shift.

"Please bring fresh water."

Suddenly it was all over. What started out to be a wonderful wedding trip had turned into a frightful nightmare.

A short time later two boys brought a small tub of water and sweet-smelling soap. "I need a cloth and a towel, if you will please," she called as they backed away.

When she was alone, she removed her shift and sank into the tub.

Tears streamed down her face, and she quickly scrubbed them away along with the remainder of the dirt and grime of the journey. She dried herself on the scratchy, linen towel and rolled the hated crinoline into a ball and put it away before she dressed in a light-weight morning dress of yellow cambric trimmed with green.

She wore no stockings and put on the sandals she had purchased at an exclusive shop in New York City a short time before. She rolled her soiled clothing into a ball and slammed her puka luggage shut.

She felt the tears forming again and wiped them away angrily. The rattle of cutlery and dishes reached her ears, so she followed the sounds to the club's dining room.

Looks of surprise fell upon her, then a young Indian boy came to her table and said, "Good morning, memsahib."

"Coffee and a bowl of cereal." Her voice sounded alien to her ears.

"Cereal?"

"That will be sufficient."

The boy brought her a bowl of gruel and a cup of strong, black coffee. He handed her a chit to sign, and she wrote "Kathleen L. Skye" in bold letters.

"And is there a carriage than can take me to the railway station?" she asked when she looked up.

"Yes, memsahib."

"And I'll need my luggage brought around."

The boy folded his hands, bowed, and backed away.

"Wait," she yelled. "Where is Captain Skye?"

"I don't know where the sahib went," the boy told her.

"Do you mean he left?" She asked him, and the boy simply looked at her without any expression.

Kitty finished her breakfast, choking down the tasteless gruel, not knowing when she could afford at eat her next meal. Christian had left her alone at a frontier station in India in the 1850's. She had to find her way back. The rupees wouldn't last long ...not nearly long enough for a voyage to America. Her American bills were useless. She'd have to sign chits and hope Christian Skye didn't learn of it until he had to settle up. Her mind was working quickly now. . . planning her strategy, trying to make every move stretch her limited funds.

The sun sliced into her like a razor while she waited on the platform for the train that would take her to Bombay. She had missed the early train loaded with goods headed for the West, so she moved beneath a shelter from the sun and waited on a hard, wooden bench.

She tried to remember her geography. It was a large country...a subcontinent. How long would it take to reach a seaport? She leaned back and shut her eyes. The heat had already sapped her energy, and she had barely slept at all the night before...her wedding night. A painful reminder of it slipped into her mind, but she erased it as quickly as it entered. Time passed slowly, and she must have slept, for she awakened to a deep growl.

"Where do you think you're going?"

Kitty opened her eyes and Christian Skye's face was terrible to see. One eye drooped and the other blazed. He had a bruise on his cheekbone and a cut on his chin.

"I'm going home."

"So that's how it is?"

"I'll not be treated like a useless piece of trash by you, Christian Skye, or any other man who ever lived on this planet. I trusted you. You betrayed me and walked out on me on our wedding night."

"That I did." He sat down and put his head in his hands.

When he raised his head, he looked into her eyes and said, "Forgive me, Kitty. Come away with me to the vale of Kashmir. 'Tis cool and pleasant there."

"I'll not be treated ever again like you treated me last night, Christian Skye."

"I'll not ask it of you. Just come with me."

He did not touch her during the journey up into the valleys of Kashmir. Her heart ached, and she grew angry then full of hurting again. He treated her with respect, but she was longing to have it out with him. Instead, he said very little and appeared to be in deep mourning. She knew instinctively that he was thinking of Emma...the wife who died...the wife he had once loved. He had never forgotten the English girl he had married.

"He grieves for her still." Her heart did crazy things when she looked at him, so strong and so handsome, his eyes filled with pain..

Something raw and painful twisted inside her, and she couldn't swallow a bite of the food he brought to her.

When she shivered with the cold in the hills, he purchased a woolen embroidered Kashmiri shawl for her to wear on her shoulders.. She tried to thank him, but the words choked in her throat. For three days, she fought back the anger. On the fourth, the beauty of the vale of Kashmir lay before her. Christian brought her a cup of hot tea, and tears sprang into her eyes. Her face worked uncontrollably, and she buried her head in her hands and wept miserably. Christian turned and walked away without speaking.

He had rented a lovely houseboat on the lake for a month, but he spent his days on the ponies while Kitty walked along the mountain trails alone. She didn't care that the houseboat was filled with elegant Victorian furniture and all the trappings of a comfortable English-style home. At the end of three days, she packed her luggage and waited for Christian to return.

When she heard his footsteps coming along the path to the houseboat where they lived but rarely spoke, she braced herself for what she was about to say. The sun still cast her gold into the hills before sliding away into the west. It would be the last day she would see the magic of Kashmir.

When Christian walked onto the houseboat, he paused before he opened the door.

"Good evening, Christian," she choked out and tried to smile when he entered.

His eyes showed no emotion, so she continued, "This isn't working out for us, Captain Skye. Surely you know that. In an expression common to the times in which we're living, our union has never been consummated. There's not a clergyman alive today who will recognize our marriage as legitimate. I'm not certain about the formalities one must go through in order to annul our marriage, but. . ."

Her words began to warm her and she continued, "I can't find it in myself to remain your wife any longer." She lowered her voice. She was an attorney once more, and she found herself eager to continue. "Not while you are continuing to grieve for Emma Skye. I can't deny the fact that I came to India searching for someone or something I lost long ago.

She lowered her voice. She was in control and found she was eager to continue. "Christian, not in this life or any other has my soul in its search for happiness been so damaged and hurt. I'll begin my journey back to America early tomorrow morning, but before I go, you must know this. Perhaps I've always loved you, and when our lives together have ended here, I shall search for you again one day. Perhaps then Emma cannot come between us."

CHAPTER NINE

"Don't leave me, Kitty. Please don't leave me. 'Tis my fool's pride and jealousy that's keeping us apart." His voice cracked at the end. He looked into her eyes and she saw the misery and hurt lying there.

Her eyes filled with tears while he continued to speak in broken phrases, "'Twas Emma that caused it...came out to India to be my bride. On the ship coming over, she met another...carried another man's child on the day we were wed. Couldn't touch her, Kitty. She was never my wife but in name only. She grieved for the other until the day she died."

She could not speak, shocked by his confession.

"Now, I understand. Oh, Christian, my dear, dear Christian. We must not let the past destroy us. In the Gita it is written, 'Love knows no bargaining. Wherever there is any seeking for something in return, there can be no real love, it becomes a mere matter of shopkeeping. Nor does love fear, for true love casts out all terror.' Emma and Luke have nothing to do with us. They, to borrow your expression, were the gnats on the elephant. Emma wronged you in a way that is unforgivable. Luke wasn't good for me. Yes, he hurt me...angered and hurt me, but if he hadn't let me go, I would never have had the courage to search for you. If Emma had been faithful, you'd still be married to her today."

"And did any other hurt you, Kitty?" He stepped close to her, and she looked up and saw the amber flecks in his eyes. The sun caught the red in his dark hair.

"Aye, there was a certain officer...a captain in John Company. His name, if I remember it correctly, was Skye."

She saw a smile spread across his face and the corners of his mouth relax. His eyes were dancing with pleasure and surprise.

"And there was a certain witch, a beautiful witch who charmed her way into old Skye's heart, creating a foolish monster...a monster filled with jealousy...not daring to believe that she loved only him."

He took her in his arms there on the houseboat on a lake in Kashmir.

While she lay contentedly in Christian's arms, she teased, "And after Emma died, you never...never found another woman you'd marry?"

"Oh, I've been as eager as any of the young lads in our regiment when the fishing fleet arrived." He nuzzled her neck and chuckled with contentment.

"The fishing fleet?"

"It happens during the six months of winter, the season when the young damsels from London and all the fine schools in England come out on the P and O Lines. We call them 'the fishing fleet' for it is understood they come to fish for husbands and adventure. The fishing is good. Our men want to meet English women, and it is all quite proper. They come out to stay with relatives or friends, and everyone enjoys an endless round of sporting and social activities. The ones who don't marry and return to England are called 'the Returned Empties'."

"And Captain Skye never got himself caught by a girl from the fishing fleet?" She giggled and he pulled her to him and kissed her.

He released her and said, "It took a clever witch from another century to snag Old Skye in her net."

"My handsome husband had better help me unpack my clothes and take me out to find something to eat before I starve."

"What am I to do with my pretty witch? She's turned me into a mass of quivering jelly. Oh, my ranee...my marahanee. . .my queen!"

The bazaar filled with stalls overflowing with scrubbed potatoes, crisp radishes, translucent onions, carrots and every imaginable vegetable newly-harvested lay spread out on mats, and chickens and lambs hung on hooks in the meat market. She chose a chicken and asked where to find the street where wheat products and spices were sold.

"Have you ever eaten curried chicken and vegetables, Christian?"

"They're Indian dishes. We don't go into the villages, and our cooks have been trained in the English culinary manner for years."

"I'll not add too much curry, just enough to season it properly. You'll like the chappattis I'm baking for you."

"Imagine marrying a witch who cooks Indian," he laughed as she handed him the potatoes to carry.

He watched her chop vegetables while the chicken simmered and smiled when she kneaded the unleavened flour so she could shape the dough into chappattis. When she was finished, he came up behind her and drew her into his arms.

"Oh, my Ranee, do you think you can ever forgive me for being such a heartless fool?"

"Captain Skye, a fool? No more than Mrs. Skye, I'll wager. If our married life continues with highs and lows like it has begun, can you imagine how wonderful it's going to be when we settle our difficulties and make up?"

"I promised to love...honor...and cherish you if I remember the words correctly, and I almost lost you."

"And I promised to 'obey' and it rankled my twentieth century mind. I never obeyed anyone in my entire lifetime."

"I could see that well enough," he laughed.

Later she served the curried meal on an English blue and white flow-blue platter.

"Spicy like my Maharanee. A burra meal, fit for a prince of India!"

"Fit for my prince of India!" Kitty looked into his eyes over her cup of tea.

"What have you done to me, Maharanee? I'm completely daft over you."

The next day they arose early and looked toward the mountains hidden by the mist rising from the water. Poplars along the edges of the lake stretched high into the sky, and ducks sang a lively chorus beside the houseboats.

"'Tis a wonderful day, my Maharanee, a day for discovering what lies beyond our little boat. What do you want to do first?"

"I want to see the remains of the Mogul pavilions and gardens."

"There's a mosque on Lake Dal where a holy hair of the Prophet Mohammed is kept. The relic was brought here by a holy man who gashed his arm and concealed the hair in his wound in order to bring it here safely they say. The place is so sacred birds never fly over the chapel and cows never turn their backsides to it."

"A wonderful story!"

"And true no doubt. You'll not be offended by the sight of a saddhu?"

"Saddhus, the holy men of India who wear no clothes. It is something alien to the rest of the world that seems right in India."

By noon the snow-capped cones of the Himalayas appeared against a sapphire sky. Scores of children and beggars had cried "Baksheeh! Baksheeh!" and held out thin, dark hands to them. Crowds of pilgrims filled the pavilions of the Mogul princes and a procession of flagellants made a weary pilgrimage to a shrine higher up in the mountains. Their clothes stiff, they carried whips made of metal chains with small razor-sharp blades at the ends with which to whip themselves. Women wearing black from head to toe floated by.

"I feel like a tourist," Kitty told Christian.

"We are strangers in a strange and beautiful land. England is not here in these streets of India."

A saddhu, barefooted and ash-smeared, walked toward them. He appeared tired and hungry, and Kitty was surprised that he was so young.

"He's hungry, Christian. Give him the fish and chappatti I could not eat."

Christian took the food to him, and the saddhu bowed and thanked him.

An aged Indian man paused before a garish red shrine beside the road and performed his pujah, unconcerned about others who passed by.

"So different from the cantonment where England survives untouched by time and India," she commented.

"Was it here?" Christian asked her, and she knew he was trying to remember where they had first loved.

They bought sweets from a street vendor and ate sweet cakes wrapped in gold leaf. "Maharanee, our souls have become one again. We can never be separated ...not by time or distance."

"And when death comes to us our souls will await the day we are brought together again."

"I couldn't find it within myself to bring happiness into my marriage with Emma...didn't know why."

"And the child?"

"Couldn't raise a child in this country. I sent him to his grandmother Fletcher in England, the least I could do. A young woman, one of the 'returned empties,' took him home. He never knew. Thinks to this day I am his father."

"Would you ever have him know the truth?"

"No, Kitty. I'd not do that to the child. He was born to my name."

Kitty took hold of Christian's hand and pointed to the scene before them.

"Wait, Christian. I want to keep this sight forever in my mind, the row of houseboats floating against green islands, the snow-capped mountains rising beyond the lake, and Akbar's fort of Hari Parbot shimmering in the distance."

"Capture it in your heart, Kitty. Take it with you wherever we go, but tell me truthfully, is it the sights of Kashmir or old Skye himself you want to remember most?"

"Foolish man! You knew the answer before you asked," she laughed.

The sun captured the red in his hair, and his eyes invited her to enter the houseboat. The sounds of a sitar wailing until the notes reached a high frenzy wafted across the water. Kitty was reminded of Mogul gardens in the town of Rainawari, of Srinegar in the hills beyond the Chenob River before it fell into a deep gorge, the Ganges plain in the wintertime with the sound of wild ducks crying to their mates, of the temples of Mahabalipuram, of the ancient city of Fatephur Sikri, and a small cottage beside the sea at Madras. She had marveled at the palaces of the princes of Mysore and all of the wonderful places that had pleased her mother and father so well. The music of the sitar cried in a wild song and then ended with a rapid crescendo of sounds.

The next day was their last in the enchanted land of Kashmir. A dhoti from the village brought their freshly-ironed clothing, and they packed their luggage. Late in the afternoon they walked through a light, drizzling rain around the lake. Then Kitty remembered the lotus bud she had found that was about to burst into bloom.

"It will be in full bloom. We must see it before it vanishes."

They raced to the place where it had thrust up its lovely pink bud, fully expecting to see it in full bloom.

"Where is it? Where did it go?"

"Come away, Kitty." Christian's voice was low and gentle. "Come away, my love."

They joined a company of worshipers making their way through the foothills to a holy shrine in the mountains. At Simla they would part company with those making the pilgrimage, and Captain Skye would resume his duties with John Company. Kitty would become the wife of an English officer. She had no idea about the duties the role demanded of her, but she knew if Christian was there, she would find contentment, whatever they were.

Traveling on the frontier had its own special risks, so they held to government roads, dodging camel caravans, donkeys, sheep, elephants, and their followers. They passed through a village where a tiger had killed a man the night before. The villagers were frightened and begged Christian to stay.

When they reached English stations where the Union Jack flew bravely, they stopped for the night, and the pilgrims camped outside the gates for protection. Sometimes the posts were barely fortified, and Kitty secretly sighed with relief when they stopped for the night within a walled fortress. The fact that Christian had armed himself and rode his pony on ahead reminded her of the dangers from robbers that faced them on the trail.

A week later they rode into Simla, unloaded the pack animals, and went to the club for refreshment.

Caroline Bradley had been watching and waiting for them to arrive. When they stepped onto the verandah of the polo club, she came to them with tears streaming down her cheeks.

"It's Edith, Christian," Kitty told him. "Something has happened to Edith."

"Yes, it's Edith. She died at Lucknow shortly after you left," Caroline told them.

"Oh, no," Kitty cried and Caroline took Kitty in her arms. "I'm so sorry, Christian. She was buried in the churchyard the same day. We came on to Simla the next. It is what she wanted."

Caroline blinked away her tears and brightened, "But I have good news to tell you, Christian. Your son has arrived from England."

CHAPTER TEN

*K*itty looked at Christian and saw the shock on his face in the twilight. She knew what he was thinking...felt it creep into her and settle there like a hard lump of clay.

"Where is the boy, Caroline?"

Kitty felt the coldness of his voice reach into her and twist itself around her heart.

"He's with our children...a delightful child. It seems his grandmother died, and your brother William sent him here. It is what Colin wanted." Caroline tried hard to keep her voice steady, but even so, Kitty knew it was difficult for her to speak.

"Thank you for looking out for him," Kitty said before Christian could speak.

"We've been on the road for days. Has our cottage been prepared for us?" Christian asked.

"We thought you would like to change here at the club. Azziz has been waiting for you. Kitty may go with me, and then I'll take her to your cottage. But be warned, it is small."

Kitty soaked with her knees against her chest in the small tub. "What is he like...Christian's son?"

"He's a dear child, a bit small for his age...a golden-haired boy with beautiful blue eyes...almost too pretty for a boy. He's rather shy, but well-mannered and bright."

"I see."

"He and the children have hit it off marvelously." Caroline's voice did not betray her emotions.

"Strange...I'm a step-mother all at once, and I don't even know the boy's name."

"His name is Colin...Colin Skye, but you must hurry, Kitty. Christian will be waiting." Caroline handed her a coarse towel.

Her maid had arrived earlier and had already laid out her evening dress, slippers, and a new crinoline. Kitty completed her bathing and then stepped from her bath. Allie brought her underclothes to her. She fastened the buttons, tied the string that held the crinoline in place, and then held the dress for Kitty to slip into.

When Kitty was fully clothed, she said, "I feel like I'm still on the horse, trudging along mountain roads, and absolutely starving."

"And how did you find Kashmir? Is it as beautiful as everyone tells me it is?"

"Even more beautiful. You must see it!"

"You're in love! I knew it!" Caroline clapped her hands.

She shrugged both shoulders and shut her eyes. "Madly! Insanely! Marvelously."

Caroline laughed and told her, "I knew it the moment you met Christian. It was love at first sight. I could see it in your eyes...and in Christian's, I might add."

"I searched for him until I found him. You have no idea how I found him." She knew in that moment she would not return. She would remain with Christian until their lives ended.

"Come, we'll go to your cottage, if you're ready." She handed Kitty a warm wrap.

Caroline appeared to be overanxious as they hurried along the dimly lit street. "Watch your step, Kitty. There are drop-offs along here." She took Kitty's hand and held it until they reached a small house with lights streaming from the windows.

Christian waited for them at the door. He was wearing an immaculate winter uniform and boots that glistened. He had shaved and held out his arms to Kitty. "Welcome home, love." He held her in his arms and kissed her, disregarding Caroline Bradley. "We have dinner prepared for us, and our guests are waiting. Are you ready?"

.Caroline opened the door, and the guests cried out, "Welcome home!" A banner blazed across the wall and three musicians played a rousing number.

Christian grinned and led Kitty into the small house. Dinner had been prepared by Christian's cook, and the servants stood in the background smiling as he took Kitty by the hand and introduced her to the men with whom he would be serving. They, in turn, introduced their wives.

"You know Colonel Oliver and Maria."

"Welcome to your new home, Kitty Skye." Colonel Oliver actually beamed at her while Maria smiled warmly and offered her cold cheek.

"You're looking well, my dear," Maria told her.

"We had a wonderful vacation," Kitty said. "Kashmir was beautiful."

When they were all seated at the table, Colonel Oliver raised his glass and offered the first toast, "To the queen, God bless her."

Christian next proposed, "To my wife., God bless her." He placed just the right emphasis on the word "her."

Her heart swelled with love and her eyes answered him.

Charles shouted, "Here! Here!" and they drained their glasses.

When the door closed on the last guest, Christian took her in his arms. " 'Twas a fine gesture, but I thought they would never leave!"

Christian stroked her hair. "Was it in Simla in some long-forgotten past we loved like this, my sweet Maharanee?"

"Perhaps, my love. Everything we do together, we've done before. Falling asleep in your arms is like floating away in time."

He said nothing more, but she knew instinctively that he was still awake.

"You're thinking about Edith. She knew at once about us."

"Aye, Kitty. That she did."

"She, too has broken a time barrier...somewhere in time. I do hope she finds happiness as I have done."

"Don't leave me, Kitty!" There was panic in his voice. "Never leave me. I couldn't live without you now."

"I'll never leave you, my sweet prince, and if we're ever parted, I'll know you immediately when we meet again. There's nothing about you that will escape me."

"You're a determined witch," he chuckled and drew her closer.

"Yes, Captain Skye, and don't you forget it. Where do you suppose I'll find you centuries from now?"

"Heaven, most likely."

She awoke and reached for him, but his side of the bed was empty and cold.

"Christian!" she called out.

She heard him putting aside his paper, and he came to her and held her in his arms. "You don't look very witchy this morning, my little Ranee. I thought you were going to sleep all day."

"Why didn't you wake me?"

"Couldn't bear to. You were sleeping so peacefully. Put your robe on, and we'll eat breakfast together before I report for duty." His papers were scattered where he had been reading, and he pushed them aside so she could join him at the table.

"'Tis a lovely day. Wait till we see Simla in the daylight. I'll report in, and we'll see it together."

"You're forgetting something, Christian. Or are you pushing it from your mind?" She put her hand upon his.

"What, Kitty?"

"Colin...Colin Skye. We must find him, you know, and bring him home."

"What are we going to do with the child, Kitty?" he exploded.

"How would I know? I've never been around children, except for Olivia's. They were living terrors."

"It's just like Will to send him here. What are we to do?"

"The boy wanted to come to you, Christian."

"It's a terrible place to raise a child...sickness...the heat...scorpions... snakes. The cantonments are no place for children."

"Would you send our children off to England?" she asked quietly.

"Now, don't borrow heartaches before they are due, Kitty."

"We must send for Colin," she insisted. "It's the only right thing to do."

"He's not my child!" His face turned red and he appeared ready to explode.

"Of course not, but he's been your responsibility, and he thinks you're his father...the only one he's ever known, and he's just a child...a boy of ten."

She rose and placed her arms around him and drew his head against her. She stroked his head gently and said, "You're so strong and good, my darling. We must not let Emma come between us again. Put those thoughts out of your mind. The child bears your name and believes in you. We cannot cast aside that trust without destroying ourselves."

He took her hand and kissed the palm. "You're so good for me. How did I ever live without you? I'm being mean-hearted and selfish...not wanting anyone, even a child to come between the two of us."

She nuzzled his neck. "No one can ever come between the two of us."

"I'll send Azziz for the boy. I don't have half a mind when you're near me." His voice rumbled from deep inside him, protesting her hold over him, but he smiled at her and drew her onto his lap. "Here I am idling about, forgetting about duty and mundane tasks. Why, Kitty, my darlin', I dare say you'll have me forgetting my orders. I may even forget to practice my shots."

"Heavens, not that!" She kissed him, and for a moment she forgot everything else.

"Here's breakfast," he said.

"Will I ever get used to your servants falling all over us?" She got off his lap and seated herself beside him.

Christian roared with laughter.

"You'll begin playing 'housey-housey' with the women here in Simla and forget about old Skye slaving away with the regiment in no time at all. When I return up the line you will have become accustomed to having servants with us everywhere we go."

"Up the line?" It was another expression she did not understand. It seemed he was always explaining something to her about the military.

"On active duty on the Northwest Frontier."

"Will you be called out often?"

"The most frequent complaint we hear from the women is that the men are seldom at home...off in the line of duty somewhere. Is it any wonder so many of them return to England when their children go off to school?"

"I'm not going to like that 'up the line business'." She buttered a muffin and spread it with jam.

"Nor I, Kitty."

"Am I supposed to remain behind and simply be a dutiful little wife... waiting impatiently for you to return while you go gallivanting off into the countryside?"

"Unless you want to brave the wilds of India...hardly a place for a woman."

"Nothing could be worse than being away from you. Do they permit camp followers? Women in your regiment? I'll join up so I can be with you."

Suddenly he sobered and looked at her.. "Do you realize that I was one hundred and twenty-eight years old the year you were born?"

"Cradle robber!" she laughed.

"And what is that supposed to mean?"

"Old man!"

She dressed warmly after Christian left her to report to Colonel Oliver. The sky lay close to the ground and a damp chill hung in the air.

She tried to read Christian's newspapers but could not focus on the meaning of the words. He had given instructions to his cook and the housekeeper and the water carrier. The servants ignored her and went about their tasks. One made beds, another swept floors. She knew enough to let them do the work assigned to their caste. Until she learned the difference and could handle the language fluently, she would let Christian run his household.

Christian had explained it as found in the Gita.. "And do thy duty, even if it be humble, rather than another's, even if it be great. To die in one's duty is life. To live another's is death."

She walked to the window and saw nothing but the morning hidden in mist. She glanced at her watch. Christian had been gone an hour, and the loneliness filled her completely. Suddenly it occurred to her that she had not thought of her parents' deaths since she married Christian and began to wonder if they, too, had found each other again. It was a comforting thought.

The front door open quietly, and Azziz bowed to her. "Memsahib," he addressed her.

Then she saw him...a slight child, frightened and obviously shy.

She tried to speak, but her heart stood still. Emma's child!

He stepped toward her and spoke in a small, crisp voice, "My name in Colin Skye."

"My name is Kitty Skye...same as yours." Her voice shook from her.

"Then you must be...must be Father's wife. How do you do, Kitty?"

He came toward her and held out a small, limp hand.

She took his hand solemnly, her heart racing. "How long have you been here in Simla, Colin Skye?"

"I came with the Bradleys. They're my friends."

"Of course."

Azziz held out a hand written note to her, so she took it and read.

"Kitty darling, Old Oliver has seen fit to put me to work. I'll be detained until tea time. I love you madly. C. S." She smiled and put the note in her pocket.

"Your father will not be here until tea time. What shall we do, Colin, until he arrives?" She smiled.

"Would you like to see Simla?" He smiled and his eyes sparkled. "I can show you the bazaar and the pavilion." He waited quietly for her response.

"How nice of you to offer."

Azziz disappeared, and Kitty found herself alone with Colin. He seemed small for a boy his age. His hair had been combed and his shoes had been shined. He waited respectfully for her to make the next move.

"Is there somewhere we can find something to eat in the town? Or should we take something from the kitchen?" She wondered how they could make the cook understand what they wanted.

"It doesn't matter. I'm not hungry."

"Then let's be off. You're certain we won't get lost and not find our way back?"

"I know my way about."

"Very well, then." She didn't tell Colin she had wanted Christian to explore the town with her, but this child appeared to be waiting for her to make the first move.

When they stepped into the street outside the cottage, she saw a steep dropoff below her.

"Careful, Kitty Skye," Colin warned, and she suddenly felt like an old woman.

Then the sun broke through the mist, and she saw the tiers of the town built one upon the other with streets clinging precariously to the mountainside. She looked up and saw the street above their cottage and another cottage above that on the cliff. Steps at the end of the street climbed the mountain to the street above.

"What an incredible sight!" she cried. "It's like a many-layered wedding cake with all colors of frosting. I had no idea it would look like this."

"The bazaar lies below the cottages," Colin explained to her. "The cantonment is beyond that. I like to sit above the parade ground to watch the men marching to mess and going through their drills. Will Father be there today?" He lifted his face to hers for an answer.

"Probably so, Colin. You spoke to Azziz. Did you study Urdu in England?"

"A little. I was just beginning when Grandmother Fletcher died."

"I see."

"Look, Kitty! A dog that does tricks."

A boy no larger than Colin put his dog through its paces on the street. The dog climbed upon a stack of boxes, danced on his hind legs, and jumped through a hoop. The boy grinned and Kitty gave him a coin.

The boy with the dog followed them. Together they chattered in Hindustani and English. She let them show her the sights, the bazaar where bright, sleazy goods filled the streets to overflowing. They dodged bullock carts and the street behind the carts filled with people at once. She followed the children through the bazaar, to a pavilion and park, and then on to the parade ground where men of horseback paraded under colors.

"Do you see my father on the parade ground?" His voice sounded anxious.

"No, Colin. He is not there. He's an officer, you know, and he may have administrative duties to take care of today." She, too, felt the disappointment Colin had revealed. When they returned to the steep streets leading up to the cottages clinging to the mountainside, Kitty felt drained. The boy and his dog had parted company down below where they waited to earn another coin.

"What do we do next?" Colin asked.

"I'm ready for tea. You've exhausted me completely. The altitude and climbing mountain trails is too much for me. I'll rest awhile when we get home and then change for tea. Perhaps you can find something to read."

"Will Father come to tea."

"Yes, if he can get away that long."

She saw a frown form between Colin's eyes and asked, "Is something wrong, Colin?"

"Will he be angry?" Colin's voice held anxiety.

"Angry?"

"Angry with me for coming here?"

"You wrote to him regularly, didn't you?"

"He didn't answer.".

"Do you mean he never wrote to you?"

"Hardly ever."

"I see."

"And he never sent gifts at Christmas time?"

"He sent money to Grandmother Fletcher."

"For gifts?"

"For support," Colin said as if reading her mind.

Colin opened the door of the cottage and held it for her.

"I'm going to lie down for awhile. Make yourself at home, Colin. Maybe you can talk cook out of something to eat."

She sighed and shut her bedroom door behind her.

CHAPTER ELEVEN

Kitty awoke to the sound of rain falling softly as it does in the foothills of the Himalayas during the summertime. She did not mind the cold rain, but she knew what lay below them on the river plains where there would be flooding. She heard Christian's footstep on the porch before he swept into the cottage, shaking himself when he removed his coat. Kitty marveled again that in spite of his strength, every move he made was with gentleness when he opened his arms to her and caught her close to him.

"Perhaps I should have planned something special," she began, "but to be honest, my darling, I wanted for us to be alone after tea time."

"This could be habit-forming, Love. I've grown addicted to our time alone. 'Twas a busy day...picking up the pieces...getting back into a routine was difficult at first. Married life has become a luxury for me. . .but enough of this! I have a surprise for you!"

"A surprise!" She took his arm and they walked toward the dining room.

"It will be along shortly," he grinned down at her.

Then Christian froze. Colin Skye jumped to his feet with fear written across his face. Neither made a move toward the other. Neither spoke.

"Christian." His name dragged from her while she felt herself draining out on the floor. "This is Colin...Colin Skye."

An awkward silence fell into the room, one she was unable to break. The houseboy bustled in with hot tea and small ginger cakes, and Kitty sank into a chair. Colin waited for Christian to seat himself beside Kitty, and then he quickly sat down at the opposite end of the table.

"Sugar, Colin?" Kitty did not recognize her own voice when she handed him a cup of tea.

"Two lumps and cream, please." Colin spoke in a small, wavering voice.

She poured Christian's tea and passed the cakes to Colin. He took one but did not taste it. Her hands were shaking, and she saw that Colin's shook, also.

Christian drank a full cup of tea quickly and set his cup in the saucer. Then he glared at the child. "So...what possessed you to come out to India without a word to me, Colin? Surely your grandmother made arrangements for you to remain in school."

"Yes, sir." He did not lower his eyes as Kitty thought he might under Christian's onslaught.

"So you took it upon yourself...didn't wait for the fishing fleet?"

"Yes sir...that is no, sir." The child was obviously shaken.

"And how is my brother Will? Did he encourage this madness?" Christian leaned forward, and his voice thundered across the table.

"Uncle Will...and Aunt Harriet, too, they thought. . ." Colin was close to tears.

Christian sighed heavily. "I thought as much. So what are you going to do? You're too young for service. Stand up, boy!"

Colin jerked to attention.

"You'll never make a soldier."

"I can try, Father."

"Well it's back to England for you. You'll need years of schooling if you're to be any use here. You'll need to go through Addiscombe, and then my lad, they just might make a man out of you. Sit down. Finish your tea. What was Will was thinking about." He turned to Kitty, and she reached for his hand under the table and gave it a reassuring squeeze.

"May I be excused, sir?" Colin Skye looked devastated.

"Yes. Yes, boy."

Colin raced from the room to the door that opened onto the street. Kitty heard the door open, and she wondered where the child was going. Darkness would fall soon. She was genuinely upset. Then Colin returned and asked, "Kitty, may I please go to the Bradleys?"

She breathed a sigh of relief. Colin had obviously been trained to ask permission to do things.

"Yes, Colin, but you must return before dark. Azziz has your things put away in your room."

When the door closed behind Colin, Christian roared, "What are we to do with this child?"

"Christian! He's only a little boy, and if I might add, he's quite a mannerly child."

"You don't say? And what do you know about children?"

"Not very much, but I do recognize a child who is intelligent and has been trained to do the right thing. And what do you know about children?"

"Children? Not so very much, but I know a witch when I see one. I remember a witch from America who came to Lucknow one night, forcing me to face up to my duties at last in Kashmir." He roared with laughter and pulled her onto his lap.

"You didn't seem to mind...not one bit, if I remember correctly."

"What was a poor man to do?"

They heard a disturbance at the front door, and he dumped her off his lap and pulled her into the front room of the small cottage. He watched her face as the movers set the huge piece down. It dwarfed the room.

"Oh, my dear Christian, how did you know? A piano. Oh, my!"

While she ran her hand over the fine mahogany case, Christian said, "You're not the only one in this marriage who has extra-sensory perception, my girl! How did I know? How did I know how you would sing, even before you played the first note? How did I know how you would feel in my arms, even before you forced yourself on me and made me hold you in my arms and kiss you there in my office at Lucknow? It's all part of who we are." He laughed with her, delighted with her pleasure with the lovely instrument.

She ran her fingers lightly over the keys and turned to Christian, "I know a thousand love songs to sing to you...songs my father taught me... ballads from the second World War and others from the fifties and sixties and seventies."

She began to play and then sang, "There'll be blue birds over the White Cliffs of Dover. . ."

Tears sprang into Christian's eyes, and it was all she could do to keep her own from flooding down her cheeks.

She lay in his arms listening to the rain fall on the roof. "He's just a lonely, little boy...a desperate, little guy wanting more than anything in the world to please you. Do you think there is enough love left over to share with him?"

"He's not my child! It just doesn't seem right."

"Did you love Emma once, Christian...before you knew?"

"I dreamed about bringing a wife out to India for years...wrote and asked her to be my wife."

"Did you love her?"

"I don't know, Kitty. It seemed the right thing to do, and I had known her all my life."

"And when you learned, you shut her out...you shut her out like you tried to shut me out."

"What are you saying, Maharanee? I distinctly remember how it was. It was an ultimatum you gave me." He was laughing softly and cuddling her close. "You do have a way about you that struck me the moment I laid eyes on you."

"Will you shut out the boy?" She lifted her lips to his before he could answer.

He was quiet, and she knew what he was thinking. It was a topic they had gone over once before. She didn't know how he was going to deal with it.

"He looks like Emma, doesn't he? Same blue eyes, blond...small?"

"Her eyes...yes they're in the Fletcher family."

"And Emma is dead."

"I killed her, Kitty. I never knew her as my wife, and I killed her."

"No, Christian. She died after childbirth. She had no will to live any longer. It happens when a woman is honor bound to marry another. She was grieving for him. And now the boy is here. He has no one to love him and reeks with loneliness. Your brother didn't want the boy, and his wife must have agreed with him! His grandmother must have cared, but Christian, she is dead, and the boy came here searching for you...the same as I did. Don't you see?"

"It's a heavy responsibility you're laying on me, my darlin'."

"Was I a heavy responsibility, you wonderful man."

"No, 'tis joy you have brought into my life, Maharanee." He was quiet a moment and then said, "I'll be kind to the boy."

When Colin returned shortly before darkness fell, he went at once to his room. Christian put aside his paper and went to his door, "Colin," he called out to him.

Kitty heard a muffled voice coming from within the room. Christian opened the door and entered.

When they emerged, a short while later, Colin's face was shining. Christian put his hand on the boy's shoulder and said, "Colin will be with us until the fall term begins, Kitty. Would you care to join us in a game?"

"I'll play soft music for you, Christian. See that you play fair...both of you."

She smiled when she heard Christian cry out after Colin won. "This is just the first round, my boy. Just you wait!"

Colin doubled over with laughter.

He called out to her, "Oh, Kitty, I haven't told you the news. We'll be stationed at Lucknow again when we leave Simla in September."

"Luchnow? Lucknow... Christian! That's where so many died during the Sepoy mutiny!"

A chill crept into her. Christian had unleashed a memory from the recesses of her mind. It sprang out like a coil unfurled and tumbled into her heart.

"What are you saying, Kitty?"

"There was a mutiny...I can't remember when. I was never good with dates."

CHAPTER TWELVE

*A*zziz brought the invitation from Colonel Oliver, bowing to Kitty when he handed it to her. Kitty folded her hands and bowed to him and then opened the envelope and read aloud to Christian and Colin.

"My dear Mrs. Skye, I shall be very pleased if you will reserve dance number three for me at the ball to be held Saturday night the sixth day of July at the Governor's house, Simla. If you will please join me near the dias at the beginning of this dance, I shall introduce you to His Excellency. Please give Christian my best regards. Mrs. Oliver has reserved the fifth dance on her card for Captain Skye.

With my regards,

Colonel Lionel Oliver"

"Lionel Oliver!" Kitty burst out laughing. "Will he actually expect me to call him Lionel."

"What's so funny about that?" Christian asked.

"I've never known anyone with that name. My father had a Lionel model train set when he was a boy. He kept adding track and trestles and all sorts of depots and buildings throughout his lifetime until he had our basement completely covered with track. There must have been a hundred miles of it. He'd bring little boys and old men in to show off his Lionel trains. We spent hours together watching the trains roar along."

"Is the train still in your house in Kansas?" Colin asked.

"Yes, I suppose so. He and some of his friends got together every so often and talked 'Lionel' trains all his life."

"May we see it when we go to America?"

Kitty shook her head as though trying to set the time straight in her mind. "I think not, Colin, but I can tell you more about it sometime."

How could she explain to Colin that he was older than her great grandparents, and that it would be impossible for him to go with her to America?

"What if I forget and call him 'Old Oliver'?"

"Well, Kitty darlin', you have arrived, as they say. Oliver has requested the third dance, an honor to say the least."

"Don't sit there smiling so smugly, Captain Skye. Tell me what you are thinking.""

"You do know how to dance the gavotte, don't you?" Christian still smiled.

"The what?"

"It's the colonel's favorite, always reserved for the third dance with the most beautiful young lady at the ball."

Panic struck her. No one ever danced the gavotte. Or did they? Kitty felt herself growing weak.

"You know very well I have never danced the gavotte, Christian. No one dances the gavotte today. Is this Maria's idea of a practical joke or yours?" Her eyes blazed into his and for one brief moment she thought they were about to have their first quarrel over a silly dance card. She began laughing at the thought of it.

"Don't worry about it. Lionel will teach you, I dare say. It's a French dance in three-quarter time...quite lively with fancy footwork."

"Christian, you're teasing me. Say it's a joke."

"'Tis no joke, Kitty." Colin spoke up from his end of the breakfast table.

"I'm going to be ill.'"

Christian laughed his slow, rumbling laughter that rolled from deep inside his chest like thunder rolling across the sky.

While they dressed for supper at the polo club that evening, Kitty said, "I'll fall flat. I know I will. Why can't we just dance a slow waltz?"

"Because it is the third dance, and Oliver has requested you for his partner. I'll waltz with you later. I'll hold you very close."

"You wouldn't dare!"

"Oh, wouldn't I now?" His eyes danced playfully.

"Did you give instructions to cook for Colin's supper?"

"Azziz," he raised his voice, and Kitty knew when he spoke in Hindustani to his bearer that he had taken care of the matter.

Then he turned to tell her, "We're going to the club with the Bradleys and the Milfords. Now I promise you to behave properly tonight. But you don't know how you tempt me."

"I'm covered from head to toe and wearing this silly cage that won't let my skirts cling anywhere. What nonsense! As though someone would see my body. I'll not wear a corset, no matter what."

"It doesn't matter how many petticoats you wear, you'll look good to me. Fasten my belt tighter, Azziz."

Kitty was finally becoming accustomed to having Azziz and Allie in their bedroom while they dressed and undressed. At first she wanted to hide behind a screen when she removed her clothes, but Christian just laughed at her modesty. She couldn't imagine why lovers only held hands when they were courting, and after they were married permitted another woman and another man to undress them. It didn't make sense to her, but that was India and that was the British way of doing things in India.

When she began laughing at the thought, Christian broke away from Azziz to chase her around the small room. Allie tried to step back out of the way and plopped backwards into Christian's bath water. She gasped, then drew herself out of the water without a change of expression and stood quietly with her back to the wall until Christian had finished kissing his wife. Then Allie stepped forward to fasten the string of pearls Kitty would wear.

"Will you teach me, Christian? You do know how to do the gavotte. Say you do."

"I'll be on duty. Not a chance. Sorry!" He chuckled to himself.

When they emerged from the room, Colin looked up from the corner where he was reading a book.

"Kanwar will prepare your supper, Colin. If you need anything, call for Azziz."

"Thank you, Father. Does Azziz play ving-et-un?" He laid his book aside.

"More than likely. Now be a good lad. Kitty and I will be home around ten."

"Good-night, Colin," Kitty told him.

"Good-night, Kitty. Good-night, Father."

Kitty was to discover yet another side to Christian Skye at supper that night. While Charles Bradley and Thomas Milford and their wives relaxed with them over glasses of Scotch before supper at the officer's club, someone mentioned the failed strategy of Harold at Hastings.

Then Thomas Milford asked Christian, "Do you still remember the names of all the kings of England?"

Christian began reciting their names in order. He drew a deep breath when he reached Alfred the Great, then continued until he reached Victoria. He raised his glass and said, "God save the queen!"

"Marvelous!" Maggie Milford cried and clapped her hands. "And do you remember Shakespeare? You quoted entire scenes from memory when. . ."

"I prefer lighter verse now," Christian said. "Elizabeth Barrett Browning put it this way, 'The little cares that fretted me, I lost them yesterday among the fields, above the sea, among the winds at play.' Since Kitty has become my wife, I seem to have no cares at all."

"What a lovely thing to say!" Caroline cried, and for a moment Kitty thought she was going to cry.

Colonel Oliver and Maria rose to go upstairs to supper, so the six of them rose to followed them in the order of their rank.

"Remember Kitty, you and Christian are to come to our house for tea on Thursday. We're entertaining all of the important people in Simla."

"What do the children do?"

"Mrs. Marshall has planned a puppet show for the children. Colin's invitation will arrive tomorrow morning along with yours. I just wanted you to know."

The next morning Christian left early to parade to mess with his regiment. It was not required of him, but he told Kitty it was necessary in order to maintain discipline among the Indian troops under his command. So Kitty and Colin were left alone until tea time.

When they sat down for breakfast together, Kitty asked, "Colin do you know the steps to the gavotte?"

"I learned them at dancing school." He looked up at her with distress, suddenly realizing why she was asking. "Oh, no! You wouldn't!"

"Oh, yes, I most certainly would. You've got to teach me. Now finish your breakfast quickly We have work to do before Saturday night, my little man."

"Do you mean we must practice the steps for five whole days?"

"You bet your sweet life we do, and if you can teach me before then, you may have a special treat. What would you like?"

"I'd like to go fishing with Father. Can you arrange it, Kitty?"

"If you can teach me the steps to the gavotte, I'll speak to him about it. That's the best I can do. Now, the music, I understand, is in three-quarter time. Let's get the tempo right and we will begin."

She went to the piano and began to play a waltz.

"Faster...faster...a little faster," Colin called from the dining room. "There. That is about right. It has to be done quickly. Would you like to begin slowly?"

Kitty shoved the furniture aside and began humming.

An hour later, she fell into a chair with a heavy sigh. "Do you think I will ever learn, Colin?"

"It would be easy if I were taller...or if you were my size."

"If I were your size, I'd not have to learn to do this. It's almost drill time at the post. Would you like to watch your father drill his men on their horses? It's quite exciting."

"Could we really?"

She had come to love the pageantry and horsemanship as the officers put their men through their paces. The band played, the banners flew, and the men sat erect and splendid on their mounts.

"You have earned a treat today. If we hurry we might not be too late for the drilling."

"Jolly good! You'll need your hat and coat and gloves. Don't forget the gloves this time, Kitty."

"Promise me one thing before we go. You'll not tell your father I'm learning the gavotte."

"You're going to surprise him? What fun!" Colin struggled into his coat and Kitty straightened a sleeve turned wrong side out.

"And surprise Colonel Oliver, too, I dare say, if I'm guessing correctly."

Azziz entered the front door of the cottage while Kitty was putting on her hat. He broke into a broad smile.

"Memsahib," he bowed and handed her two envelopes, one addressed to Captain and Mrs. Christian Skye and the other to Colin Skye.

"Our invitations, Colin." She smiled while he read his invitation to the puppet show and then looked up at her with his eyes glowing.

"It comes with the dropping of cards," she explained solemnly.

"Of course, my grandmother was quite strict about the cards," he said in a matter-of-fact tone of voice.

"Imagine that!"

By tea time the air had become soft and fragrant. Azziz undressed Christian when he returned and poured water over him in his bath while Kitty finished dressing.

"Kitty," he began, "Do you remember what happened at Lucknow? You mentioned a Sepoy revolt. Do you know the reason? Do you remember when it happened?"

"Please, not now." She was thinking of Azziz and wondered if he would ever turn against Christian one day.

"Azziz knows everything I do. He has been my bearer for thirteen years. You may speak freely with him." He relaxed and leaned back in the tub while Azziz lathered his dark hair.

"I can't remember all of it. The name Lucknow struck a chord in me. There was a siege. Dates were never my strong suit in history. It could have happened in the twentieth century. I'll never be able to pull a date out of the hat."

"There have been pockets of resistance among the Sepoys. There are some men among the English troops who insist on calling the natives unforgivable names in spite of everything we can do to discourage the practice. The Mussalman especially is hurt when he is addressed by an unacceptable title."

"Why do they insist on using names for them which demean them?" she asked.

"It is inevitable, but in spite of the fact that missionaries have tried to Christianize the Hindus, widows still fling themselves on their husband's funeral pyres. The Sepoys resist Christianity...and in the army we do not try to make them conform. We must lead our native troops with harsh discipline from time to time, however, to keep them from stepping out of line." Azziz rubbed him vigorously with the coarse linen towel.

"To keep them in their places. It won't work, Christian. They'll resent the role to which they have been relegated. The English came as conquerors and subjected the natives to their rule."

"My own troops will never mutiny...of that I am convinced, but in some regiments the officers rub their Indian troops raw in their efforts to force Christianity and harsh discipline upon them." He held his arms out for his shirt.

"One cannot force another to become a Christian. It comes with the Holy Spirit working from within," she argued.

"I know. I'm perfectly aware of that fact. And how did you spend the day, Kitty?"

"Colin and I trooped down through the bazaar and to a special point above the parade ground where we could watch you drilling your men. It was quite spectacular...the band playing...bugles blowing commands... flags flying...sabers flashing and all the while your horses performing beautifully."

"Performing beautifully is not the way it is done in battle, Kitty. We must maneuver swiftly and with precision, but that is not all there is to it. Remember what happened in the Crimea? Our losses were stunning, all because our men did not have sufficient food and clothing."

"There must be a better way than going to war."

"Men settle matters with fists and knives and bayonets and cannon, Kitty. It is the only way we have ever known to end disputes when it's all said and done. You know it is true... two world wars!" He was fully dressed, wearing the colors of his regiment proudly.

"You're beautiful, Christian Skye!" Her eyes grew dreamy.

"Watch it, girl! You're dressed for tea and time is growing short. Quit looking at me like that." He moved swiftly to grab her, but she was quick and side-stepped him.

"We could stroll through the town? It's a lovely sight."

They quickly fell into a routine...breakfast together, tea at four, changing for supper and going to the polo club...parties and outings for Colin with the other children at the foothills retreat.

By Saturday night a derzi had completed Kitty's new ball gown made up in rose with gold and silver threads and tiny crystal beadwork sewn on the silk fabric. Her slippers matched in a deeper shade of rose and her silk stockings were dyed to match. Allie had worked golden threads and beads into her hairpiece, and the effect of gold and beadwork created a shimmering effect. Kitty was pleased.

When she slid into the gown, Christian's voice thundered, "Maharanee, you're beautiful...the most beautiful woman I've ever seen."

"And you are my handsome prince! Do we dare go to the ball. I'll fall in love with you all over again."

He placed her fine woolen Kashmiri shawl around her shoulders and touched her lips lightly. "We'll go to the governor's ball in the carriage down below, but mind your manners."

"I feel like Cinderella. Must I leave promptly at midnight?"

"We'll dance till morning and then it's parade to church. "Tis a hard life, Kitty! Your dance card is already filled, thanks to Maria. I insisted on every other dance or I'd leave the regiment and take you back to England."

"You wouldn't!"

"No, Kitty. I'll not go back till I'm ready to retire...years from now."

The ball room and rooms adjoining it at the Governor's house had been converted into a fairyland, Kitty discovered when they arrived. Chandeliers shone brightly, and the ballroom floor glistened. On the dias the governor and his wife were splendid in white and dashes of red and blue sashing.

Christian introduced Kitty to the officers and their wives, the ones she had not yet met, those with whom he had seen service in the war against the Sikhs in the Northwest and those with whom he had served on cantonments up and down the Grand Trunk Road. He had done duty with Major Addison in the far Northwest at Peshawar near the Afghanistan border and with Lt. Brown at Dum Dum Cantonment outside Calcutta. When she looked about her at the grand array of ball gowns and men dressed in formal attire with white ties and colorful sashes, she suddenly realized that there was not a native officer present.

The orchestra was hidden behind ornamental shrubbery and flowers, and precisely at eight o'clock they signaled the beginning of the ball by playing the introduction for the quadrille. The governor and his wife stepped from the dias to the center of the floor. Sets formed and Kitty at once found herself going through the unfamiliar formal dance routine.

When she and Christian came together, he whispered, "Remember the Gavotte."

When the quadrille ended, the partners promenaded slowly around the room while waiting for a lively English country dance to begin. Thomas Milford bowed and Kitty curtsied.

"What dance is this?" she asked when the music began.

"It's Scottish, from up near the border. Would you like refreshments?"

"Yes, if you will please lead the way. Old Oliver is on my card next. I'm scared half to death."

"He'll limber up after a few drinks and will be ready for the most exciting dance of the evening."

He held out his arm to her, and they went to a room off the dance floor where the tables groaned with assorted drinks, various ices, cakes, turkey, ham, and tiny sandwiches.

"A glass of punch for me, Tom." She laughed. "Perhaps something stronger would better brace me for the gavotte with Colonel Oliver, but then I'd simply fall on my face."

Tom Milford poured from the punch bowl and said, "Here's to you, Kitty," and downed his drink. She swallowed hers slowly and waited for the tension which had gripped her to fall away.

"I haven't eaten since tea time."

"Better eat some ham and a sandwich, Kitty."

When they returned to the ballroom, they followed the other couples around the room until they reached the dias where Colonel Oliver waited. Oliver bowed to her and she returned his bow with a curtsey, grateful that her knees didn't crack.

She was shocked when the music began, for he led her into the gavotte with great speed and vigor.

Midway through the dance, she found herself enjoying the gavotte immensely, and when it was over, Colonel Oliver smiled and said, "Christian said you didn't know how to dance the gavotte. He was mistaken." He held out his arm, and then he remembered he had forgotten to introduce her to his Excellency. They walked slowly around the room, following the couples ahead of them until they reached the dias.

"Your excellencies, may I present Mrs. Christian Skye." The next moment a drop of hot candle wax fell on his bare head, and he cried out, "What the . . .!

He reached for the top of his head, and Kitty saw Christian coming to claim her for the next dance.

Then she was in Christian's arms, looking up into his eyes and watching the golden flecks dance with delight. He didn't hold her close during the waltz, but he threatened her. " Kitty. I can't believe what you just did." All the while he smiled, and she saw the red in his hair glistening beneath the chandeliers while they waltzed about the room.

At three in the morning the ball was over. She had waltzed fifteen times. She had danced the galop and the polka more times than she could count and had surprised Christian by dancing the gavotte.

Returning in the carriage with the Milfords, Christian roared, "All right, Kitty. Who taught you the gavotte?"

"Well, you see it's like this. Colin would like for you to take him fishing in one of those mountain streams, and I wanted to learn the dance. We struck a deal. I'd ask you to consider a picnic and fishing trip if he would teach me to do the dance. He really got a raw deal out of it, I'm thinking."

Tom slapped his legs and began to laugh. "You've a smart wife, old boy!"

Christian drew Kitty into his arms, and said, "Can you imagine six times around?"

"You didn't kiss!" Maggie cried out in a shocked voice.

"No," Christian drawled, "We wouldn't have gone that far." He gave Kitty a little squeeze.

Again Kitty felt herself trying to adjust to the fact that Maggie Milford was a modest Victorian woman who had never been kissed until Tom proposed. She then remembered that marriages were arranged between Indian families when she was in India with her parents. Their guide had refused to marry the young woman who had been chosen for him. She had been covered from head to toe the first time he saw her, and because her bare feet were too dark, he refused to marry her.

Christian began laughing and Kitty asked, "What now, Captain Skye?"

"I was just thinking how my household is conspiring against me. A man doesn't have a chance! By the way, Kitty, did Colonel Oliver ask you to call him Lionel?"

"But, of course."

"And you did?"

"I almost called him 'Lionel Train'."

Maggie asked, "Whatever gave you that idea?"

"Just a little secret Christian and I laugh about, something from my far and distant past."

"I asked Kitty about the Sepoy mutiny again, Tom. Perhaps it won't come in our lifetimes, but all the same I am going to warn Colonel Oliver."

CHAPTER THIRTEEN

Kitty and her parents had visited the Woodstock School at the hill station of Mussoorie during the seventies. At that time it had become a private Christian international school, and Kitty knew with the certainty of a sixteen year old that she'd return to teach there one day. Only forty miles from the Chinese border, Mussoorie, like Simla, provided a delightful respite from the heat below on the Ganges River Plain. There the red dirt swirled, and the heat of midsummer rose like a furnace.

In spite of the fact that Christian was determined to send the boy back to England to finish his education, Kitty was reluctant to part with him. True, the boy tormented her unmercifully, but by the first of September she had to admit she cared deeply for the child. To send him back now would leave a void in her life she had never thought possible. Perhaps there was an English school in India where he could finish his education.

"It is the way things are done," Caroline Bradley told her. She was returning to England with her children, and did not change expressions when she said, "Charles and I knew when I came out to India to marry him that I'd return to see that the children are educated properly. You'll understand when your time comes. Besides, we are together only a few months of the year, all told. The children are too young to put away in boarding school, and we cannot simply let them grow up in this heathen country. Separation is unavoidable. I'll write often and Charles will work hard for a promotion while we're apart. He has a leave coming in two years, and he'll come to England to be with us then. God has prepared me for this."

Kitty could not believe Caroline would leave her husband for years, but she learned that Maria Oliver's son Robert was graduating from

Addiscombe and would be coming to India in October. Maria had returned to England for twelve years in order to see that her children were educated properly. Now, their youngest was graduating with honors and was preparing to join his father in India,

Maggie and Tom Milford's children were young. She would leave India, she told Kitty, when her oldest child Warren was ready for school.

All around her the story was the same, and the wives faced the separations with apparent stoicism. Kitty wondered silently if the women had simply endured their lives with their husbands because duty demanded it of them and because it was the thing that was done. She could not bear to think of years without Christian.

Then it was time to leave Simla. Winter came early in the hill country, and Kitty found herself preparing for the long journey down to Lucknow. The friends she had made were going different ways--Caroline Bradley back to England, Maggie Milford to the Dum Dum cantonment outside Calcutta, Elizabeth Smith to Peshawar, and Martha Tuttle to Cawnpore. Kitty had played Housey-Housey, a game similar to Bingo, with them all summer. Together they had gone on picnics and explored the twisted mountain trails with their children. Now, it was time to part, and for the first time since Kitty had returned to India, she realized how alone Christian must have been when his regiment split up with continuous promotions and separations. He knew acquaintances all up and down the Grand Trunk Road. At Lucknow he'd find old friends again, and they'd play polo and cricket. Then they'd all go to the club for supper and dancing afterward.

Azziz had packed Christian's clothes, but he insisted on packing the purchases he had made in Simla. "There is a dullness to life in the barracks, Kitty, that drives the troops mad. Young men can't afford to marry, and they spend endless hours with nothing to do but stare at the walls when they are not on duty." Christian tried to explain to her how the only space a private or a corporal had to call his own was around his bed. His trunk held his sole possessions, the most precious were the letters from home. The best he could hope for was a promotion. Those came slowly.

Kitty watched him moving, noticing his supple movements and reveling in the sound of his voice.

"The fishing fleet will be in when we reach Lucknow," he told her.

"The unmarried officers will have their pick of the young ladies. The ones who marry will find companionship for a season, then when the children are older, they must pack up and go back to England, the loneliness will begin all over again."

"Do all men send their families off to England?" She turned to him with shock written on her face.

"It is the way things have to be done. It is the rules of the game unless they have married Indian women as some have chosen to do. Then one forgets how dark they are, and you must admit Indian women are very beautiful," he told her while he packed the morocco bound volumes of Shakespeare.

"Christian Skye! If I didn't know better, I'd think you were a twentieth century man for all your Victorian ways. Men the world over have always been the same when it comes to women, I'm thinking."

"You will have your admirer with us at Lucknow, Kitty." His eyes teased her, while he put the lid on the box and began to bind it with a heavy water-resistant paper coated with wax.

"Which one?" she laughed.

"I'll be under Oliver's command again. They are accompanying us as we travel there."

"And Maria will be pulling her rank on me all the way." Kitty didn't know whether to be pleased about it or not. Maria had her faults, but she seldom displayed them publicly.

"Will Maria approve of the split skirts I had my derzi make for me so I can straddle my pony?"

"'It will be a long, hard ride. It makes sense to prepare for it in a sensible manner. Besides, I can't see you sitting prim and ladylike in a sidesaddle over four hundred miles down to Lucknow."

"It's not the way I learned to ride. For once I'm going to forget that this is the nineteenth century."

When it came time for the Bradley's to part, Kitty saw Caroline's stoic facade break. Tears rolled down her cheeks when she and her children set off with a party heading down to Delhi to begin the long journey back to England. She knew Caroline was fond of Charles and wondered secretly how they could bear to be separated so long.

"Be of good cheer, Caroline," Charles told her. "It won't be long till I get my leave. Before you know it, I'll be in England. Tell my parents not to worry about me. Now be a good, brave girl." He kissed her lightly on her cheek, and Kitty waved to her as the group of travelers going down the mountain trail moved away. Caroline gathered her children to her and waved bravely.

The contingent of travelers going to Lucknow was considerably larger than the small party with whom Caroline traveled down to Delhi. Each officer had from four to twelve servants, and the baggage train alone would reach several miles in length, Christian had told her. Her colorful rugs, brass, and china had been packed and were being taken along, but she had to leave the piano behind. She had enjoyed singing and playing for Christian and Colin while they played Cribbage or Beggar my Neighbor. Perhaps they would find another piano someone in Lucknow had to leave behind.

Christian thought Colin should accompany Caroline and the children back to England, but Kitty convinced him that Colin should stay with them at least until the Return Empties went back to England before the hot weather set in again. To be quite truthful, she could not bear to part with the child who had come into their lives. She realized, too, that Christian had grown fond of Colin, and she suspected that he no longer reminded him of Emma.

So, she and Colin would ride behind the troops but ahead of the baggage wagons, bearers, and foot artillery. Christian had purchased the two ponies with polo in mind, and Colin had quickly learned to handle his chestnut pony with ease. Kitty was pleased when Christian noticed and praised his ability to handle his pony so well.

"How many days will it take to reach Lucknow?" Colin asked her when he turned his pony over to the groom at the stable.

"A month...maybe more. It will still be hot when we reach the plains, I'm afraid." She ran her hand over her black pony she named "Zorro."

Colin watched the groom lead his pony away. He turned to her. "I think I shall call my pony 'India.' Her coat matches the dust of India."

"A splendid choice," Kitty told him.

"Will Father be with us all the way?"

"He'd better be with us, or we'll get lost."

"It will be a jolly good outing then, Kitty."

"Yes, it will be a jolly good outing."

That evening Christian put away the game earlier than usual. " 'Twill be hot on the plains, Colin. Do you think a fine English lad like you can take the heat and dust?"

"Will I get to ride India all the way?"

"Afraid so, trooper. Now, it's off to bed with you. We'll be up before sunrise in the morning. 'Twill be a long, hard day on the road."

"Just a while longer, Father," Colin pleaded.

"That, son, was an order. I'll wake you at four o'clock, and you'll have to step lively if you're leaving with the artillery."

"Nice try, Colin. Better luck next time," Kitty laughed.

When they were alone, Christian sighed. "Ahhhh, Kitty! You've brought such pleasure and contentment into my life. Soldiering has never been so good. You've spoiled me." He took her hand and kissed it.

"I keep thinking about Caroline and the other women returning to England."

"Aye, 'tis sad, the partings. Poor old Smith is being sent to Peshawar. 'Tis a miserable, unhealthy place where European and native troops are all crowded in together so that the station will not be vulnerable to attack from the Afridis and other robber tribes from the mountains of Afghanistan. His wife will have to spend her summers at hill stations. Tom Milford's not happy about being stationed at Dum Dum...too large and an old cantonment. At least Charlie is going with us to Lucknow. We do get on well."

"You're planning ahead...worrying about whether Colin and I can make the long journey down along the Grand Trunk Road at the end of summer...afraid I'll not be content to spend summers at Lucknow with you, but I'll tell you this, Captain Skye, where you go, there I go, also. All I ask is to wake up each morning and know you are there."

"Aye, Kitty."

"The girls in the fishing fleet are going to be terribly disappointed when they arrive at Lucknow this year."

"How so, my love?" Christian asked as he drew her into his arms.

"Why, the prize they dreamed of catching has been caught." She kissed him lightly.

"Aye, 'twill be a great disappointment, 'tis true. The girls will all be returned empties when they discover Old Skye has been bewitched and has left the fish market without so much as a glance to look the catch over. When word gets out, they may not even come out to India this year."

"Conceited idiot!" she laughed.

"You'll pay for that remark, Milady!"

A chill wind crossed the mountains as Kitty mounted her pony in the early gray of morning. Wrapped in woolens against the cold, she lifted her eyes upward, but the early morning hid the mountains in a dense fog. The snow scapes wore gray veils and the twisted trail with sheer drop-offs waited beneath her.

She looked ahead of her where Colin's pony pawed the earth, eager to be off. The boy, cradled in innocence and knowing no fear, had no idea what lay ahead. His eyes danced with anticipation.

Colonel Oliver galloped alongside and called to her, "All set, Kitty?"

She smiled and raised her hand. He went on down the line calling out orders. Suddenly, the horses ahead of Colin began their descent from Simla, and Kitty nudged Zorro forward. Buffeted by a cold wind blowing in from the mountains, the train of animals and men on foot moved slowly along the twisting trail.

When the horses ahead of Colin stopped and pulled off the road into a clearing, the sun came out, and Kitty gazed below her on a scene of such incredible beauty it took her breath away. Wild and empty, the mountains below melted into grassy hills. Low-lying clouds floated below them on the landscape, and in the distance a serpentine river, shrouded in trees, twisted and turned.

The beesties hurried off to carry water, and someone started a fire.

She dismounted and joined Maria and the other women in the party who sought the seclusion of the trees and bushes alongside the trail.

Christian joined Kitty and Colin under the spreading trees for the noon-time meal. At nightfall they camped along the trail with their cots set up in tents alongside their traveling companions...the women and men in separate campsites. Although she was weary after riding all day, she longed to have Christian near her, but he explained that it was necessary for him to sleep with his men to maintain discipline.

And so it was that they fell into a routine, steady travel during the mornings, a period of rest at noon time, and sleeping under tents after the evening meal. Five days later they arrived at Meerut with the dust of five thousand summers swirling around them and the heat of late summer rising up to hit them in their faces.

Colonel Oliver had wired ahead for quarters for Christian and Kitty at Meerut, and when Kitty fell into a tub of lukewarm water at the end of the day, she sighed, "This is pure heaven!"

"You've done well, Kitty," Christian told her.

"We've only begun."

"Aye, 'twill get no easier now that we're picking up a full detail of Indian stable helpers, grooms, and grass cutters who will forage for the animals. We'll have to travel slower with so many to slow the march. The days will be hot, but perhaps the nights will be cooler in a few days."

"Will Colin be all right with Charles and Azziz? I feel guilty sleeping in a real bed with a mosquito netting."

"He'll be fine. The lad has spunk, I have to hand it to him."

"He was so pleased when you invited him to ride at your side when we entered Meerut."

"You think so, Kitty?" He poured water over her head and she rubbed soap into her dirt-caked hair.

"Couldn't you tell? More water, please."

"I thought he might like to ride at the head of the column," he laughed deeply.

Kitty realized that he was glad she approved of his thoughtfulness.

She shook her hair and stood up in the tub. "Your turn, Christian. I feel almost human again."

"And your looks have improved greatly, I might add, but then I have always loved you even when you're covered with the dirt of travel."

She stepped out of the tub and told him. "Your turn."

His deep rumbling laughter told her what she was longing to hear. Five days in the constant company of others without as much as a simple touch from Christian. She had wanted more than anything at the end of the long, tiring days, to crawl into his arms to rest, but he had slept with his men, and she with the women in a tent together.

She poured water over him, rubbed his back, and washed the red dirt from his hair.

"I do believe my man is under there somewhere," she teased.

"Were you expecting to find someone else perhaps?"

"Funny man. No wonder I love you so."

Later, after they dined and danced at the polo club at Meerut, she lay awake in his arms.

"You're not sleeping, Love," he said.

"I'm remembering...remembering my loneliness before I returned to India and found you. I had searched everywhere for you. How did it happen, Christian? Will I suddenly be snatched away again? It is the thing I dread most of all."

"Maharanee...oh, my sweet Maharanee...don't even think it. 'Twould be the end of me to lose you!"

"Hold me, Christian. Never let me go!" A sob broke from her throat and his lips claimed hers with a fierceness that told her he'd been haunted by the same thoughts as she.

CHAPTER FOURTEEN

They set out from Meerut before daybreak the following day in order to travel during the relative cool of the morning. By mid-day the poisonous dust of the plains swirled around them. Parched fields and the ever-present herds and those who peopled the river valley and tried desperately to eke out a living there stared while the military train rolled along the Grand Trunk Road through India. It was not a new sight to the people of the villages. The British had built the road and had run the telegraph lines, but they continued to stare while small boys dashed among the cattle to rescue their dung in order to fashion it into cow patties for their fires.

By mid-morning the ground shimmered with heat, creating an optical illusion, and the relentless dust rose into the air choking their lungs and caking their faces and burning their eyes. Those who lived in red, mud and cow-dung plastered houses with floors of glazed cattle urine, had nothing but one community well from which the women carried water on their heads in huge, brass containers. Here the sun blazed for a full six months year after year, and when winter ended the monsoon and floods which often covered their simple homes inundated their houses.

Kitty and her parents had flown from Calcutta to New Delhi when the rivers were flooding in July. Entire villages lay under water with only the rooftops of the mud bricked village houses reaching for air above the water of rain-swollen rivers. They had wondered then what had happened to those who lived below where miles and miles of water spread over the land in every direction. Now, she knew, the monsoon had ended and the dry season had returned. The rivers had returned to their courses. The people returned to their houses and began all over again.

By noon of the sixth day, Colin's fair skin had turned the color of the red earth. If he ever regretted not returning to England with Caroline Bradley and her children, Kitty never knew of it. Tired, thirsty, hungry, with tiny sweat droplets trickling down his dust-choked cheeks, he shrugged off his weariness the moment Christian threw himself on the mat with them when the column paused to rest.

Christian's eyes sought Kitty's at once, "You all right?" He poured water over Colin's head and gave him a playful slap. "We'll rest awhile then push on toward Aligarh. Have you ever tasted fresh coconut milk, Colin?"

Kitty tried to smile through her weariness while Christian tapped a coconut he had bought from a boy along the route. He poured the milk into a cup and they drank it. Then Christian cut off slivers of the hard meat for them to eat. The grooms watered the horses and ponies while all around them their cutters searched for dry grass to cut for the horses and ponies.

Someone screamed when the makeshift tent next to theirs was unrolled, and Kitty saw Maria Oliver standing in the hot sun, her body shaking visibly.

Christian rushed to see what the commotion was all about, and when he returned, he explained, "A krait made its bed in their tent-roll overnight."

"It's the most deadly snake in all India!" Kitty cried.

"True, but the men killed it straightway. Poor Maria was frightened out of her wits."

"May I see the krait, Father?" Colin asked.

"It's a small thing. Come, we'll see if they've carried it off.."

Kitty threw her pith helmet upon the ground and fell beside it. While she watched a peasant plowing his rice field in the distance, Azziz brought her a bowl of mulligatowny, a spicy soup no one had bothered to heat, but she shrugged it away.

When Colin and Christian returned, Colin told her, " 'Twas no longer than a foot and all red and black and cream colored. Such a pretty thing!"

"And deadly. Don't forget that, my boy," Christian reminded him.

Kitty closed her eyes and leaned back against the pole holding their tent above them, listening while Christian patiently explained about the dangers of cobras and scorpions and kraits to Colin. She was awakened by the cry of a peacock. She'd been dreaming and the cry, so like a baby, startled her into consciousness. Colin had fallen asleep, and Christian studied a map.

She heard a young boy whistle to his water buffalo while he drove them toward the river to cool their great bodies in the water.

Then, sooner than she would have liked, Christian rose and helped her to her feet. "Time to go, Ranee. Can't believe you're so pretty...all dusty and growing as dark as a Dravidian."

"I'll be a withered old prune when we reach Lucknow."

"We'll be camping beneath the stars for the next three nights, and then we'll stay in fine quarters at Aligarh and at Fategarh."

"Air conditioning, Christian? Running hot and cold water and showers?" she asked hopefully.

"Not yet, Kitty. You've been spoiled too long. Why I'll wager your Mustang was even cooled."

"Indeed it was!" She saw Zorro waiting patiently for her.

"And next you'll be telling me you would make this entire trip in a day's time."

"Absolutely. Once my parents and I left Denver in the Rocky Mountains at daybreak on the sixth day of July and drove across the parched country. We arrived at home before sunset...a trip of just over four hundred miles through a Kansas heat wave without once feeling the heat. Want to know the truth of it? I'd not exchange one second of this miserable, dirty, back-breaking, heat-filled journey with you beside me at the end of it at Aligarh for that one day of racing through Kansas."

"The heat has affected your brain, Ranee. There's no doubt of it." His eyes smiled into hers, and she wiped the dust from the crease in his chin.

"Just daft over one tall, old soldier with a superb body and eyes that tell me he is mine."

He put his map into his bag along with his orders, and kissed her quickly. "Aligarh," he whispered and then mounted and rode away to the head of the column of the mounted Horse Artillery.

She and Colin mounted their ponies and waited for the horses ahead of them to begin moving forward. Behind them the bullock carts carried their tent and supplies and the men and boys raced along on bare feet when the column moved out. Yet, she knew when they pulled up to camp for the night, the tents would arise as though by a miracle from the dust-laden trail, and Allie would be there to lay out her light gown for the night, and her fresh divided skirt and blouse would be there the next day. By some magic the khas tutti, a screen of grass matting would appear to provide a flooring for the rope beds and bedding rolls. Colin would spend the night in the men's camp, and there would be hopeless giggling and chattering among the women about the krait in Maria's tent until she fell asleep with the mosquito netting forming a cage around her. The stars above them would appear so close after the dust settled, she could almost reach up and touch them. Then the night smells of animals and people and cow dung fires and incense would filter into her senses. The sounds of India would be around her, and she'd fall asleep quickly, knowing Christian and Colin were safe in the men's camp along the Grand Trunk Road.

That afternoon they met a long caravan of camels traveling toward the northwest. The animals plodded along slowly, carrying goods to Delhi. Withered women draped in black and wearing dangling gold bracelets and earrings led the animals while the men and children drove goats along behind them. The women smiled and shouted greetings, and the children came to her crying, "Baksheeh!"

After three days of travel, a cool wind blew across the plains like a benediction upon the weary travelers. Her pony picked up his ears and snorted, and Colin ahead of her turned and raised his hand. She let out an old yell from her girlhood days, "Yahoooo!" and Colin returned it. Maria gave them a look of disapproval, but Kitty only smiled.

As they neared Aligarh, a mass of humanity and animals filled the road leading into the city. The villages of the countryside they had passed through that day gave way to throngs of people. Merchants in the bazaar reminded Kitty of her mother's shopping expeditions throughout India in the seventies, and a deep melancholy filled her. Since she had found Christian her life had been too full to think of her parents except during moments when a forgotten memory stole into her. Then it all came rushing back and flooded over her. The pain of their deaths returned again, and for the first time in many months she accepted the way things were, grateful for whatever force it had been which returned her to an India her parents had never known. As the horses ahead of Colin continued to march smartly through the crowded city to a destination she could not know, she thought about her past and how she had never taken time to consider the why of her existence until this moment. For the first time she was not working at some task, striving to achieve impossible goals. From an early age she had been driven by a competitive spirit to succeed, to be at the head of her classes in school, to be the valedictorian when she was graduated, to earn a scholarship, to win honors while other girls her age were thinking of marriage. She had not taken time to discover why it was she worked so hard to succeed but had been driven by ambition throughout her college days...to graduate summa cum laude...to go on to graduate school and to finish law school at the top of her class. Then she had gone to work with the same frantic ambition, succeeding...always winning...never losing. Never losing until Luke Filbey told her, "I'm moving out, Kitty."

In that moment she knew all her discipline and hard work had gained her nothing...not love...not peace of mind...not even a sense of accomplishment. The missing factor that would make her life worth living had never shown itself to her. The flow of adrenalin which had kept her going had left her.

Now, Kitty had found the spark that made her existence worthwhile. She had discovered something she had only dreamed about...a dream, stolen out of time. This night in Aligarh, she'd lie in Christian's arms, and they'd talk far into the night. What she had been striving for all her lifetime...another whose soul matched hers completely was beside her. Am I living on the edge of borrowed time? Oh no, God! Please, don't take me back. There's nothing for me there.

CHAPTER FIFTEEN

*K*itty felt the masses crowding in on the military company moving through Aligarh. A small child, barely able to walk, wandered along the crowded street, holding out her hand and crying, "Baksheeh."

She considered her own mother then. Louise Kincaide had graduated at the head of her class, and during World War II she worked in a munitions plant and saved her money to go to college to study math and physics and art. When the war ended, she enrolled at the University of Kansas and was well into her junior year when she met Richard Farrell. It was love at first sight, and Louise Kincaide tossed it all away to marry, move to the Flint Hills near Junction City, Kansas, and became a full-time housewife.

Kitty, during her teen years, truthfully believed that her charming father was brighter and far more intelligent than her mother. Although her mother later finished her degree and began teaching algebra and geometry at the local high school where Kitty later was graduated with honors, it was Mr. Carson who taught the tougher classes...trigonometry, calculus, and physics. It wasn't until much later that Kitty was hit with the realization that her mother could have taught circles around dull Mr. Carson--with her eyes closed...could have taught in the university, except for her second class status...a married woman whose husband taught history and coached the football team at the local high school. Mr. Carson coached basketball and for his ineptness in the classroom he was paid a higher salary than Louise Farrell who prepared her students well for the advanced courses.

Kitty stumbled upon the fact that her mother quietly went about making Richard Farrell the star-performer in their family. He was well-known in his home town...had been the captain of his football squad in high school, a fair student, and one of the heroes who came home after World War II was over. Truth was, Kitty admitted later, he did not distinguish himself during the war. Discharged with the rank of corporal, he went on to college on the G. I. Bill and moved on to teach in the same high school from which he graduated in 1942.

Dick Farrell became one of the "good old boys" of the town. He loved to talk sports, hunted pheasant and quail, fished the lakes of Kansas, and played poker once a week with his cronies. He actually had little ambition, but he enjoyed life and adored Louise and his daughter Kitty.

It was Louise Farrell who read the professional journals and kept his career on track. It was she, Kitty remembered later, who had proposed that Richard apply for the grant to study in India for a year, and it had been Louise Farrell who wrote his application for the Fulbright fellowship and typed it out on her old portable Royal. She asked nothing for herself. That, Kitty could not understand.

So Kitty had fought against the possibility that she'd fall into the same trap, and she had succeeded. That is, she had almost made it work until she suddenly became aware that she had missed out on one of the greatest of all adventures, loving the one for whom she had been destined. Life with Luke Filbey held no joy. The acquisition of fine antiques, a beautiful apartment, a boat, the cabin in the mountains, and two cars meant nothing. She would have grown old with only her hollow victories to warm her memories.

Now, she understood...had come to understand why her mother had sought nothing for herself except the pleasure and joy Richard Farrell brought into her life. They had been totally devoted to each other, and when Louise Farrell lay dying, Richard, too, began to die. She should have seen it coming.

"Kitty, dear," Louise Farrell said before she died, "I know you will finish the novel I have started, but I had hoped you would find happiness... the real happiness I have known."

"Oh, Mom, that kind of happiness doesn't exist in the world today. Men are totally ignorant of really loving."

"You must search for it, honey...it is there...somewhere...you must reach out for it. I promise you God intends for you to find it."

Remembering her mother, Kitty's eyes filled with tears, blurring the image of Colin ahead of her. She let her tears for her mother fall freely.

Her tears flooded down her cheeks, but she didn't brush them away.

She felt them cleansing her heart...washing away the guilt and grief she had pushed into the back of her mind...the joy for the woman she had become. At once she felt closer to her mother than she had ever been when Louise Farrell lived. Peace and acceptance filled her. She knew her face had turned red and splotchy with her tears racing through the dust on her face. Her nose turned red like it always did when she cried, and her eyes burned. She had no handkerchief, so she bent over, blew her nose between her fingers and pinched it off as she had seen her father do when they were out in the fields.

The noise she made startled Colin, and he turned in his saddle ahead of her. When he saw her crying, he fell back beside her.

"What is it, Mum? Why do you cry?"

It was the first time he had used the endearing term...had always called her "Kitty", and it touched her heart.

She tried to smile. "I cry sometimes when I'm very happy."

Later when she and Colin were alone with their luggage while Christian made arrangements for their rooms at the hotel, Colin took her hand and said, "Why were you happy, Mum?"

"Because I love you and Christian so much...and..." Her voice broke and she felt very close to tears again.

"And?"

"My mother wanted me to find the happiness I've found, and she died without knowing."

"I wonder if my mother wanted me to be happy?" He turned his innocent, blue eyes to her. His hair was bleached out, and his face had turned ever darker.

She put her arm around him and drew him close. She could feel his frail body melt against her, could smell the dirt of his body, and then kissed the top of his head.

"Our mothers must know how happy we are or heaven would be a very sad place."

She looked up and saw Christian smiling when he came toward them. "And what are you two conspiring about this time?" he laughed.

"Just reminding each other how happy we are to be here with you."

"Well, now, that makes three of us...all three of us, dirty and tired and hungry and happy. We'll stay here until my regiment from Lucknow joins us. Time enough to get our clothes laundered and ironed. The remainder of the journey will go quickly."

"Smashing!" Colin cried.

"You'll be in Charles Bradley's room down the hall, Colin. Change into something clean and respectable, and you can go to supper with us later."

Charles joined them and said, "Come along, son. You're getting a good bath and a change of clothes." He looked over Colin's head and winked at Christian.

Azziz had prepared their baths and Allie had laid out her last clean dress for the evening. Christian dismissed them, and at last Kitty sighed. They were alone. Laughing together, they fell into each other's arms on the bed.

"I never thought I'd be happy with a woman who had a dirty face!" Christian chuckled. "Or one whose tears had streaked her cheeks." His kiss sought hers. "I want to know about the tears, Ranee," he told her. "You're not sorry?"

"One has time to think while riding along. I have nothing to be sorry about. You've given me much to live for."

"I think of you, wonder what you're dreaming. I think about holding you in my arms. Are you sure you're not sorry you came?"

"Never! My tears were for my mother...suddenly understanding through my own life why she was happy and wished the same happiness for me. I never knew until I met you what it was to love. The empty longing is not there now. My mother's life is repeating itself through me, and I've accepted the fact of her death at last. Then Colin called me 'Mum' and I cried again. No one has ever been so richly blessed."

"I was afraid you had suddenly realized what a poor piece of dirt you married. That would indeed bring on a flood." He nuzzled her neck softly.

"You're lying, Christian Skye. You know very well that this moment is all I live for! Why else would I ride that stupid animal for four hundred miles from Simla to Lucknow?"

"You're too easily satisfied, but I never knew it could be like this... loving you like I do."

They fell asleep full of contentment, and when Kitty awoke, it was dark, so she slipped out of Christian's arms and bathed, letting the lukewarm water soothe her tired body. She had come to terms with her life and had no regrets.

When they left their room to join Charles and Colin, Christian paused and drew her into his arms. "Luke Filbey was a fool."

"Of course, he was a fool," she laughed, wondering what had prompted him to mention Luke.

"And I almost let him make a fool out of me!" Christian exploded.

"And I was so angry about that...ready to toss in the towel and go home."

"You very well couldn't have done that." His eyes blazed into hers.

"And why couldn't I?" she challenged

"Because I loved you so much. That's why!"

Kitty doubled over with laughter and Christian laughed with her. They were still laughing when Colin opened the door and stared at them.

Charles stepped up behind Colin and put his hand on his shoulder and said, "They're just a couple of crazy fools, son!"

The remainder of the journey toward Lucknow passed uneventfully and quickly as Christian had promised. When they arrived, Christian insisted that he and Kitty live in one of the cottages instead of at the Registry where other officers and their wives lived. The cottage walls had been draped with linen and the floors were covered with slick floor cloths. Kitty knew, at once, she had to get to work in order to make their first real home a respectable place in which to live. While men from the town plastered the walls, she and Colin went into the bazaar within the cantonment searching for furnishings--beds, wardrobes for their clothing, a wicker sofa with brightly colored cushions and deep comfortable chairs, a Queen Anne dining room table with chairs and a china cabinet to match. When the walls of the cottage had been freshly white-washed the next day, she hung bright curtains at the windows, spread out the rugs and bedspreads she had brought with her from Kashmir, and filled the cabinet with blue and white Staffordshire pieces. Last of all she and Colin filled her big brass jugs with freshly-cut flowers and stood back to admire their work.

"How does it look, Colin. Will your father be pleased?"

"There's only one thing missing, Mum," he told her.

"What is that?"

"The piano."

"Perhaps I should have bought the guitar, you know, the Asian one with the long neck. I can learn to play it and sing for you."

"Could you teach me to play?"

His blue eyes sought hers, and she hugged him. "I'd love to teach you to play it, but we must begin serious classes at once. We have work to do, my lad. I have no intention of sending you back to boarding school in the springtime like an ignorant ninny."

"Do you mean I will have a tutor?"

"No, Colin. I'd not trust anyone else to teach you. We'll begin your lessons at once, and you'll soon learn that I'm without mercy when it comes to your education."

"Do you mean it, Mum? You will teach me yourself?"

"And why not, my dear boy? I'm not totally illiterate, and I can teach you things your other teachers have never dreamed possible."

"Things not in books, Kitty? Things you learned when you lived in America?"

It was as close as she had come to telling Colin about herself and how she came to be in India in 1856...as close as she would ever come to telling him that he would die long before the year she was born. In spite of everything, she suspected that he knew she was special in a way he couldn't understand, in the same sense that Lionel Oliver knew.

When she thought about Colonel Oliver, she wondered if he had purposely appointed Christian to oversee the judicial matters in the province of Oudh. That position meant that he would often be traveling about the countryside to listen to complaints and to settle disputes among the native farmers. He knew Kitty would not permit Christian to leave her behind, that she would sit beside him under banyan trees and under improvised shelters while Christian handed down his verdicts.

Sometimes she caught Colonel Oliver watching her strangely. Did he suspect?

After they had been at Lucknow Cantonment for two weeks, she asked Christian, "And what are we to do about Colin while we are jaunting about the countryside hearing cases?"

"Is there any reason why he can't accompany us? 'Twill do him good to get a feel for the countryside...to learn history and court procedures first hand. He can take his books along and while we're hearing weary complaints, he can study."

"I was hoping you would suggest that." She kissed him lightly on the cheek.

"We'll live in the tents while we're knocking about in the countryside. 'Twill be fine to have you with me, Ranee."

"And what about sleeping arrangements?" She slipped into his arms and ran her hands up and down his back.

"Whatever made you think of that?" He chuckled deep and kissed her a quick peck on her cheek as he often did when they discussed important matters that concerned themselves. "Colin will sleep in the tent with Azziz and our new cook.".

"You're anxious to be working again," she said.

"Aye. You know me well." The amber flecks in his eyes shone brightly in the lamplight in their room.

"As well as I know myself," she said.

"Aye, Kitty. 'Tis a constant wonder to me."

"There's magic in our love, Captain Skye. Do you feel it?"

"Aye, Kitty,, my love," Christian moaned. "My own Maharanee. What did I ever do to deserve our love?"

"We must have done something wondrously well in another lifetime, my darling," she said dreamily. "Do you realize that you are the only person I have ever known to whom I can say anything, and you don't think it's foolishness. 'Tis marvelous! I love every part of you ...your body and mind...so beautifully made."

"Ah, my Maharanee...you've reached into my soul, you know. We have no secrets between us...nothing that can ever part us. We are one... one body in our minds and souls possessing each other. I think I knew all along, all those lonely years, that you would find me one day...one in body and spirit...as God intended us to be. Do you remember our first kiss?" He propped his hand under his chin and looked down at her in the moonlight.

"It was like an electric current shooting through me."

"It was the scent of you there in the hot office with your tears falling. I knew it at once. It fair drove me crazy till I had you in my arms."

"But after we were wed, you never touched me again," she murmured and half-closed her eyes.

"Wanted nothing between us...I went wild to think you might have loved others the way I loved you. When you told me you were leaving, I knew then it didn't matter. I knew...I knew there had never been anyone like the two of us together."

His lips possessed hers before she could tell him how foolish he had been. He smelled of smoke and musk and India...the scent of him she knew so well.

Chapter Sixteen

Throughout the month of October, Christian and Kitty traveled from village to village in the province of Oudh. Colin took along his books, his pens, paper, and inkhorn in order to continue his studies. When Christian suggested that Colin enter the school in Lucknow, Kitty objected fiercely, saying, "La Martiniere may be the finest school in India, but there are things Colin must know that only I can teach him."

While Christian patiently heard the cases which were brought before him and occasionally asked Kitty's legal advice, Colin worked diligently at his studies until late in the afternoons when he begged to join the village boys tending goats and cattle. In no time at all he had mastered the Urdu language, quite by accident, and Kitty was well pleased by the progress he made with his studies.

By the middle of October their tour of duty had ended, and the last of the fishing fleet had arrived along with the catalogs. Colin promptly took over the Christmas catalog and began to devour the pages. He marked each toy with his pen.

"We called them 'wish books' when I was a girl," Kitty told Colin. "Let me see what you want for Christmas."

He looked at her sheepishly. "I've marked all the things I have always wished for."

Kitty took the catalog from him. "A sled. But there's no snow...and ice skates! Metal soldiers and sailors...sets from every regiment. Drums and fifes and bugles. Uniforms...marbles. . ... sets of cards...games. I do declare, Colin, your catalog looks like mine used to look. Every page marked. What fun!"

"I know Father cannot buy all of it," he apologized.

"But it's such fun to think he might," Kitty said as she turned page after page.

In the end Christian sat down and made out the order for sets of artillerymen and light horse regiments.

"We must have a uniform made up for him with your colors, Christian. You know how he loves to dress up." Kitty's mind was racing ahead again.

"Aye, Kitty. You'll tend to seeing that it's done." Christian sounded pleased at Kitty's thoughtfulness.

"And what can I give him? Something he can take back to England."

"You'll think of something, Kitty. It's still two full months off."

"'Twill be here before we know it."

So the order was sent off to be filled and returned in time for Christmas, and Kitty was reminded again of the days when she wished for impossible things in the Sears and Roebuck Christmas Catalog, knowing full well she'd be lucky to find just one of the things she'd marked under the tree on Christmas morning. How she had dreamed! Then on Christmas morning she always slipped down the stairs very early to wait patiently for her parents to wake up. She had shaken the packages wrapped in brightly colored paper and tied with ribbons until she knew with a certainty what each held for her, but she was not quite sure.

"Kitty?" her mother had called to her.

"I'm waiting to open our presents. Is Daddy awake?" Her heart raced, and she could barely contain her anxiety any longer.

"Come, Richard. Don't shave yet. I'll plug in the coffee pot and we'll open the presents." Her mother had not dressed but wore an old gray chenille bathrobe over her nightgown.

Her father appeared in his floppy house slippers and an old, red, velvet robe, his hair uncombed. He was yawning and complaining, "Can't a man sleep late just once."

"Sit here, Daddy. You can open your present from me. I made it for you all by myself."

"Let me wake up first, honey. You go ahead and begin while I drink my coffee. Try the one wrapped in silver paper first." He pointed to it with his pipe.

So Kitty unwrapped her gifts while her parents watched, their faces glowing with love.

"Now, Daddy." She had wrapped his gift as well as her small hands could, but somehow the paper had not come out right. The bow fell off before she handed it to him, and she slapped it back in place. Finally, he made a great speech about what the gift could be. Then he removed the bow which would not stay in place with a flourish, and he removed the paper, complete with loads of scotch tape to hold it together. From the box her mother had kept over from last year, he lifted the white scarf.

"What have we here! Oh! Oh! Would you look at this, Louise! A nice wool scarf...a scarf with my own initials. How thoughtful!"

Kitty saw the initials she had struggled to embroider...saw where the threads had been ripped out time and time again until the fabric was almost threadbare.

"Do you like it, Daddy? I made it all by myself."

"You did? Well, now isn't that something. Louise did you see this?" Her father draped the scarf around his neck, and Kitty saw it was far too short for a tall man to wear, but Richard Farrell thanked her profusely and told her he'd never seen anything so nice. She guessed he liked it and wondered if he would ever wear it to church.

"We made something for you together, Richard. Help me bring it out, Kitty."

Kitty rushed to help her mother bring out the deep yellow section house trimmed in brown which she and her mother had made to install along his model train tracks. Kitty had watched her mother cut out the scale model house and glue it together, and she had helped make the tiny shingles they glued in place on the roof. It rested on a cookie sheet with cotton spread under it.

"This is just great, my girlies! Simply great. When did you ever do this without my knowing about it?"

"It wasn't easy," her mother smiled knowingly.

"Well thank you very, very much." He then drew a small box from the pocket of his robe and handed it to her mother.

"And this is for you, Honey."

Kitty could have sworn his eyes were misty.

Her mother opened the small gift, and when she discovered it held a ring box, she opened it quickly and gasped. "Richard, you didn't!"

"I told you I'd buy you a proper ring one day. Let me put it on your finger."

He took the gold ring with its single sparkling diamond from the box and put it on her mother's third finger left hand. He kissed her and said, "Now, we're officially engaged. No more cigar wrappers for you, sweetheart."

Her mother was crying.

It was much later when Kitty was in college that she realized how poor her parents had been when they married. They had struggled to get ahead, and the ring with its small diamond was symbolic of better times, not signs of wealth by any means, but a promise kept.

"Mum, you're awfully quiet," Colin spoke in a small voice.

She hugged him to her and said, "I was remembering, remembering a day long ago when I was your age and didn't know how little of the world's wealth my parents possessed. I wished for a bicycle all my very own every year, and when my parents could finally buy it for me, I was too old to care. You do understand that your father isn't made of money, that we don't always get everything we want?"

"I know that, Mum."

"We have to save for your passage back to England...your education... our leave in a couple of years...all on a soldier's pay. Oh, but I must not spoil the time we have together now with things like that."

"I'll not fret when it's time for me to go, you'll see. I can be brave."

Tears sprang into Kitty's eyes. "Let's not think about it now."

Parties. . .parties. . parties. The season was made for social events. The crisp autumn weather came as a welcome relief to India. Officers played hard polo and enlisted men practiced their shots. Gone were the searing days of summer...the blazing sun...the insufferable heat. Out came winter uniforms and cashmere and woolen garments.

The weary soldiers who had waited for the young women from England to arrive saw their futures brighten. Picnics, balls, dinners, teas, riding parties, and special entertainments of every description filled every waking moment. Kitty had never seen such feverish courting, all very discreet with blushes and eye contact and very little else. By the middle of November, the engagements began to be announced and weddings followed quickly.

When Christian set out for a small station in the province at the end of November, Kitty was relieved that they'd be alone and could leave the frenzied activities at Lucknow behind them. They worked hard during the days but still dressed for dinner, observing a long-established custom even though they were oftentimes far from a station in an obscure village. Their servants set up tents and served supper on collapsible furnishings, as usual, and after supper Kitty sang while Colin and Christian challenged each other with games.

The season was filled with the squawking of waterfowl overhead, and with cooler dry weather settling in, flowers bloomed in profusion. When the sun settled behind a blazing horizon, she and Colin often joined Christian while he strolled down a country road. They were the English, the English who conquered the proud Sikhs of India and made them subjects--fierce Hindu warriors and unwilling Muslims. Were it not for the English in India, the Hindus and Muslims would be enemies, but now the English was the enemy. They tolerated English laws, served in the army, and became servants, but they did not accept Christianity or adopt English customs. When night fell, they went back to their gods Shiva and Mohammed. Hindus stood before the elephant god, a monkey god, or a huge black stone bull and performed their pujahs, cleansing themselves of the English. Muslims prostrated themselves before Mecca, the birthplace of Mohammed, asking forgiveness if their hands had come close to the Englishman's pork. The Hindus ate no beef, considered their cattle sacred.

Toward the middle of December, Christian had finished his circuit throughout the province and returned to Lucknow until the first of the new year, January 1857.

Kitty was glad to return to their cottage in Lucknow, relieved but couldn't decide why she was relieved in seeking the safety of the walled cantonment. Christian, she knew, was anxious to rejoin his regiment, to spend the mornings drilling his men on the parade ground and to play polo before tea time in the late afternoons.

"I've grown soft, Kitty, need to get back in shape. That desk job in the villages fair made an old man out of me!" He removed his sword and laid it aside.

Kitty rubbed his back with a fragrant oil. "You're all tense and your muscles are tight," she told him.

"Inactive too long. Oliver will have to find someone else to take his desk job next season!"

"He asked for you specifically, didn't he? He will expect you to take it again."

"Aye, but 'twas a fool that agreed to do the job. You were a great help to me, Kitty darlin'. Do you reckon old Oliver knew you had experience with the law?"

"I'm certain of it, though he never spoke of it. In the heat of not knowing where I was from or how I came to be here, I am positive I told him. I'm sure he remembers. He's a sly one."

"That he is!"

"Perhaps you'll be able to convince him otherwise in another season." Her hands went around his waist to help him unfasten his waist band. She had convinced Christian that Azziz and Allie did not need to share the few moments they had alone before tea time.

"'Twill take some doing to convince your Lionel Train, Ranee," he chuckled.

"And if I'm not able to accompany you to hasten the work?"

"Not able?"

She wiggled into his arms and whispered, "I have something to tell you, my darling."

She felt his reaction to her words reach into her. He took hold of her arms with both hands and held her out from him. His face had grown pale and his eyes moistened.

"Oh, my, Ranee. What have I done?" His voice had suddenly turned to a hoarse whisper.

"If what I'm thinking is true, you've given me a precious gift."

She bent over to remove his stockings, and he lifted her to her feet.

"Oh, Ranee, my darling Ranee."

"Captain Skye," she stood straight and looked into his eyes, "are you going to do something foolish and faint?"

She almost laughed aloud, but she saw his anguish and drew him into her arms and said in a soothing tone. "Oh, my darling, don't you see. It is a new life...a part of you and a part of me, something we've brought about together. I'm surprised it didn't happen sooner. You're so strong...so wonderfully powerful. It was bound to happen."

"Oh, Maharanee. I don't deserve you.

The weather during December was crisp and clear with a soft blue haze from cow dung fires hanging in the air throughout the Lucknow cantonment. A week before Christmas the mail order arrived and Christian told Kitty he had hidden Colin's gifts until Christmas morning.

A flurry of holiday parties, engagements, and early marriages gave the season an exciting air. Colin could barely keep his mind on his studies while Kitty put the finishing touches on a brilliant red sash for Christian to wear with his uniform. She embroidered his initials above the fringe at the end in black silk thread, but she still had not found a suitable gift for Colin.

Colin was waiting for Christian to finish playing polo and asked Kitty for the third time, "What time is it, Mum?"

Suddenly Kitty knew. She'd give Colin the watch. It was not one of the new digital watches which ran on small batteries which would need to be replaced in a couple of years, but a stem-wound serviceable old watch with a stop action, a second hand, and gem stones set at the hours. It was a large ladies' watch, entirely suitable for a nineteenth century young man to wear. He would have something of hers to carry with him when he returned to England, certainly a watch like none other in England, she imagined. Should it ever need to be repaired, a good watch maker could repair it. So after they attended church services on Christmas eve and after Colin had gone to bed, Kitty wrapped her gift for her son.

Kitty was awakened by Colin's singing in the living room, so she and Christian quickly flung on their robes and joined him there to open their gifts to each other

When Colin opened his present from Kitty, he cried, "Oh, no, Mum. I can't take it."

"Yes, Colin, you must. I want you to be prompt to your classes, and you'll soon be going on to Addiscombe to work toward your commission, and you must never be tardy. I have no use for it here. India runs on her own slow time. An hour late is nothing."

He flung his arms around her and cried, "I promise to use it wisely." Christian smiled over Colin's head, and Kitty saw that he was deeply moved.

"Now, my gift for your father." She smiled and handed Christian his gift.

Christian felt the crimson sash and saw his initials embroidered neatly above the fringe. He started to speak, but something caught in his throat. Finally he said, " 'Tis a thoughtful gift I'll treasure always."

"I made it especially for you, Christian."

"Aye, I thought as much when I first saw what it was," he told her and took his gift to her from the deep pocket in his morning robe.

Colin lay on the floor with his mixed regiment spread before him.

"Hold out your left hand, Ranee. Wanted it to be of gold and precious stones, engraved properly," he said and slipped the ring on her third finger.

"And what is engraved on the inside, Christian?" she asked as she admired the ring he placed on her finger.

"One soul," he told her.

"I'll wear it always, my darling," she said in a voice for only his ears.

"The church bells are ringing," he told her.

"Reminding us to thank God for our many blessings."

"Come, Colin. We must dress for church. You will have all day for the 8th Light Dragoons, the llth Hussars, the 13th Light Dragoons, and the 17th Lancers to fight the charge of the light brigade in the Crimean War."

Charles Bradley joined them for dinner after church services were over, and when he had finished eating, he excused himself, offering a lame reason to be off.

"What's eating Charles?" Kitty asked. "He seemed to be an awful stitch to leave us."

"Guess he's uncomfortable around a happy family." Christian offered weakly.

"I thought we'd make this Christmas day without Caroline and the children more bearable for him."

"He's other things to keep his mind occupied."

"What things, Christian?"

"Don't press me, Kitty. 'Tis not something we talk about."

"You cannot tell me!" She heard her voice rising.

"No, Kitty. You'd think ill of Bradley."

"Christian, what is going on? Why must you start something you can't finish? There's nothing that vexes me more than a tale half-finished!"

"Charles and Caroline never had what we have, Kitty."

"What does that have to do with Charles leaving as soon as he eats? What does he have to do on Christmas day that's so important he leaves his friends as soon as soon as he has eaten?" She knew her voice had a sharp edge, but she could not help it. She felt her eyes blazing, and even though she knew instinctively what was coming next, she didn't want to hear it said aloud.

"Don't excite yourself, Kitty."

"I'm not exciting myself! And I don't care what Charles Bradley does with his afternoon." She was screaming at him.

"I should have known the fool wouldn't stay."

"He has another woman," Kitty knew even before she spoke.

"Aye, 'tis true...a woman he had before he wed Caroline."

"An Indian woman."

"Aye."

"I should have known." She sucked in her breath with a sharp sound.

"It is a thing that is not frequently done. . . something we don't talk about."

Kitty was breathing heavily. She felt herself gasping for breath.

"How many English men in your regiment, Christian?" Her voice hardened.

"Don't trouble yourself with those thoughts, Kitty. It isn't safe to get yourself so wrought up."

He rose to console her, but she would have none of it.

"And you, Captain Skye? You never married after Emma died?"

"Kitty. Keep your voice down?"

"Bang! Bang! Swish! Swish!" Colin cried as the charge of the light brigade began on the living room floor.

"You would have to pry." His eyes blazed, the amber flecks dancing, his face contorted.

She felt her anger creep higher and higher, her face flaming.

"I trusted you...had no idea how it was."

Christian turned from Kitty, put on his coat, and left the cottage.

The cold silence of the dining room sliced into her.

Her stomach turned and she grew clammy and cold.

Then she remembered his saying, "One forgets how dark the women are. Some of them are quite beautiful."

She was past crying.

"What is it, Mum?" Colin stood at the open door staring at her.

"It is nothing, Colin. I'm not feeling at all well. I think I'll lie down for a bit."

"I'll see if I can find Father."

"No," she snapped.

She felt herself heaving inside...sobbing without tears...straining and heaving, feeling betrayed, old, and unwanted. She closed her bedroom door and flung herself across the bed. During the night she awoke hurting and went to lie on the sofa in the living room where she huddled for the remainder of the night. Somewhere between dawn and daylight she awoke with a sob deep inside herself. Colin found her there early the next morning and raced away to find someone to care for her.

CHAPTER SEVENTEEN

*K*itty opened her eyes and with a rush it all came back to her. She smelled something medicinal and wondered what it was. She hurt all over and when she swallowed, a strangling sound came out of her throat, as though someone were choking her. It didn't matter. She had lost Christian. She didn't want to live any longer...wanted to die and forget she had ever loved him.

Then a quiet rage came over her, and she began to shake. She pulled the blanket over her head and began to sob with anger. She choked and the dry heaving returned again. She licked her dry lips and tried to go to sleep, to block out the memory forever.

"Kitty," she heard someone speak her name. "Kitty, would you like a drink of water?"

When she heard no other sound, she lowered the blanket, but the brightness of the room hurt her eyes. She covered her face again and lay still until she dozed off again.

She struggled to rise and Colonel Oliver came to her side. "Lie still, Kitty. Let me wet your lips."

"Where am I?"

"You're in the infirmary. Colin went for the doctor. We brought you here." He wet her lips and held her head up so she could swallow the water he held to her mouth.

Her feet were elevated, she realized, and her head sank back. It didn't matter. She lay back exhausted.

"You'll be fine in a day or two," he said

"Oh, sure. I'll be just wonderful, you know. How long...how long have you been here? What day is it?"

"Today is the 26th day of December, the day after Christmas."

"And yesterday was Christmas Day?" She groaned, remembering.

"Just rest, Kitty. You need to rest."

"I need to get out of here...must return, Lionel. Please help me. I must go home."

"Where would you go, Kitty?"

"Cannot stay here. . .must return to Kansas." She knew she was rambling on and on. "Won't someone help me? Won't anyone listen? Where is the force that brought me to India? Call it back."

Colonel Oliver let her talk until at last she lay back exhausted.

"Do you want to see Christian now?"

She came back with a jolt. "I never want to see him again as long as I live." Her voice sounded harsh and raspy to her own ears.

"Don't judge him, Kitty. I've never known Christian to do a dishonorable deed in his life."

"It's all the same to me."

"Kitty, don't accuse Christian Skye without cause. I know for a fact that he's never had anything to do with the native women. I've tried to keep my men away from them, but they're always there...willing to please... and. . ."

"Say no more! You needn't make excuses."

"You must not let this upset you, Kitty."

"I'm not staying. Just as soon as I can get out of this bed. I'm strapped in...standing on my head...can't move!"

"It's time for tea, Kitty. What would you like?"

"What I need right now is something to take me away."

She could hear him laughing when she closed her eyes.

Colonel Oliver left her and an orderly appeared. "Mrs. Skye, let's see if you can sit up now." He loosened her restraints. "Easy," he said.

He helped her to sit upright. She ran her fingers through her hair and asked for a wet cloth. Her hair felt matted and plastered to her head.

"This isn't your usual line of work, private," she said.

"No, M'am. Would you like to sit in the chair? Colonel Oliver will be back shortly."

"Yes, and could you bring me a comb please," she said as he eased her into a chair beside the bed. She felt as though she were old and infirm like the old ladies she had visited in the nursing home where her mother died.

When Colonel Oliver returned, he was carrying cups and a pot of tea. "Tea time, Mrs. Skye!" He poured a cup of tea and handed it to Kitty. "To your health, Kitty!"

"How long have you been here?" she asked.

"Since early this morning. You gave your son quite a jolt."

"Poor Colin. Where is he now?"

"I took him to Maria. He's alright."

"Thank you." She knew she could not ask about Christian Skye. Didn't want to hear his name.

"I'm glad to see you looking better." He downed his tea and said, "You have a visitor."

"I don't want to see Christian Skye!"

"It's not Christian."

"Very well, then. Perhaps I can persuade whoever it is to help me get out of here."

"Give yourself time, Kitty," he said when finished his tea and rose to leave.

She felt the effects of the tea warming her. "Sure, I'll give myself all the time in the world."

Lionel Oliver patted her hand and said, "There's a bright tomorrow, Kitty. I promise you."

The tea on her empty stomach worked wonders. She felt giddy and wondered why she wasn't crying.

When Charles Bradley entered the room, he shook hands with Colonel Oliver as he was leaving.

Kitty watched as he poured a cup of tea and drank from it. He didn't speak for what seemed an eternity.

"Guess we need more than tea and biscuits today, Kitty." He sounded confused.

She watched his face but did not answer.

"You're new to India, you know, but somehow I feel you know more about John Company than any English woman who ever came out to India," he told her. "But, of course, you're not English. I keep forgetting. What made you stay, Kitty?"

"Where is he?"

"Who knows? Still sleeping it off in the officers' mess no doubt."

"I don't want to see him. I'm not staying. You must help me get away, Charles."

"You know I can't do that," he told her.

"I'll not stay and listen to his tales any longer."

"You'd drive him away from you with guilt when he hasn't done anything?"

"Guilt? It's your double standards, Lieutenant Bradley.". Her thought pattern became scrambled. She looked at him and asked, "Have you no conscience at all, Charles?"

"You don't understand how it is for a man stationed in this forgotten place...the loneliness. . .the awful sense of not belonging to anyone... Caroline and the children in England...a furlough years away."

"Oh, I understand perfectly." Her head was reeling.

"Christian has not . ."

She cut him off, "Don't try to protect him."

"He loves you, Kitty."

"Like you love Caroline! Ha!"

"As my wife...not like Christian loves you." He rose to leave. "Don't do this to him, Kitty.".

She felt her tears falling while his footsteps echoed away in the infirmary. She glanced down at the ring on her left hand and took it off. Then her eyes fell upon the two words "one soul" engraved inside the ring, and she returned it to her finger.

Dusk had fallen and she had climbed back into her bed, feeling miserable and forsaken. Her body began to shake, and she called for the orderly to bring another blanket, but no one came.

When she heard steps in the hall, she called out, "Orderly, can you bring me another blanket, please."

"It is only I, Kitty."

She knew that deep, rumbling voice and drew herself into a tight knot.

"Go away. I don't want to see you...ever again. I'm leaving this place just as soon as I can get out of ..."

"Not until you've heard me out, Kitty."

"What is there to say?"

"There is nothing to say, but you'll hear me out, Ranee." His voice fell and she heard a sob escape his throat.

"Why couldn't you tell me how it was?" She wanted to simply tell him that she meant to leave in a normal tone of voice but she couldn't say more.

"Kitty, I didn't lie. I should have told you...never wanted you to know how things sometimes happen...didn't want to hurt you."

"I told you everything...how Filbey and I met...lived together...how he walked out on me...how I never truly loved him."

"And I judged you harshly for it. I'm sorry."

He went to her bedside and gathered her into his arms, pinning her into the blanket so she couldn't move. "I was afraid, Ranee...afraid you'd leave me if you knew how things sometimes happened."

She could hear him sobbing into the blanket that held her captive.

"You knew very well I'd not stay!" she tried to free herself from his tight grip.

"Don't struggle, Kitty. You'll hear me out and if you leave me, I can do nothing about it. I'm not making excuses. You know I never touched Emma. After she died, her wardrobe woman came to care for Colin until I sent him to his grandmother in England when he was a few months old. I knew then I'd never marry, for the girls who came out with the fishing fleet did not interest me...too flighty and silly and pretending to be everything they were not. There was no one I could trust for a long while, but I never knew why until I first saw you. That's all there is to it."

"There was not another?"

"No, Kitty. And now you know everything." He released her and slumped into the chair beside her bed.

She lay with her back to him on the narrow bed.

"I can't blame you for wanting to go, Ranee. I've brought you nothing but misery."

She rolled over to face him, and even in the fading light within the room, she saw the misery etched in the lines of his face. One soul...one soul aching...hurting...grieving.

"I need you so, Christian," she said in a small voice, or was it something inside her crying.

He stared at her a long while before he knelt beside her bed and took her in his arms. "Can you ever forgive this weak clod of a man for hurting you so, my dearest Ranee?"

"Hold me in your arms, Christian. Hold me close."

She felt her grief sliding away from her as surely as it had come.

When the orderly came into her room, he found Christian lying on the narrow bed with Kitty cradled tenderly in his arms. They were both asleep, so he shut the door and tip-toed down the hall.

Early in January Christian told Kitty, "The new Enfield rifles are arriving. At last we can replace the old 'Brown Bess' with one with a longer range and greater accuracy."

"The Enfield?" Her face registered shock.

"What is it, Kitty?"

She felt the blood drain from her face. "Does the Enfield require a greased cartridge?"

"Aye, but how did you know?" He looked at her strangely. "The cartridge must be bitten off at the end of its paper by the rifleman before he inserts it into the gun barrel?"

"Oh, no! That's it. The greased cartridge with the paper covering."

"Aye."

"We must send Colin home at once. It's the greased cartridges that will start the Sepoy mutiny?"

"I don't see. . ." Christian began.

"It's the grease, don't you see? It was the grease that started it all. I remember it now. The revolt began because of the grease. The Hindu will not defile his body by allowing any part of the tallow from cow to touch his body. The Muslim Sepoys will not touch pig fat. Either tallow or pig fat will cause the loss of caste automatically and will bring about ostracization from family and friends to the native troops. It was a terrible mutiny... reaching into all the posts along the Grand Trunk Road. It brought about warfare between the Indians and the English."

"I must warn the magazines at Ft. William where the first of the new rifles have arrived. Are you certain of the extent of the revolt, Kitty?" Christian questioned her, but she knew from the look on his face he knew she spoke the truth.

On January 29, 1857, the inspector-general of ordnance and magazines at Ft. William wired the stations. "Enquired at arsenal as to nature of composition used. Found instructions received from Court of Directors: mixture of tallow and beeswax."

"The damage has been done" Christian told her. "Outbreaks of mutiny have already begun amid rumors of Dum Dum's greased cartridges."

"Maggie and Tom are there."

"Yes."

"Can we send for Maggie and the children?"

"'Twouldn't be safe to travel."

Then she thought of Colin. "We must send Colin back to England before the revolt spreads any further to the cantonments."

"Aye, but he cannot take the route near Meerut where the mutiny has begun."

"Has Lucknow taken any precautions?"

"Our Sepoys are loyal."

"Christian, you cannot trust any of your Sepoys...even Azziz."

"Kitty, don't let a small revolt near Meerut upset you."

"It was not a small revolt...Delhi...Meerut...Cawnpore...Lucknow... Lahore. Those are just some of the names I remember. There were terrible massacres."

"We'll send Colin away at once."

Chapter Eighteen

Colonel Oliver sent Charles Bradley off into the province to judge cases in January. It was a wise move as far as Kitty was concerned, and she marveled at Oliver's expertise in making the decision.

In the meantime Christian prepared for spring maneuvers in the countryside near Lucknow. Kitty knew Lionel Oliver had purposefully kept him near the cantonment in order that he could spend time with her and Colin, for Colin would be returning to England soon, and she found herself dreading the day they'd have to send him home.

As for Christian Skye, their relationship had deepened, and she found herself loving him even more since she almost lost him.

"Did you truly wish yourself back?" His voice broke when he whispered that question, and she knew he spoke in desperation.

"It was only my hurting that longed for it."

"Aye, Ranee, but you must never wish for it again. How would I ever find you? I don't know how to break the time barrier."

"Nor do I. Hold me close. Tell me that you love me once more."

"We must quit saying we're sorry, my Maharanee. We must look forward and forget the things that have hurt us. We have our entire lives ahead of us. Nothing...nothing can ever come between us again." He laughed his deep, rumbling laughter and the golden lights in his eyes shone. She knew in that moment that nothing could ever part them.

The sun was falling beyond the horizon, and Kitty said, "Must we continually keep up appearances? I'd love to cook supper for you and Colin and spend a quiet evening alone...just the three of us. Send the servants away and we'll while away this evening with our son."

"He's a good lad."

"You love him, too."

"Aye, we'll miss him."

Kitty began smiling and Christian enfolded her in his arms. "You know what you do to me. 'Twas the tears that were my undoing that day. Once I held you in my arms, I knew my bachelor days were over. The warm scent of you...ever so sweet. I knew I was done for."

"Captain Skye, you do have a way with words. You could sweet-talk me into anything."

"I hear our boy returning from practicing his shots. He must enjoy our last evening together.

Colin would be leaving the next day. She had counted the days off one by one, dreading the parting, trying to memorize his actions, his sunny smile, and the way he frowned when he studied.

"I'll be ahead of my classmates when I return to grammar school, Mum."

"That means you'll finish early and can return to us all the sooner."

"You'll come to England next year on Father's leave."

"We promise," she told him, "and we'll write often."

"Then, I'll work hard for you. You'll be proud of me."

"We're proud of you now. Would you have your father bursting his buttons off?" Kitty looked over his papers and said, "Your handwriting has improved greatly, I'm proud of you."

"And you've told me things about science Mr. Gray doesn't even suspect."

Christian looked at him soberly and said, "Remember you're not to talk about rockets or space ships or computer chips or any of the other things your mother has told you about. They will come in the future. They're the things men only dream about. To tell them for facts accomplished will bring down the roof."

"I'll go to America one day when I'm grown," Colin stated.

"If you live to be a hundred," Christian told him, "You may see some of the things your mum has told you about."

"It will be 1946. I'd like to live that long, if only to see what happens then."

Kitty handed his arithmetic papers back. "Only one error in long division, Colin. A small thing, the decimal point, but a large error in the end."

"I hurried so I could catch Father playing polo."

"Ah yes, a major distraction, your father." Kitty smiled over his head and winked at Christian.

His brown hair caught the sunlight and picked up the tinges of red. She knew his confident walk, the quiet manner he ordered the servants about, the way the amber lights danced in his eyes when he teased her.. "A major, major distraction," she added.

The hours passed quickly, and it was time for Colin to leave them. His puka luggage was packed, he had told the Indian boys he played with goodbye, and now he waited for the carriage that would take him away...away on a long voyage back to England. A Corporal Wyeth from Christian's unit would accompany him on his long journey to Bombay.

The carriage rumbled down the street toward the cottage where Colin and his traveling companion waited.

"Keep your chin up, son," Christian told him.

Colin flung himself into Christian's arms. "I'll be brave, Father."

His eyes filled with tears when he looked at Kitty. She had meant not to cry, but she held him close and said, "We love you, Son. Write often."

They went with Colin and Corporal Wyeth to the carriage. He broke away and climbed into the carriage. Corporal Wyeth shook hands with Christian, Azziz put his luggage into the rack, and Colin called out to Kitty. "I love you, Mum."

"Be careful, Son. Take care." Christian called to him.

They watched the carriage roll out of sight, and when it was gone, Kitty knew a part of her went with the child.

"Oliver gave me leave to be with you today, Kitty," Christian told her and she knew his voice was straining over the lump in his throat. "What would you like to do?"

"Could we saddle our horses and ride out into the countryside...just the two of us?"

"It can be arranged."

"I want us to be together...to be sad together because our son is returning to England. He seemed so small. Did you notice?"

"Aye, Kitty."

"And so brave."

"Aye, that he was."

"We'll miss him so."

That afternoon they rode out into the countryside. The weather couldn't have been finer. The late winter sun of India was shining, their horses were spirited, and they shed their sadness. The sun disappeared quickly at this time of the year, so they headed back toward the city, and when they approached the outskirts of the town, Kitty cried out, "Christian, a lotus blossom! It's lovely...all pink and waxy and perfect."

"A good omen, Kitty. Never dreamed we'd come to love him," Christian said.

She put her hand in his and looked into his eyes.

They heard the crack of a rifle and the blossom split from its stem.

"What is. . .?"

"Quickly, Kitty."

They reined their horses away from the lily pond and kicked them forward at a gallop. When they reached the gate of the cantonment, Christian slowed his horse and permitted Kitty to ride into the fort ahead of him.

"What did it mean?" Kitty asked him.

"That is what I intend to find out."

"Colin? Will he be safe?"

"'Twas an isolated shot. See...all is quiet now."

For a short while, the fort at Lucknow experienced no troubles with the Sepoys. Then word came about the fall of the East India Company at Delhi. Men raced away to aid the defenders at the Red Fort, but Colonel Oliver insisted that Christian and his men stay to defend Lucknow if that need came. When word came that Meerut had fallen, they knew the mutiny was spreading. When the attackers came over the wall, Kitty heard the fighting near the school. She grabbed her purse and hurried toward the Registry where Christian told her to go in case she heard the guns firing.

"Christian! Christian!" she cried aloud, but the big 12 pounders were firing and the air was filled with smoke. The roar of the heavy artillery deafened her, and she saw men falling in the distance as she raced on.

"Christian! Christian! Christian!"

Then she saw Azziz where he had fallen. His hands clutched the crimson sash Kitty had given to Christian, and she bent to retrieve the sash. The air cooled and chargeed with electricity as the monsoon swept in.

CHAPTER NINETEEN

Somewhere in the recesses of Kitty's subconscious state she heard voices.

"She's coming around."

"Kitty. It's Olivia. Do you hear me?"

"Stay beside her, Mrs. Stewart. Call me if you see any change."

She felt herself blissfully slipping back into the darkness which had claimed her.

When she opened her eyes later, she saw someone sitting beside her bed. Whoever it was appeared to be asleep. She felt the pain that reached into every part of her body and wondered briefly what had happened to her. She moved her feet to discover if they were still there. She wiggled her fingers and brought her hand to her face. Something was terribly wrong with her.

"Water," she choked, and Olivia Stewart sprang to her side.

"You're alive! Nurse! Come quickly!"

The nurse took her blood pressure. Then she thrust a thermometer into her dry mouth. When she removed the thermometer, someone's voice spoke low, "You may take a little water now. Careful, you're all wired up with I V's."

Kitty sipped water slowly through a straw, but she soon lost interest in the liquid seeping into her mouth and let it run down onto her chest. She shut her eyes, too exhausted to open them again.

"I'm here with you, Kitty."

"Olivia?" she whispered.

"I'm here, Honey. You've had quite a jolt," she heard Olivia saying somewhere in the haze in which she found herself.

Then Kitty asked, "How...how did you get here?"

"I came as soon as I got word that you had been found. Rest now, Kitty."

"Crazy world. First me and now you."

She had no way of knowing how long she had been asleep, but Olivia was still beside her bed. She had been trying to reach the Registry, and then everything blacked out.

"Christian," she whispered.

"Christian?"

"Where's Christian?"

"Christian?" It was Olivia asking about Christian again.

"Christian Skye. Have you seen him?" Kitty heard her voice rising.

"Christian Skye, Kitty?" Olivia asked.

"My husband! He's here somewhere. You must find him...see if he's safe."

She felt herself drifting off, but thinking about Christian brought her back with a start. "Where's Christian, Livy?"

"I haven't seen him, but if I do, I'll tell him you want to see him."

"All right, Miss Farrell. Let's take a look." It was another voice, one she had never heard before.

The nurse rolled her off a hard bedpan, and Kitty felt a million shards of pain piercing throughout her body.

"Strange, very strange. We've never seen a case quite like this before." It was a man's voice she heard. "There's no evidence of bodily damage. The CT scan showed nothing unusual. Yet, she seems to have gone through severe trauma of some sort."

"She's looking for someone, Dr. Ault. Who do you suppose Christian Skye can be? I have never heard of him."

Kitty struggled to bring her eyes into focus on the doctor's face.

"Where is he?" She had to find Christian.

Then the pain swept through her again and again, springing from deep inside herself. Yet, it was not a physical pain but an unbearable sadness.

"You have had a severe shock, Miss Farrell. Can you tell us what happened?"

She heard herself moan.

"Kitty, do you know me? It's Olivia. I'm here with you."

Olivia's voice penetrated her numbness, but she did not want to listen to the grating sound of her words. "What day?" she asked.

"June the sixth," Olivia answered.

"I have to find Christian. I was trying to reach him. Sepoys were coming over the wall. " She cried out.

"What do you think she is talking about, Doctor Ault?" Olivia looked at the doctor.

"I have no idea. Delusions...perhaps drug induced!"

"Oh, no! Not Kitty! She never touched drugs."

"I was trying to reach the Registry!" She shuddered with a sudden memory.

"Don't excite yourself, Miss Farrell." The doctor shone a light into her eyes, and he shook his head. "We may have to send her to Topeka," he told Olivia in a low, confidential tone.

"No, you can't send me back. I must find Christian. Olivia, have you searched everywhere for him?"

"There, there. It's alright." Olivia's motherly tone soothed her and she began to relax. "I'll see if I can find him."

Kitty saw the doctor and her friend exchange worried glances and wondered what it meant.

"Where am I?" Suddenly the electric lighting, the hospital bed on which she was lying, the nurse's uniform, Olivia's dress, were strange to her.

"You're in Riley County Memorial."

"Oh, no! No!" Kitty shuddered and buried her head in her hands.

"What is it?" the doctor asked.

"I've returned." Her voice rose and she looked about frightened.

"Where have you been?" Olivia began to pace the floor.

"Say it isn't so. Please, tell me you came to India to find me, Livy."

"India? You went to India!" She stopped pacing and drew a deep breath after she exploded.

"I tried. I tried...no telephones...no fax machines...you'd not even been born yet." Kitty wanted to explain why she had not let her best friend in the world know where she had gone, but for some strange reason, Olivia did not understand.

"What in the world are you talking about? I hadn't been born yet? Doctor, I'm afraid you're right." Olivia looked at the doctor helplessly.

"You don't understand, Livy. I arrived at Lucknow in the middle of the night on the sixth day of May. The next day I met Christian." She knew instinctively Olivia would not understand and said no more.

"You, poor kid. Doctor, is there anything you can do for her?"

"No. She's hallucinating. We'll have to determine what it was she was taking before we can treat her."

"She never. . ."

Kitty began sobbing and Olivia held her close. "We'll talk about it later, Honey."

"We were married. See my ring. Look inside." She tried to wrench the ring from her finger. "It is engraved on the inside."

"Your names?"

"One soul...we were one." She twisted the ring off and handed it to Olivia.

"We really can't handle these cases here," the doctor said. "I'll make the necessary arrangements."

Olivia followed the doctor into the hall, "She's just not that kind of person. I can't believe that she'd become involved in..."

Kitty heard Olivia's voice drifting off down the hall. She was too numb to cry...hurting too much to care.

When Olivia returned to Kitty's room, she straightened her bedding and gave her a glass of orange juice to drink. "We're transferring you to Topeka for evaluation."

"Why?" She didn't taste the orange juice, didn't want to think about anything.

"Just for a series of routine tests."

"You think I'm stark, raving mad. Is that it?" She wiped her mouth with the bed sheet and tried to sit up.

"No. Nothing like that. How are you feeling?" She took the glass of juice Kitty handed back to her and set it on the bedside table.

"Has Colin written?"

"Colin? Colin?" Olivia's bright hazel eyes fixed on Kitty's face.

"Our son. We should have heard from him. Did he reach England? He promised to write."

"What on earth are you talking about now?"

"Aren't we in India?"

"You're not in India, Kitty. This is Olivia. We're in Kansas." She spoke slowly, trying once more to make Kitty understand.

"Livy? Why aren't you in New York?"

"I came as soon as I got the word they had found you."

"Found me? I wasn't lost. I was with Christian just before they came over the walls. Then he left quickly. I don't know what happened to him."

"Of course, dear. I understand." Her voice was soothing.

"You'd better get back to work. Ted will can you. What are you doing here?" Kitty shook her head to clear it.

"Someone finally found you sitting alongside a country road. Your shorts were torn and wet. It seems you wandered away from your car. They called me at once."

"Christian will never forgive me...must find him. He'll never understand...will think I willed this to happen. He needs me."

"And when I got here, I knew you needed help."

"Must find him. Do you hear me?"

"The highway patrol found your car. You were nowhere in sight. I came out to Kansas as soon as I could. They searched for you. You had simply vanished off the face of the earth without leaving a trace." Olivia reached nervously for a cigarette, remembered she was in the hospital and put the package back in her purse. "Someone, I don't know who he was, finally found you."

"I'm trying to tell you. I was in India. We were married in May of 1856 and went to Kashmir on our wedding trip. Christian was so funny. He was jealous of Luke Filbey. Can you imagine that? But we made up in Kashmir and in Simla and in Lucknow and all the points between." She sighed, remembering, and then continued, "Had to send Colin away before the mutiny began. Don't know if he's alive or not. Such a dangerous time to travel. He is such a dear, sweet boy. The lotus blossom should have been a warning to us, but we stayed on. 'Twas those greased cartridges that started it all." Her hands began to tremble. She knew she was talking too much, that Olivia could not make heads or tails of what she was saying. Somehow it did not matter.

"Nurse!" Olivia called out. "We need a tranquilizer here."

Kitty heard the nurse running into the room and saw the instrument in her hand.

"No! No! Let me tell you about it," Kitty demanded in a hysterical voice. "Cawnpore and Lucknow are under siege. Delhi has fallen." She continued talking. "The entire northwest frontier is under...under... under. . ." Her words dwindled away for the injection was doing its work.

She awoke as she was handed up into the ambulance. Olivia was still with her, and Kitty asked, "Where are we going?"

"We're taking you to Topeka. Just relax, Dear. It isn't far."

Someone inside the ambulance said, "You've been tripping all over the place, Miss Farrell!"

The statement angered her and Kitty spat out, "The name is Skye!"

"Sure, kiddo. Whatever you say, Sky, Moon, or Stars. It's all the same."

"I'll follow you," she heard Olivia tell the driver before she simply gave up and slid back into whatever state of half-consciousness she had fallen into.

Her head had cleared somewhat by the time the ambulance reached Topeka, and Olivia was with her when the assistant wheeled her into a private room.

"I shouldn't be putting you out like this," Kitty said.

"Nonsense! After all you've put me through already, this is a piece of cake. We'll have you out of here in nothing flat. You're as healthy as a race horse. Besides, I needed a vacation. Luke is coming out on Friday."

"Luke Filbey? Why in the world is he coming here? Sorry, I'm going in and out again."

"It's a good sign."

"If you say so. My head is seven stories high. Was that in a song we used to sing?" She giggled and felt nonsensical things running through her mind.

"You're funny?"

"Is that why you're taking me to the funny farm? I hurt something awful! Was I hit by a truck or a train?"

"You're fit as a fiddle physically. It's something else. The MRI didn't show anything. Guess we'll know soon enough. Are you up to tough questions?"

"No, as a matter of fact, I'm not up to questions at all. By the way, you look awful, Olivia. You'd better get some sleep."

"I'm checking into the hotel just as soon as you're under control here. Then I'll see you bright and early tomorrow morning."

Kitty held out her hand to her friend. "Will I ever find him again?"

"Christian?"

"Aye, Captain Christian Skye . . . my husband." Tears sprang into her eyes.

Olivia patted her hand and the nursing staff took over. She saw Olivia's familiar face vanishing and longed to reach out and hold her hand.

The next morning her head had cleared, and an aide brought a box filled with red roses to her room. She handed a small card to Kitty and said, "Someone must think you're pretty special. I'll see if I can find a large vase to hold all of them."

Kitty took the card from the envelope and read, "Keep your chin up, Baby. I'll see you Friday. Love you, Luke."

She felt no emotion. "Is Olivia Stewart here yet?"

"I don't know. I do see breakfast arriving. Are you hungry?"

Kitty remembered where she was and thought about Christian. Waves of sadness swept over her, and she did not answer. She longed to be alone... to sort out what had happened. More than anything else, she wanted Christian with her, holding her in his arms, telling her he loved her.

"You're looking much better this morning." A young nurse, who couldn't be more than twenty, breezed into the room. "Would you like to wash your face and hands before you eat breakfast?"

"Yes, and can you help me go to the bathroom. My legs feel like Jello. Guess I'm a little dizzy, too."

"Of course." The lively young woman had red curls which she tied back with a black ribbon. Her arms felt firm beneath her. Kitty gasped when she saw the gleaming fixtures in the immaculate bathroom. She had all but forgotten such things existed. The tap water was warm to her touch. She knew instinctively she could drink from the faucet without boiling the water.

"Here you are. If you need help, just call for me. My name is Alicia."

"Thank you, Alicia. I'm fine. I'm just fine."

She had no reason to look to see if snakes had invaded her spotless stool. No red dust had filtered into the immaculate room. The tile glistened. She breathed a sigh of relief.

"Mrs. Stewart is here. Is everything alright?" It was the voice of Alicia calling to her.

"Good morning, Kitty," Olivia called to her. "Breakfast looks good."

Kitty washed her face and lathered her hands with the sweet-smelling soap. She let the water from the faucet run over her hands and smiled.

She dried her hands on a plush towel with a soft feel to it. Then she opened the door and shuffled to the chair beside her table.

"Let me brush your hair. It looks like a rat's nest," Olivia told her.

"I brushed Edith Skye's hair. She enjoyed it so. My it does feel good," she said and felt her tears about to spill over.

"Now, for the food." Olivia lifted the cover over the plate and steam arose. "Scrambled eggs and sausage. Grits, toast and jelly. Enough for a harvest hand. It's too bad I have eaten already. And I see you have roses!"

Kitty made no comment, but she tried to eat. "I've brought you something to wear. A blue skirt...a pretty blouse...sandals...and underwear. Couldn't remember if you were a 'B' or 'C' cup. You have an appointment at eight with a Doctor Dewey Goddard. Do you want me to go in with you?"

"By all means. I might say something totally ridiculous. Has my hospitalization expired? I have a feeling this is costing me a bundle, if it has."

"I couldn't let it lapse...knew you'd be looking like something the cat dragged in when we found you."

Kitty laughed and put her fork down. "Real coffee, at last. I'll never drink tea again as long as I live."

"That's my girl!"

The receptionist at the desk rose and smiled. "Good morning, Miss Farrell. It's good to see you. Come this way, please."

"I feel like an idiot," Kitty said. "Do we have to go through all this again."

"We haven't gone through anything yet," Olivia reminded her.

Dr. Goddard looked up through his glasses and rose from his desk where he had obviously been studying her case. He took Kitty's hand warmly and began talking about the Kansas weather and whether she was interested in sports.

"I had begun to learn about polo. My husband. . ."

"And now let us begin at the beginning. Where were you going when you had car trouble near the second Fort Riley exit?"

"I didn't have car trouble. I simply pulled over during a thunderstorm."

"Did you see anyone while you were waiting for the storm to let up?"

"No."

"I see. What happened after you pulled over?" He looked up at her over his glasses and waited for her to answer his question.

She tried to explain the sensations she experienced before and after the thunderbolt hit close to her, but the words sounded hollow to her.

"So what made you think you were in India?"

"I know I had reached India; there's not another place like it on the face of the earth."

"Tell me what happened when you arrived there."

She wondered what he was thinking when she began talking. Suddenly she felt better talking about it to someone...just anyone. Besides, this doctor appeared to be genuinely interested in what she was saying, so she told him everything that had taken place that first day.

"And you spoke of a Captain Skye. Was he in the English army at Lucknow."

"Yes."

"What was your relationship with Captain Christian Skye?"

So Kitty talked on and on, but when she tried to tell him about the wedding trip to Kashmir she choked up and began to cry.

"Now tell me how it was you found your way back to Kansas? What was happening in Kashmir?"

"We weren't in Kashmir when the mutiny began. We had to send Colin away for I remembered that the Enfield rifles which replaced the old 'Brown Bess' used greased cartridges."

"Just a moment. You did not return to Kansas from Kashmir?"

"Oh, no. We spent the summer months at the Hill Station of Simla, and in the fall we went down the Grand Trunk Road to Lucknow. There had been no really serious troubles with the native troops in the immediate past, but it was biting off the paper on the greased cartridges which brought on the revolt by the Sepoys."

"Who were the Sepoys and what did the greased papers have to do with the revolt and your returning to America?"

"The Sepoys were the Indian troops. They secretly hated the English, and when the cartridges were greased with animal fat...no one knew what kind of fat was used actually...it was defiling to Hindu and Muslin alike."

"I see. What happened at Lucknow?"

"It began at Meerut and Dum Dum. The Native Cavalry refused to use the greased cartridges." Her hands were shaking visibly. "A court-martial and long sentences were handed down to the 85 leaders of the rebellion at Meerut. They were shackled in leg irons and marched down the line in the scorching hot sun. The remainder of the native troops were horrified, and the next day the mutiny began at Meerut. After the 85 ringleaders were freed by Sepoys many Europeans were killed."

"Do go on."

"The news reached Lucknow over the wires. Many thought the revolt would be an isolated occurrence. Christian was certain his troops would remain loyal. I tried to tell Colonel Oliver, but Lionel didn't believe the rebels would go far in the blazing, hot sun. When the mutineers marched on to Delhi, they were joined by the populace and the uprising was a terrible thing. The king re-established his authority, and they killed every European in Delhi. When they tried to take the magazine, an officer gave his own life, and took the lives of 300 of the attackers, also. We knew when this news reached Lucknow that the mutiny had spread all along the Grand Trunk Road...from Dum Dum at Calcutta to Peshwar in the far northwest."

"Were you at Lucknow when the mutiny began?"

"Aye."

"Can you tell me what happened when the word of the revolt reached Lucknow?"

"When the attackers came over the wall, Christian shouted a warning for me to go somewhere, I think he meant for me to go to The Residency, where I would be safe, and he rushed off to join his regiment. The six and 12 pounders were firing and the air was filled with smoke and the roar of the heavy artillery. A violent thunderstorm hit Lucknow during the fighting while I was running toward The Residency which had been heavily fortified. Can't remember if Christian told me to go there, or if I thought he might be defending it. I found his sash...the crimson one I gave him for

Christmas in the hands of his Muslin bearer. A bolt of lightning crashed near me. You know the rest.."

Dr. Goddard lifted his eyes from his note taking. "And you have no memory of returning?"

"None whatsoever."

"In what year did you say the mutiny began? Was it May of 1857?"

"Yes, doctor."

"That will be all this morning. I'd like for you to build up your strength. Walk in the gardens...get some rest and eat a good lunch. You'll see to that, Mrs. Stewart?"

"By all means, Dr. Goddard."

"And I'd like to see you again at three. By the way, Miss Farrell, or should I call you Mrs. Skye?" He folded his notes and placed them in a manila folder.

"Call me Kitty."

"Would you recommend a good book for me to read about the Sepoy Mutiny of 1857, Kitty? Perhaps you know a good novel?"

"I'm sorry, I barely remember studying about the mutiny myself. Some of it came back to me in bits and pieces when it happened, but both my father and mother wrote about it. I don't know of any books in print."

Suddenly she realized he was baiting her, attempting to find out if she had been reading about the mutiny in a steamy romance.

"Thank you. I'll see you at three." He opened the folder and was scribbling on his pad and barely glanced at her.

"Kitty!" Olivia cried when they were alone on the elevator. "What in the world were you saying? Was there actually a Captain Skye?"

"Yes! Yes! Yes!" she sobbed. "And it's all over. I am here and he is there. I can never find him now."

CHAPTER TWENTY

"**D**o you feel like walking?" Olivia asked Kitty. "I need some fresh air. There's no way you could have gone to India, or at least if you did, it wasn't the way you said it happened and no way was it when you think it happened. Who have you been with? Did you meet some jerk and simply take off without telling anyone what you were up to? What did you do after you left New York?" Olivia was shaking. She reached for a cigarette, realized they were on an elevator in the hospital and put it away. " Kitty, level with me."

"I know it sounds impossible...but, oh, maybe I should just tell Dr. Goddard I made it all up, was attacked by a no-good guy who beat me half to death and dumped me along the road. It would make more sense."

"I don't know what game you're playing, but you'd better tell me the truth before I get really mad." Olivia pushed the wheelchair off the elevator and into the lobby. "Come on. We're going for a walk, and you're going to tell me where you've been and what you were really doing."

Kitty felt wobbly on her feet, but she made a great effort to walk. Olivia did not offer to help her but marched through the automatic door tapping her cigarette on her fist as she went. When she realized Kitty was in trouble, she returned and offered her arm.

"Sorry, Kid. I guess you've been through a lot. Didn't mean to yell at you, but you know I have a short fuse. Now, let's have it. Who are you protecting? Whoever it was gave you a beating. I intend to get to the bottom of this one way or another. He'll do time for this."

"It's not important. This whole thing is getting out of hand. Just as soon as I can manage on my own, I want to go home."

"Now that's the first sensible thing I've heard you say since I got here. Are you O. K., need any help?" Olivia lit her cigarette and took a deep drag.

She sank onto a bench in the garden area. "Let's sit here for a little while. It is pretty here and so clean. I could sit here forever."

"Level with me. How are you feeling?" Olivia blew smoke and put her package of Camels in her purse.

"I've got to get moving. Can't simply sit here and feel sorry for myself, hurting and wishing. . ."

"Wishing what, Kitty? What were you trying to tell me?" Olivia looked at her intently.

"It has escaped me. Guess I'll get my thought patterns straightened out in a day or two. Sorry to put you through this, and I haven't even told you that I'm glad you are here. I wanted so to let you know where I was... tried to make them understand."

"I don't for one minute believe you went to India...at least not in 1856. You're going to drive me crazy with a tale like that."

Kitty looked down at her feet. "If you think you're daft, how do you think I feel about this?"

"Luke will be here tomorrow. He's taking off early Thursday and flying out Friday morning. You do want to see him, don't you?" Olivia took one last drag on her cigarette and looked about for somewhere to put the butt. She ground it out on the sidewalk and then picked it up and put it in a tissue and put it in her purse. "They'd probably arrest me on the spot if I threw my cigarette away here."

Kitty laughed. "That's the first time I ever saw you worry about a thing like that."

"Come on, tell me what you're feeling about Luke? You can tell Aunt Olivia."

"Nothing. Absolutely nothing."

"He knows he was a fool. . . wanted to call you, but I told him to wait. Then you up and left and they found your car alongside the road and you were missing. He nearly lost his mind."

"Luke Filbey?"

"Well, he's alive and well...not living in the nineteenth century. Kitty, why did you leave? Why didn't you call me?"

"Maybe I have amnesia and don't remember a thing that happened."

"Now, at last you're making sense. For a while I thought we were going to have to lock you up."

"Will Dr. Goddard buy that story?"

"Twice as fast as the one you told him this morning. I'm glad you're here at last. We need you with the company as soon as you've had some rest."

At three o'clock they returned for a second session with Dr. Goddard. He was late returning to his office, so Kitty and Olivia sat in the outer office and read magazines. Kitty found several issues of news magazines and tried to learn what was happening, but she could not concentrate long and dozed in her chair.

"The doctor will see you now," she heard someone say and sat up.

"Are you ready?" Olivia gave her a hand.

"As ready as I'll ever be. Is it necessary to go through all this? All I want to do is go home."

"Right this way." she heard someone say. "Did you have a good lunch?"

"We ate in the cafeteria dining room and then took a nap. Afraid I'm wearing Mrs. Stewart out." It was chit-chat, something Kitty had never mastered. She knew she was regaining her strength and was no longer hurting physically, in fact, the pain had never been physical. She had simply been crying deep within. She thought of Christian again and a stabbing pain reached into her and twisted around in her insides.

When they entered the small consultation room, they waited again until Dr. Goddard tapped lightly on the door. He entered carrying her file and sat down facing her.

"And how are you feeling this afternoon?" He looked into her eyes with the little flashlight he carried.

"Much better. We walked and ate lunch in the cafeteria and took a nap. I don't know which did the most good."

"Follow my finger with your eyes," he told her and she tried to focus on his finger moving from left to right. "And when did you first go to India?" The doctor was looking into her eyes again, and she found it next to impossible to answer with her head thrown back. Then he was watching her face for her reaction to his question and was sitting so close she could smell the fragrance of his aftershave.

"I was only sixteen. My parents and I spent a year in India when Dad was awarded a Fulbright fellowship to study there."

"What did your parents do for a living?" He moved back and picked up his pad again.

"They were teachers."

He was writing again.

"Let me see you walk. Follow the black line on the floor."

Kitty found it impossible to put one foot in front of the other without tipping over. "My equilibrium appears to be somewhat messed up, doctor. What does that mean?"

"It's to be expected. I spent three hours at the library," he told her. "I found very little about the Sepoy Mutiny, but it did happen, just as you said. You had the date right, and Lucknow was under siege for many months."

"Did many die there? What of the officers and their wives?"

"The account I read gave no names to speak of, but many did die. The mutiny was finally brought under control by the Europeans. Tell me again about Captain Skye."

He had a pleasant voice, one which inspired confidence, but she was cautious now about how she should answer him. "Perhaps I had a dream. I have had many dreams so real that I could have sworn something really strange actually happened. Sometimes I wake up angry at someone for something they didn't even know about. My dreams are often quite real."

"Kitty, one does not dream the trauma you have gone through. Something unusual happened...something real."

"Perhaps I have amnesia and the dream became mixed in my mind."

"It is possible. Would you describe a lotus blossom for me?" His eyes were almost closed.

"The lotus blossom?"

"Yes, you spoke of a lotus blossom. Can you describe it for me?"

"Actually it's a water lily...except quite large and waxy appearing, the loveliest flower I have ever seen."

"What color is the lotus?"

"Shades of pink...appearing fragile but quite strong."

"Did you ever taste the fruit of the lotus?" He peered at her over his glasses.

"Heavens, no! Why would one ever eat the fruit of a lotus? I'm not sure the lotus even has a fruit."

"May I see your ring?" He changed the topic under discussion suddenly and held out his hand.

She removed the emerald her father had given her. He studied the ring and asked her to tell him about it.

"There's nothing to say. My father bought it for me when we were in India when I was sixteen. Emeralds are quite inexpensive in India."

Then Dr. Goddard asked to see the band with the smaller stones. She slipped the ring from her finger and he studied the two rings.

"And this is the ring Christian Skye gave you?" He held the gold band up.

"Yes. It is my wedding ring." Too late, she knew she had revealed more than she had intended.

"I see."

"It may have been just a dream." She looked him in the eye and hoped he would not pursue that course of conversation.

He handed both rings back to her and wrote something he saw in the two rings on his pad.

He turned to Olivia. "Mrs. Stewart, how long have you known Kitty?"

"Since we were in college. We worked in the same law office in New York City. Kitty had an unfortunate affair with one of the vice-presidents of the company and quit in order to return to Kansas. She appeared to be completely exhausted by all of it."

"What did you hope to accomplish by leaving the law firm, Kitty?" His voice was soothing.

"My parents had both died within a week. I did not take time to settle the estate properly...unfinished business. And it's like Livy said, I was totally exhausted."

"You had a considerable sum of money in cash with you when you pulled off the highway. What happened to that money? Is there a possibility that you were robbed?"

"Yes, there is that possibility. I may have suffered a concussion. My purse is in my room. I don't know what is in it now."

"Now, about your rings. May I keep them overnight? I'll return them tomorrow morning."

"Doctor, Luke Filbey will be here in the morning." Olivia spoke hesitantly, and Kitty could not see what possible difference it would make to Dr. Goddard. She was certain she could care whether he came back into her life or not.

"What time do you expect him to arrive?"

"He'll be here at seven-thirty." She took off her wire-rims and rubbed her eyes.

"Good. I'd like to see him as soon as possible."

"Get a good night's rest, Kitty. Oh, by the way, Mrs. Stewart, may I take you out to dinner tonight?" He rose and held the door open for them..

"Why, yes. I'd love to go out to dinner." She was smiling.

"I'll pick you up at seven at your hotel."

She had eaten her meal in her room and had turned on the television set above her bed when a nurse came in to take her temperature and blood pressure. She handed Kitty a small paper cup with two small pills in it and a glass of water. She watched while Kitty took the pills and then wrote on her pad.

Before the nurse left the room, Kitty began to feel drowsy.

She awoke early the next morning and went to the bathroom. She turned on the water and adjusted the temperature of the water before she stepped into the shower.

She washed her hair and felt the shampoo she had lathered into her hair going down her body. Then she thought of Christian Skye and slid down to the floor of the shower while the water rained down on her.

"Miss Farrell! What are you doing?"

Someone turned off the water and strong hands lifted her off the floor of the shower. "Someone help me get her back in bed," she heard a voice calling.

Kitty let them help her.

She continued to sob while someone wrapped a towel around her and helped her into a hospital gown that tied in the back. Someone else was towel-drying her hair.

"You should have called," a voice scolded her. "We would have helped you."

Suddenly, the room was filled with people. Someone said, "Bring the hair drier in. I'll dry her hair for her. Do you feel like sitting, Kitty?"

"Yes, I'll be alright."

By ten o'clock, Kitty had been dressed in the new skirt and blouse. She felt helpless among strangers who were intent on helping her.

"Has Mrs. Stewart been here this morning?" Kitty could not keep the edge of annoyance from her voice.

"Yes, she asked if you slept well, then left."

Kitty heard a knock at the door and a familiar voice asked, "May I come in?"

"Come in Mr. Filbey. Have you had coffee? We're finished now. Will you take Miss Farrell up to the fourth floor?"

Luke Filbey did not answer but stood looking down at Kitty. "How are you, Baby?" he asked at last.

She sat on the edge of her bed and simply stared at him. They had once lived together, but he could have been a stranger. She knew the way his salt and pepper colored hair grew thick near the back of his neck and thinner on the top of his head. She knew the solid feel of him. He had a fine tan from sailing, and the hair on his arms had bleached out as it had been when he last held her. She knew how he would smell...clean and fresh. The irresistible boyish charm was still in his eyes. His voice had not changed.

He came to her and put his arms around her and drew her to him. "I should not have let you go!"

"'Twas a mid-life crisis hitting, Luke. What was I to do?"

"Where did you learn to talk like that, Kitty?" He pulled back, unbelieving.

"Thank you for the roses, Luke. You were always thoughtful." She purposely did not tell him she had slipped into Christian Skye's speech pattern unknowingly.

"Answer me, Kitty."

She could see his face, recoiling from the first words she had spoken to him.

"I'm sorry, Luke." She shrugged. "I can't explain."

"I know. I know." He looked at her as though seeing her for the first time.

"You can't know. No one knows."

"We're trying to help you, Honey. The doctor is baffled by your case. Are you well enough to go home? He may release you today if you are up to going out to your farm. Olivia and I will stay with you until Monday morning...longer if you need us."

"I'd like that."

"That's my girl! Are you ready to see the doc? You have an appointment at ten-thirty, and you have five minutes to make it. I'm to take you in the chair. Want a fast ride?"

Olivia and Luke waited for her in the waiting room while she walked behind the receptionist down the long hall to a conference room. Dr. Goddard waited for her there.

"You are looking well this morning, Kitty." Dr. Goddard stood and then indicated the chair. "Sit here. Did you sleep well last night?"

"Those two, tiny pills knocked me out like a light."

She waited for him to begin questioning her.

"I took the liberty of having your rings evaluated. The emerald is a twentieth century ring from India." He handed it back to her. "The band with the stones is a typical mid-nineteenth century ring custom made, probably in India. I don't know how you came by it, but I have a gut feeling about it. I have nothing to verify...cannot explain any of this in a rational manner." He shook his head. "If you had a paranormal experience of some kind, there is nothing to prove that it happened...or didn't happen. Do you understand what I'm saying?" He placed the emerald and her wedding ring in her hand.

"I think I do."

"We have certain facts upon which we can depend. You were found sitting alongside a country road. Your clothes had been wet and muddy. Your speech was slurred and you stumbled while you walked."

"I see." She tried to comprehend what he said.

Dr. Goddard looked at her with concern. He took her hand in his to reassure her. "I want you to go home. Try to live as normally as you possibly can for awhile. I'd like to see you in a month or sooner if you have any problems. I'm not prescribing any medication except something to help you sleep when you need it, and I don't want you to take anything stronger than an aspirin once a day. Should you feel yourself going in and out, call me at once. Mrs. Stewart will find a home health nurse to stay with you for awhile, just in case you should feel yourself going over the edge."

"I'm being discharged today?"

"I see no reason to keep you here any longer than necessary. Try to put all this behind you as quickly as possible. It won't be good to go over and over it with others. Good luck, Kitty. And by the way, the money from the sale of your personal property was in your purse. You may pick it up at the office. Mrs. Stewart put it in the safe for you when you came in. Your charge cards, driver's license, and other cards of identification are there as well."

"You mean I'm gong home?"

"I don't see why not."

"Thank you, doctor. Thank you. Oh, by the way, why did you ask me I had ever eaten the fruit of the lotus?"

"Just a hunch. I was wrong, of course. The fruit produces a kind of lethargy in those who eat of it. Wondered if it had brought about some chemical effect on you. I know now that you were telling the truth when you said that you had never tasted the fruit."

"How did you know that?"

"One learns to watch for certain things," he laughed. "And besides, Mrs. Stewart assured me that you never touched drugs of any kind."

"Well, I'm relieved to hear that!" Her head began spinning, but she did not tell Dr. Goddard about that. All she wanted to do was to go home... home...home.

CHAPTER TWENTY-ONE

"Everything is just as I remember it!" Kitty dashed from room to room, touching the things she remembered. Her mother's sewing basket sat beside her chair just as it had been before she died, the artificial flowers still sat on the dining room table where her mother had placed them two years ago, her father's pipe stood in the pipe stand where he had last used it. The furniture was just as she remembered it, slightly soiled and having seen better days. There had been no particular style of furnishings in her parent's home. Her mother always laughed when she described her home as "early miscellaneous" and admitted that she hated the idea of being a slave to housekeeping. She flopped down in her mother's easy chair and shut her eyes.

"She liked to read or sew here while Dad slept in front of the television. It seems I haven't been away. And how did you manage to bring my Mustang here and put all my things away. Even the sterling and Lenox are intact."

"You must remember. Kitty Farrell was missing. I came at once, I might add, badgering law officers because they were dragging their feet. I put your things away for you, just in case you turned up unexpectedly."

Luke listened without making comments, but Kitty caught him watching her.

"What do you think, Lucas? Can you imagine my spending my life here...perfect solitude...perfect peace?"

"I have to admit it is totally in character. You always liked your space. I'd say you had plenty of that out here."

"Now that we're all settled here for the week-end, " Olivia said, "this old gal is going into town to buy food and take care of business. I'm going to deposit your money in the bank before you fool around and lose it.

Is that all right, Kitty?" Olivia took over in her motherly, businesslike manner.

"Anything you say," Kitty told her.

"You both look like you could stand a little rest. When did you sleep last, Luke?" Olivia had made out a list of things she needed to do in town and checked it again.

"I'm beat. Show me to my bed, Mamma Bear, and I'll behave myself and catch a nap while you're in town."

Olivia laughed "You're in the hired man's bedroom downstairs. Kitty and I have the upstairs rooms. Do you need anything before I go into town?" She looked at Kitty.

"I'm melting into Mamma's lounge chair. Never knew how she could fall asleep here until this very minute. Do you reckon I'm really ready for the looney bin?"

"Of course not. Whatever gave you that idea?" Olivia shrugged her shoulders and took the bills which had been wrapped in a paper bag from Kitty's purse. "I can't believe you carried this wad of bills and never lost any of it."

"When I awoke at Lucknow Colonel Oliver, or maybe it was Maria, had exchanged one of the bills for rupees, I think, and they had swapped purses with me. Can you believe Old Oliver had never seen plastic? He thought I was a witch when I told him I must have flown from Topeka or possibly that I had driven on to Denver. He accused me of carrying counterfeit bills. Isn't that a kick?"

Luke and Olivia exchanged looks, and Luke asked her, "What were you wearing when you arrived?"

"My shorts and a tee shirt...and sandals, of course. Everyone thought I had appeared in my underwear. Lionel Oliver was outraged." She laughed, remembering. "He actually put me under house arrest for not obeying orders."

"What was she wearing when they found her?" Luke turned to Olivia.

"It was shorts and a T-shirt. They cut the shorts away at the hospital."

Their voices floated over her consciousness. She was remembering going to Christian in the old, dark, muslin dress which clung to her. She smiled when she thought of his first kiss and felt herself floating away in a sea of happiness. Then the sadness struck. She turned away from them with her tears flowing.

She awoke when she heard Olivia talking to Luke in the kitchen. "Is she still asleep? I have the sleeping pills for tonight and the nurse will come out Sunday evening to get acquainted. Her husband is in the infantry in the Middle East. She's glad to get out of heavy duty nursing. I deposited the money and talked to the hospital attendants. Did I do the right thing, Luke?"

"Sure, Olivia," she heard Luke say. "And she's slept like a baby."

"It's steak over the grill for supper. How are you with charcoal?"

"My specialty."

"You start the charcoal then, and I'll wake Kitty and see if she's ready to be sociable."

The next morning Kitty awoke early, rummaged in her dresser drawers for comfortable clothes to wear, and found her favorite pair of old shorts and a red T-shirt. She put on sneakers and went downstairs where she knew someone was making coffee.

"You're spoiling me. Coffee...toast and jam!"

"You can use a little pampering, and we're having fun, you silly goose. What would you like to do today?"

She thought of Christian Skye, and for a moment she knew she would begin to cry.

"Sorry. That was a stupid thing to ask."

"It's alright. I'm going to have to face up to the fact that Christian is no longer a part of my life, but it's worse than death...the uncertainty...the not knowing."

Luke spoke up, "Kitty and I are going to explore the farm today. How about a fishing trip out to that pond I have my eye on? Could you pack us a lunch, Olivia? We'll take one of those heavy blankets I found in my room, and Kitty can rest while I try my luck."

"Wonderful idea. I have some business in town to finish while you two entertain each other." She buttered toast for Kitty and handed her two slices along with the apricot jam.

Kitty tipped her coffee cup and relished the taste of it.

After breakfast, Luke handed her a pillow, and he picked up the lunch basket, a fishing rod and reel, a can of worms he found under the big flat rocks which served as stepping stones while she ate, and the heavy blanket he had found in the hired man's room.

"Ready to go? I'm heading for that willow tree on the dam. We'll take turns using the pole."

Kitty grabbed her mother's old straw hat hanging on a peg by the back door and followed Luke toward the pond. The heat from the sun felt warm on her back, and she began to relax.

When they reached the dam, Luke spread the blanket in the shade of the willow tree and placed the basket Olivia had prepared beside it. Kitty strolled along the dam and tried to catch frogs for bait, but everything she did reminded her of either Christian or Colin. At last, she wandered back to the blanket and sat with her head on her knees watching Luke's cork dancing in the water.

Finally, he brought the rod close to the blanket and set it in a forked stick.

"Kitty, I've never told you that I'm sorry."

"'Twasn't necessary, Luke."

He looked at her strangely. "Perhaps not, but I want you to know that there was no one else...never felt about anyone like I did you. I never knew it until it was too late to say how it was with me. I told Olivia I wanted you back. And then you left New York and disappeared. It scared the life out of me."

"I never knew where I was. So strange."

"You were...you had. . ."

"What are you trying to say?" she asked Luke.

"I am confused."

"I seem to be the all-time winner when it comes to confusion." She spoke in a matter of fact tone of voice which he realized was far more rational than his own.

He looked stunned, then turned and took her hand. "I deserved that."

They were silent, with nothing more to say to each other. They watched the red and white cork bouncing in the water.

He put his arm around her and drew her to him. It was comforting to feel him close to her, but she felt nothing for him. Olivia had surely told him about Christian Skye.

"If only we could erase the last several months of our lives," Luke told her with a heavy sigh..

"I'd not exchange them for anything in the world." She felt her face glowing. If she did nothing else, she had to let Luke and Olivia know with a certainty that she didn't regret for a moment the time she had spent with Christian. She knew she would be tormented by the thoughts of what had happened to Christian until she learned his fate. She had no idea how she was going to learn what happened to him, but somewhere, in some dusty, forgotten military report, his name would appear. She would find him and know the truth.

"You loved him?"

"I know you find it hard to believe, but I loved him as I never believed I could love anyone."

"Then why did you..?"

"I have every reason to believe that we were separated for a reason neither of us could understand or do anything about. That is what troubles me so, Luke."

"Where were you Kitty?"

"I was in India during the days of the Raj."

"What is that supposed to mean?" His voice registered disbelief, and he looked at her with an incredible look of doubt.

"During the days of Queen Victoria when the British ruled India."

"I couldn't believe what you said about that Skye fellow being dead for over one hundred years. Kitty, quit looking away with that faraway expression on your face. You know it couldn't happen. Olivia doesn't believe it for one second."

"Of course, it couldn't happen." She could find no reason to argue with Luke Filbey, the attorney who was too practical to believe she might be telling the truth.

"Come on, Baby. The fish aren't biting and it's getting hot out here. Let's go back to the house and see of we can find something cold to drink." He rose and pulled in his line. "Wonder if that window air conditioner works."

He found Cokes in the refrigerator, then they went to the porch and sat in comfortable rocking chairs painted white. He made no move to touch her. For that she was grateful. He was speaking and she came back from wherever it was she had been.

"When are you coming back to New York, Kitty?" he asked her.

"New York? I don't suppose I'll ever go back to that rat race again."

"Did you leave because of us?" He asked the question cautiously.

"Yes and no. I never felt right about our relationship. Yet, I was angry and hurt and sad and all the other things a woman feels when she is dumped, but there was something I could not identify pulling me away. I called it destiny."

"Had you . . .?"

"No, Luke. I was perfectly sane when I pulled off the interstate. I was as sane as you are today. I knew what I wanted when I left New York City, and when I found it, I knew and was completely overwhelmed by it. She tipped her glass and looked over the rim of it to see his reaction.

"I'd like to stay on here with you, Kitty." He said it simply without making any moves toward her.

"No, Luke. I have already made up my mind what I have to do."

"And that is?"

"Search the records for. . ."

"For what?"

"The Sepoy revolt."

"Do you actually believe you were there when the Sepoy's . . when they revolted because of a gun?"

"Perhaps."

"And you think you will find your name written down in the 1857 books? Don't be ridiculous. You will never find what you are searching for in books."

"You are probably right, Luke. Why don't we just drop the subject?"

They sat quietly on the porch, the sound of the rockers on the wooden floor comforting and familiar.

"Will you marry me, Kitty?"

It was the first time he had ever spoken the word "marriage", and it startled her.

She held out her hand to him and showed him her ring. "I am already married, Luke. I cannot marry you."

"That ring is an antique wedding ring from the nineteenth century. It came from the Far East. Where did you find it? I know you, Kitty. If there's an antique within a hundred miles, you're sure to buy it."

"You don't want to know."

"No. I want to marry you...take you home with me...or live here with you. I want to marry you and take care of you the rest of my life."

"Not now, Luke. There are things I must learn before I do anything with my life."

"Christian Skye?"

"Aye, Christian Skye."

"How long will it take you?"

"Not long, Luke. Give me time. I can't make any decisions until I know what happened to him."

"I'm taking a week off the first of July if I can get away from New York. I'm coming out to be with you then."

"I may not be here. My search may take me to England."

"Then let me go with you."

"No. What I have to do now is something I must do alone. On second thought, you might be able to help me. You have always been good at ferreting out the truth of things in books in the most difficult of cases."

"Just let me know what I can do," Luke told her.

When Olivia returned, they had just eaten their picnic lunch on the front porch and sat staring contentedly over the bluestem. They watched a pair of red-tailed hawks soaring high in the sky and heard a meadowlark's cry. That evening Kitty and Luke wandered down the road in the twilight, and he put his arm around her. He looked up into the Kansas evening sky and said, "The stars are so close out here I feel I can reach up and touch them. Maybe I've been wasting my life in New York City." He took her in his arms and kissed her cheek.

The next evening a young woman driving an old beat-up pick-up truck drove into the yard and honked her horn. "Is this where Kitty Farrell lives?" she yelled in a rasping voice.

Olivia jumped up from the supper table and cried, "That will be Shannon Eaton!"

"Has Olivia been making bosom buddies already?" Kitty asked.

"Shannon is a nurse. She's been looking for a place to live while her husband is out of the country. Olivia thought you'd like company."

"Why didn't she ask me if I wanted company?" Kitty's voice held an edge of annoyance. "It's just like Olivia to arrange my life for me."

Shannon Eaton was getting out of the truck, and Olivia was talking a streak.

Kitty saw a vivacious red head with long legs coming toward the porch.

"Kitty, we have company."

Olivia was ushering the red headed girl into the kitchen. "Kitty, I'd like for you to meet Shannon Eaton. We met today in town at the bank."

"How do you do, Miss Eaton."

"Mrs. Eaton," the red head corrected her, "but you must call me Shannon."

"I'm beat, folks. I think I'll just hang it up early tonight," Kitty told them. She rose from the table and marched to the stairway. "Good-night everyone. I'll see you in the morning, Olivia...Luke.... Shannon."

She felt a small victory. Let the three of them as well as Dr. Goddard think she was as crazy as a bedbug.

She sat in the old, white wicker rocker with the faded blue cushion beside her bed, listening to the sounds of the electric clock. The wind had died down, and the air in the upstairs bedroom was stifling hot. She turned on her fan and opened her window as wide as it would go. Then she took off her clothes and put on a thin wrapper.

Someone knocked at her door.

"Who is it?" she called.

"It's Shannon. May I come in?"

Kitty knew she waited outside the door for her to invite her to come in to talk with her. "Come in," she called in a small voice.

Shannon was barefooted and looked like a young girl. When Kitty studied her face, she discovered small lines around her mouth and eyes.

"I'm going to level with you," Shannon began when she sat down in the wicker chair opposite Kitty's. "I know from studying your case that you aren't one who wants to play games. Dr. Goddard sent you home because he knew you'd recover in record time in your own surroundings, but on one condition."

"And that is?" Kitty gave her a defiant look.

"You are not to stay alone for awhile. That's where I come in. I'm a registered nurse. I've studied your case, and have become interested in the things you have told Dr. Goddard and Olivia. I, too, have had a paranormal experience and know what it is to have everyone doubt that you're entirely sane. When my first husband was in Nam, I awoke late one night and heard him calling my name. His voice was so clear, I got out of bed and went downstairs, convinced that he had returned in the night. I was fully awake and knew his voice above all others. I heard him calling distinctly, but he was not there. I got my folks out of bed and made myself a cup of coffee, but I could not sleep. Several days later I got the telegram. He had died on that night at the precise hour I heard him calling to me. There are things that cannot be explained logically, Kitty. I'm here to help you adjust to living in today's world. I have remarried, and Robert is serving in the Middle East. Perhaps we can help one another by being alive and adjusting to reality, whatever that is."

"So it's not just therapy, therapy, therapy. Will you help me try to find out what happened to him?" Her eyes sought Shannon Eaton's.

"How do you propose going about it?"

"There are military histories. I intend to read everything I can put my hands on here...and if necessary go to England to delve into old records to learn where he died...and where he is buried."

"And if you can't find his name?"

The clock on the wall downstairs struck seven o'clock and Kitty smiled. "Then I'll return to Kansas and try to begin all over again. Are you willing to help me?"

"You're not covered by your insurance policy unless you are hospitalized, but I'd like to get off the fast lane for awhile. Let's just say I'm on an extended vacation at half-pay."

"When can you begin?" She was back on track, beginning something that would occupy every minute of her waking hours.

"We'll drive Olivia and Luke to the airport early Monday morning," Shannon told her, "and then we will go to the library at K State to learn what we can about the Sepoy Mutiny. We'll check out each footnote on every page. Somewhere we'll find something that will lead us to the list of men who served at Lucknow and what happened to them."

"I had no idea you really believed I was there."

"Stranger things have happened. Believe me, I have seen everything."

"Then, you're on. Bring your things out early Monday morning, and we'll see Livy and Luke off to New York."

"Luke has asked you to marry him."

"Yes."

"Don't give him your answer yet."

"Do you have the sight? How do you know these things, Shannon?"

"I know men. He didn't come all the way out here for nothing."

"I have already told him that I'm married. Until I learn otherwise, I'm still very much married to Christian Skye. I must find him."

Shannon held out the two small sleeping pills and said, "Don't take them unless you find yourself tossing and turning and unable to settle down."

"We're going to get along. For the first time since I came back, I have found someone who admits something unusual may have happened to me and doesn't treat me like a fool."

"You're smart enough to know if you need something to help you sleep. I have a feeling you're smart enough to learn whatever it is you're trying to find out about your man."

"Thanks, Shannon"

"Now, I'll go down and face the tigers." She laughed and closed the door behind her.

After she had gone, Kitty closed her eyes and said, "Please, God. We must find out what happened to Christian and Colin." She put on her clothes and rejoined the others in the kitchen.

CHAPTER TWENTY-TWO

Kitty and Shannon Eaton told Luke and Olivia goodbye at the airport and went to the parking lot where they had parked the Mustang. Shannon unlocked the car.

She looked at Kitty. "What are we waiting for?" She climbed in, put the key in the ignition, and started the car.

Kitty laughed.

"It's a good sign when you can laugh. Now, don't get your hopes up too high. Remember we are in the heart of Kansas. It is very unlikely that we'll find anything that will lead us to Christian Skye immediately." Shannon backed the Mustang out and left the parking lot with a toss of her long hair.

"Librarians are the most helpful persons in the world. Sometimes they do the impossible." Kitty told her.

"I've never been one to spend time in libraries. And if we don't find anything in Manhattan? What is the game plan next?" Shannon asked as she picked up speed.

"We go on to Topeka. Does Dr. Goddard know what we're doing?"

"Yes, I called him yesterday. He sees nothing wrong with your plan? In fact, if we go to Topeka, we might stop in, so he can see how much progress you're making."

"Not just yet." Kitty had reservations about things like driving her car or making arrangements for the hotel. She didn't know why, but she hadn't gotten back into the twentieth century comfortably. In the back of her mind, the possibility existed that she might have to seek therapy if she found out what happened at Lucknow.

"Whatever you say." Shannon pulled out onto the interstate and drove toward Manhattan. "It was near here," she told Kitty, " they found you. Do you have any recollection of it at all?"

"None whatsoever. What do you know about it?"

"You were soaking wet, but the sun was shining. The officer who found you said that you looked like you had gone through a tornado. You were plastered with mud, understandably so given the circumstances. You were clutching your purse and a long piece of red fabric."

"What did they do with my things?"

"Olivia threw them away, I suppose. Why do you ask?" She turned to look at Kitty.

"The red fabric was Christian's sash. Do you know about it?"

"Oh, yes. The sash you made him for Christmas. His bearer was clutching it when you found him lying where he fell."

"We must find it. Don't you see? I must have taken it from Azziz."

"We'll call Olivia Stewart when she gets back to New York." Shannon looked down at the speedometer and said, "This little monster certainly has a mind of her own. I'm going eighty already. What we don't need is a ticket for speeding."

Kitty leaned back and tried to remember what had happened. Where was Christian? Maria? Maria's husband, the colonel? The people she knew.

The library at Kansas State University held a reasonably good selection of books about India as Kitty knew it would. She settled down at a long table with a stack of books in front of her. She meant to copy each reference in hopes of finding original sources. The third book she opened told about the mutiny in detail. She relived the early days of the rebellion, but when she read about the two Sepoys at Anarkulle who were overhead talking of overthrowing their English officers, she recoiled from the words. It had happened in early June, and Christian could not believe the severe punishment that was handed down. Yet, here it was, just as he told her about it.

The two Sepoys were arrested immediately and Neville Chamberlain, in command at Anarkulle, felt that quick and severe retribution in the presence of their own comrades was necessary. The 1st Punjab Infantry, composed mostly of Sikhs and Pathan native officers who had proved their loyalty, conducted the Court-Martial. The Subadar-Major of the Corps, Mir Jaffir, presided over the trial. The prisoners were found guilty of mutiny, and Neville Chamberlain handed down harsh punishment.

The form Chamberlain handed down, Kitty knew, was unacceptable to both Hindu and Muslim, for it dishonored the body so that Shradd could not be performed for them. For the Hindu it denied a happy transmigration of the soul to a wandering state in the other world. This belief was not acceptable in the Christian mind.

"Tis true, what happened at Anarkullee." Her voice was hoarse, and when she lifted her eyes, Shannon's face registered disbelief. "Christian did not believe Chamberlain would resort to harsh punishment."

Shannon read the account and said, "You knew about this before you read it here."

"Aye. That I did. We had word of it at Lucknow."

"Perhaps we should return to the farm."

Kitty saw that Shannon was visibly shaken, but she was determined to read on. "No, I must find out what happened at Lucknow."

"I'm afraid for you, Kitty. I can't let you do this until I talk with Dr. Goddard."

"Here is something else," she read on. "Delhi, Cawnpore, Lucknow... all in enemy hands. I was taken away while that was happening." She looked up at Shannon and saw her standing beside her.

"It's way past lunch time, Kitty. I promise to bring you back here if Dr. Goddard thinks it is advisable. Besides Olivia is going to call as soon as she reaches New York City."

Kitty felt drained. "Perhaps you are right. I have learned enough for now."

"I think you're right. We will go back to the farm and rest."

"Very well, but we haven't learned anything yet." She longed to read on, yet her insides were crying out.

"Let's just call it quits for today?" Shannon's voice was low and soothing.

"I didn't know this would be so hard."

"Come away, Kitty. There'll be another day." Shannon shut the book before her and put it on the 'return cart'. She led Kitty from the library. "We'll return tomorrow, if you wish and Dr. Goddard agrees to it. After all, he's the doctor."

"Let's see if we can get a library card and check out the books."

"No, Kitty. We can return."

It was then that Kitty guessed that Shannon knew how physically tiring the trip had been.

The telephone was ringing when they pulled into the driveway. Shannon heard it and raced into the house. When Kitty entered the kitchen, she hung up.

"It was Olivia. They just arrived in New York. You'll find the sash in the top drawer of the dresser in the hired man's room. She had it cleaned, but I think you should rest before you take a look there."

Kitty dashed to the simple bedroom beyond the kitchen and yanked open the dresser drawer. The crimson, satin sash Christian had worn when he paraded his troops that last morning lay on top of the underclothing she had worn.

She hugged the sash to her, remembering Azziz's face when she took it from him. She fell upon the small bed and cried out, "Shannon! Shannon! I need you!"

"I'm here, Kitty. What is it?"

"This is the sash I made for him."

"It's here in your file! But why did Azziz have it?"

"I don't know. I don't know." She was sobbing uncontrollably.

"I must call Dr. Goddard." Shannon spoke low, and Kitty knew another bit of information was going into her case history. "Olivia will call you when she gets home. They were just leaving the airport, and Luke was waiting. He will call you tonight."

Kitty held the sash close. Her heart cried out, "Christian! Christian! Christian!

"Put it back in the drawer," Shannon told her gently.

CHAPTER TWENTY-THREE

"How about resting for awhile before dinner," Shannon suggested.

Kitty had almost forgotten she was a nurse...a nurse hired to see that she didn't go over the brink. For that matter, the mention of Lucknow under siege and finding the sash Christian wore was almost more than she could bear. It didn't matter what Olivia thought about the matter...or whether anyone believed a word she had said. Something had happened to her, something remarkable and wonderful and horrible. For some reason she could not explain, she was yanked back to the present. The only way she could explain it in her own mind was that something had happened to Christian as well.

"Colin got out before the fighting began," she said more to herself than to Shannon Eaton. "I think I will rest for awhile. Would you like to go into town to eat tonight? I'm a lousy cook, and I doubt if there's anything in the house to eat."

"I'll wake you if Olivia or Luke calls. Go ahead and rest. I want to talk to Dr. Goddard to see what he thinks we should do next."

Kitty awoke when she heard the telephone ringing downstairs. She heard Shannon talking, and then she called to her.

"I'll be right down." She put on her slippers and shook her head to clear it of sleep.

When she reached the kitchen, Shannon said, "It's Luke," and handed her the telephone.

"Luke?" Kitty said. Her voice held a trace of annoyance.

"Wanted to talk to you before I crashed. How are things going?"

"Did Shannon tell you. Lucknow was under siege. The Sepoys held the cantonment. I wasn't able to read all of it. Maybe we can go back tomorrow."

Shannon was shaking her head. "We did plan to go back tomorrow, but Shannon says not. She must have talked to Dr. Goddard."

"Let me talk to him again before you hang up, Kitty," Shannon said.

"Better get some rest, Luke. Shannon wants to talk to you before you hang up though."

"Kitty," Luke said, "don't try to do too much just yet. Take care of yourself."

"I will, and Luke," she started to tell him about finding the sash in the top drawer of the dresser in the room where he slept but decided against it.

"What is it, Baby?"

"Nothing important. Take care. Here's Shannon." She felt the tears welling up and was glad to quit talking.

"Luke, I have a plan in mind that involves you. It's like this, Dr. Goddard thinks we shouldn't hit the books too hard just now. He'd like for Kitty to do something just for fun and relaxation for several months until she gets back to normal, and then if she's determined to read about all of that mutiny stuff in India we can dig into it. What I'd like for you to do is this. If you can find time to go to a really good library, see what you can find about a Captain Christian Skye or anyone by the name of Skye who might have been in India in the 1850s. Do you think you can do that? We might have to dig into the military archives in England to learn the fate of the men at Lucknow. I don't think Kitty will rest until we find something."

Kitty waited for Shannon to speak again.

"Chances are you won't, but just in case. It would help matters if you were to find a name...something in the references. In the meantime, what do you suggest that Kitty and I do besides sit under the air conditioner and sip sodas?"

Shannon paused then turned to Kitty. "What did you say the boy's name was?"

"Colin. Colin Skye."

She heard Shannon repeat the name then add, "He was ten years old . . maybe eleven when he returned to England. Just a minute. What else do you need to know?"

"Christian had a brother William Skye in the wool trade...northern England maybe Scotland. I don't know the name of the county."

"A brother William in wool...northern England. Oh, uh...I see. Kitty, he wants to talk to you again."

Shannon handed Kitty the telephone. "I love you Baby," Luke said. "I'd not do this crazy thing for anyone but you."

"Thanks, Luke. I know that. Bye now."

They waited for Olivia to call before they went into town to eat, and they didn't have long to wait.

"Kitty? My kids are piled around me...wanting to tell you they love you, but I'm not going to put them on the phone tonight. I'm beat. How was your day? You were in a big hurry to get away this morning. What did you and Shannon do today?"

"We went to the university library."

"I might have known."

She heard Olivia groaning on her end of the line and added, "The old witch of the north says I've got to stay away for awhile. I almost fell apart. Guess she knows best."

"Why don't you come to New York in a few days...see some good musicals...show Shannon the sights...go out with Luke?"

"Not yet. Maybe later. Besides, Luke is going to dig into the books for me."

"He'd be good at that...has a real nose for mystery. It will keep him from going berserk . . . to be doing something for you. What do you expect him to find?"

"A regimental history...what happened to Christian Skye."

"And if he does, what will it prove?"

"That I was there, not that I know otherwise. You still don't believe me, do you?"

"I'd come a lot nearer believing you were off on a jaunt with a crazy man."

"Thanks, Livy, for everything."

Olivia did not answer.

"Livy? You still there?"

"Yes, Kitty. Maybe I'd better get off and try to get some sleep. Oh, oh. Jamie wants to tell you she loves you."

Each of the children took a turn telling her they loved her, and when she at last hung up, she said, "What a madhouse! Maybe we'd better not think about New York just yet."

After a month had passed, Kitty and Shannon paid a visit to Dr. Goddard and when they were ready to leave, he said, "If you're still determined to read about the mutiny, I believe you can handle it now. I don't know what useful purpose it will serve, but it might ease your mind to know what happened there."

"Luke Filbey has been passing along information. He is having copies made of regimental lists from the archives in London. I'd like to know, exactly, the extent of the mutiny, although I don't think the history books in our local libraries will tell us much."

"Then it won't do any harm to read about it. Afraid you're stuck with library work, Mrs. Eaton." He grinned and laid his glasses on Kitty's file.

"Guess I can handle it," she told him. "I have no other wild plans until my husband returns to Kansas."

"And where is he now?"

"Saudi Arabia."

"Sure hope this build-up doesn't turn into anything bigger than a big scare."

"He never says much."

"Well, you ladies stay out of trouble. I don't want to see you again unless there are drastic changes."

"We're going sailing tomorrow on Tuttle Creek Lake. Is that on the prescribed list of activities."

"Sounds like fun, but some of us have to work." He rose and shook hands with Kitty and Shannon.

Two days later Kitty got behind the wheel of her Mustang and drove to the library at Kansas State. She read about the fate of the English officers, women, and children of the East India Company in Delhi. The same report came from Aligarh, and at Gwali.

"Kitty, why do you want to read this stuff?" Shannon was obviously repulsed by the stories.

"I can't help myself. I know the history of those events won't tell me what I want to know, but I have to learn what happened there."

She didn't look up. The events of those days did not affect her as they had earlier, and when she read about the things that had happened, it was through the eyes of one who had never been there at all.

Yet, she knew exactly how the maps at the posts throughout the Ganges Valley read, and when she heard about the movable column fighting its way throughout the monsoon-soaked countryside as it made its way toward Delhi to retake the city from the rebels, she knew what they went through to get there. When she read that the trees had been mutilated in order to provide food for camels, she knew. She was not surprised to read that cholera later ravaged the encampment at Delhi which had been under siege for almost three months.

She read on and on about the retaking of Delhi and then on to events that happened later at Cawnpore, an important cantonment from which officers and troops had been siphoned off to go to Lucknow which came under siege. All up and down the Ganges River Valley the battles raged until at last Cawnpore was attacked.

"I'm beginning to understand why I was brought back," Kitty told Shannon. "Have you found any footnotes that we should study further?"

"You've worn me out totally. My eyes are bleary and I can't even focus them any longer. Do you know what time it is?"

Kitty glanced at the clock on the wall and said, "I'm sorry, Shannon. We should have eaten hours ago. Do you suppose anything is open?"

"The library closes in a half hour."

They ate a hamburger and French fries at a drive-in before they returned to the farm. When they entered the kitchen, the telephone was ringing. Kitty raced to answer it.

Luke Filbey yelled, "Where in the world have you been? I've been trying to call you since noon."

"Well, if I'd known you were going to call, I'd have stayed at home and sat beside the phone all day."

Kitty was annoyed that he had yelled at her. Furthermore, she resented his intrusion into her life again. Luke Filbey had walked out on her once, a fact she had not forgotten. Olivia had tried to get them together again, and Kitty had no intentions of becoming involved with him ever again.

"Kitty? Are you still there?"

"Yes, but barely."

"I found something you should know about. There's a book...no longer in print and certainly not in America anywhere for I've called all over the country. I have requested that a library in London which has it to fax copies as soon as possible. Now, don't get your hopes up, Kitty, for it may not prove to be anything at all."

"What is it, Luke?"

"It's called *The Life and Times of an Englishman in India during the Days of the Raj—1860-1910.*."

"And?"

She was remembering the stories about wool merchants in England he had sent to her, none of which ever mentioned a family by the name of Skye. He had faxed her regimental histories, none of which mentioned Christian Skye. She had wondered if he was deliberately stalling. He had come to see her during the four days he had off in July. They had gone sailing and had gone fishing below the dam at Tuttle Creek. She felt nothing but a warm friendship where Luke was concerned.

Luke paused before he continued. "I called London and asked about the book, and it seems that it might be relevant to your search, but it's difficult to say. It may not tell us anything about the mutiny or anything else you want to know."

"What made you think the book might be important, Luke?" She knew he was tossing her a crumb, when she felt no inclination to have him near her.

"Are you sitting down?"

"Of course not, you idiot."

"Kitty the book was published in 1922. It's the author who may be important. His name was Sir Colin Skye."

CHAPTER TWENTY-FOUR

"Sir? Sir Colin Skye? Luke! Do you know what this means?"

"Now, don't get excited, Kitty. We don't know who this old gentleman was or if he was even distantly related to the Colin Skye you told me about. You may have just picked the name out of the air, you know. The book appears to be a reminiscence of an old man who distinguished himself in England in some manner."

"Colin would have gone to Addiscombe...would have graduated with honors and a commission. Christian saw to that before. . ."

"Go to bed, Kitty. I'm having the entire book faxed to Dr. Goddard. He'll call you."

"You're right. There may have been other Colin Skyes in England... must not jump to conclusions. Thanks a million, Luke. Have you had any more leads on the regiments?"

"Some of the lists were lost or misplaced or misfiled over the years. The microfilm is tedious to read. The retired army officer is still searching."

"Christian Skye would not have disappeared without a trace when every other officer at Lucknow was accounted for. It just doesn't make sense to me."

"I won't take time to tell you again how I feel about this search."

"Good night, Luke." She hung up. It was clear he didn't believe there was ever a person called Christian Skye.

Two days later Dr. Goddard called her. "Kitty, I think you should come in to see me to look over some material I just received."

"It's Colin, isn't it?"

"I'm not quite certain who it is. The old gentleman did spend time in India, it seems."

"I'll know when I begin reading. We're on our way and will be there by ten o'clock. If you are tied up with a patient, have your receptionist hand the manuscript to me, and I'll find a place to read."

Dr. Goddard was waiting for Kitty and handed her a ream of paper. "I was busy all day yesterday and didn't have time to read all of this, Kitty. Why don't you just begin browsing through it to see if there's anything worthwhile in it about the personal life of this Sir Colin Skye. He seems to have done well enough for himself, whoever he was."

She had no illusions about yet another old soldier's story about life in India during the days of the Raj, but she took the heavy manuscript to a small room with a library table, a sofa, and comfortable brown leather chairs.

"Shannon, this is going to be tedious work. Why don't you do some shopping while I read. We need sun screen if we're going sailing Sunday afternoon."

"Anything else?"

"You might get me another highlighting pen. This one is surely about out of ink. Do you realize that I'm probably the best authority on the Sepoy Mutiny in the United States? All of the stories highlighted with yellow ink."

Shannon laughed and gave her heavy, red mane a toss. "I'm more than willing to leave you with yet another old geezer's story. I'm probably the second best authority on the mutiny, and I'm not even interested in it."

Kitty closed the door, said a prayer, and sat down with Sir Colin Skye's manuscript. It became clear to her at once that Sir Colin wrote in the flowery language of the late nineteenth century writers with "this author's viewpoint" interrupting continually. He recounted his life in India during the 1870s in minute detail. He wrote about parading to mess and practicing his shots. He described what he wore, what he ate, and what he said. He wrote about a Miss Smith who refused to marry him after he had courted her for the entire winter season. She then returned to England, one of the "returned empties." He wrote about pig hunts, fancy dress balls, and dressing for dinner in minute detail. Then he wrote about meeting a Miss Angela Berkeley when the fishing fleet arrived the following season and of his proposal of marriage. Kitty decided the old gentleman had married Miss Berkeley, for he wrote later of three sons and the burial of his devoted wife at Lucknow.

The story didn't ring true for some reason. It was only the ramblings of an old man, reliving his days as an officer in the queen's service in India. He devoted one half page to the woman he married and his family, and wrote over four hundred pages about the army. The army was his life, more important to him than his wife and children.

Then a line stood out from all the others, and Kitty highlighted that sentence with her yellow pen.

"In my first book," he wrote, "I told about the Sepoy Mutiny and how it happened that I was not there when it began early in June of 1857." She read on further and when she reached the end of the book, another sentences shot out at her.

"Although I was sent back to England to complete my schooling, a very wonderful lady had told me what life would be like in the twentieth century. She was right about the great World War which has just ended. I've often wondered how it was that my step-mother had the foresight about the future, but everything she taught me has come to pass exactly as she predicted it would ...except for a second world war, the use of rockets, and a landing of men on the moon."

Colin! Colin Skye! You remembered. Oh, my dearest Colin...my son Colin.

She had read through the entire manuscript. Her eyes were tired. Someone had turned on the overhead lights without her knowing of it. She was crying softly.

Thank you, God. Colin made it back to England safely. Now, we must find his first book, learn more about why he was knighted. I always knew he was someone very special.

She looked up and saw Shannon asleep on the sofa in the reading room.

"Shannon!" she yelled. "Shannon, I've found Colin."

Shannon rubbed her eyes and sat you. "You found Colin?" she asked.

"I knew it was Colin...my son Colin...when he added those three lines at the end."

"You read all the way through for three lines at the end?" Shannon's voice registered disbelief.

"Oh, but it was worth it. I remember it all as if it were yesterday. And Shannon, there's another book that comes before this one. In it he tells about his first trip to India. We have to find it. Is there a telephone somewhere nearby? I must call Luke. We'll go to England and turn up the earth to find that book if necessary."

"Let the people over there search for it...advertise for it, if necessary. Offer enough reward money so that everyone in the country will empty their dusty shelves searching for it."

"You're right, as usual. We'd not know where to begin and spend months over there for nothing."

"Are you certain of what he wrote? Let me see it." Shannon came to life and said, "Let me read it."

After she had finished the short entry, she said, "We must find that first edition, advertise for it in England, offer a reward large enough that everyone in the country will clear off their old, dusty shelves."

"I hadn't thought of that. It certainly wasn't for his style of writing his book was published. I could have taught him a thing or two about keeping it simple. Pages and pages of descriptive passages. I will read them again now that I know. And to think that those three lines didn't appear until the book was almost finished."

"You highlighted them, of course." Shannon said.

"Aye, that I did."

Shannon handed that section of the book to Kitty and watched her face register pure joy when she realized what Sir Colin Skye, an old man in his eighties had written about her.

"Kitty, how did you do it?"

The next weeks were torture for Kitty, knowing Colin had written about the days he spent in India with Christian and her, so she again put the search for Colin's first book in Luke's hands. Each time he called her, he had no news of the missing book.

"Are they searching for manuscripts, too?" she asked.

"That's it, Kitty. It may be in a file somewhere, a pamphlet. Are you certain you want to go on with this?"

"Let's advertise! I'll sell the sterling and buy some stainless at a garage sale."

"And you won't have to polish it. I'll forward the reward money and have the book or the manuscript, whichever it is, sent directly to you. I've a big case coming up. The people in London will find the book if there's a copy of it left anywhere. How does 1,000 pounds for the book in mint condition sound to you?"

"I'd pay more, but that is quite a price to pay for a book. I would even settle for an old dog-eared copy with tea and gravy stains."

"Five hundred for a copy?"

"Anything. I'd even sell the Lenox and eat on paper plates to know."

"I had no idea you were that desperate. That kid must have been something! I'm buying into the screwy tale you concocted. You are driving me crazy. I'm coming out to Kansas just as soon as this big case is over."

"Thanks, Luke!"

"Yeah, Baby. What are friends for?"

Kitty and Shannon began a waiting game. Shannon for word from Robert...Kitty for the manuscript to arrive in the mail. Shannon had long ceased to be Kitty's nurse. From time to time she took a case at the hospital, but, at Kitty's insistence, she stayed on at the farm. Sometimes they drove into the base where other army wives lived. They played bridge on Monday nights and bingo on Thursday nights.

Kitty knew Shannon was purposely keeping her occupied with activities so she'd not think continually about Colin Skye's first book arriving in the mail. They joined an exercise club and reported in at three o'clock four days a week. After showering and dressing, they ate at a nearby restaurant they had dubbed "The Oil and Vinegar Place" before they went home.

Kitty often fell asleep while Shannon polished her nails and watched her favorite sit-com before the news came on at five-thirty.

"News time, Kitty!" Shannon called to her.

Kitty rose from her mother's Lazy Boy and went to the blue and white kitchen for a drink of water.

"Kitty! Come quick. Kuwait is being invaded by Iraq."

Kitty returned to the living room while the newsman reported the details.

"Robert is right there!"

"What does that mean?"

"It means that he'll not be home again for a long time. We're bound to get involved."

In the weeks that followed Shannon and Kitty were so caught up with the news coming out of the Middle East that Colin Skye's missing book was pushed onto a back burner where it waited. They were glued to the television set--waiting. Would America come to the defense of tiny Kuwait? Would President Bush convince Congress that it was in the best interest of the United States to intervene?

"We'll go to war against Saddam Hussein. Sure as the world, our men over there are going into Kuwait."

The build-up of men and materials began amid the confusion and threats against Iraq and Saddam Hussien. Kitty knew war was eminent, and Shannon tried to hide her anxiety. It was during this time of worry and doubt about the future that the book arrived.

Kitty tore open the package at the mail box at the end of the lane. The book in mint condition, its lotus blossom embossed in gold and pink adorning the cover, spoke to her from the past. It was as though Christian stood beside her. Then she read the title *I Remember* by Sir Colin Skye.

She didn't return to the house to share the news with Shannon, but deep inside she felt the glowing sensation of happiness beginning to spread. Its warmth began somewhere in the pit of her stomach and spread throughout her entire body. She raced across the autumn prairie to a place where a panorama of earth meeting sky came together as one and then dropped off into a deep ravine of brambles. Far below her the cottonwoods reached for the sky, and her neighbor's cattle sought refuge from the wind. There on that ridge where the winds of Kansas roared across the barren ground, she sat in a sheltered, secluded spot near an outcropping of rock and began to read Colin Skye's words he had written in 1910.

How old was Colin in 1910? He was ten when he arrived in 1856. That means he was forty-four in 1900...fifty-four in 1910. Strange to think that he was already old before my father was born. Oh, but my dearest Colin. This is your story...even if you never tell me what I must know, I am so proud of you...my wonderful son.

She wiped the tears from her eyes and began to read.

"I went out to India after my Grandmother Fletcher died, to find my father. Something inside me yearned to meet him face to face, to ask him how it had been between my mother and him, and why it was that he never wrote to me about her. I was only ten years old and probably hadn't even formed that idea in my head at that time, although later, I knew that is why I went. I wanted to know. I longed to visit her grave.

Her name was Emma Fletcher when she married my father. When I returned to India a grown man just out of college with my commission bought and paid for, I found their marriage recorded in the church register at Lucknow. Her grave was there, her date of death bearing the date I was born. No one had ever told me she died giving birth to me, and I was terribly upset upon learning that fact. I think I had longed to know her for all of my twenty-two years, and when I saw she had died so that I might have life, I renewed my vow to make something out of myself. I had only been a few months old when Father sent me back to England to live with my grandmother whose name was Helen Fletcher. Although I have no memory of those early years of my life, I considered India my home and knew I would return one day.

I often dreamed as a child how it would be. Father would welcome me with open arms, and I would finish my schooling in India and go into his regiment as soon as I was old enough to serve with him. Needless to say, it was a child's way of dreaming. When I arrived, Mistress Bradley told me that Father had recently remarried and had gone off to Kashmir. I knew instantly that I would not like this woman who, for some reason no one could explain satisfactorily to me, had suddenly appeared one night at a party in Lucknow. No one spoke about Kathryn's arrival, but there was a mystery connected with it that was kept from me then, and I was never able to discover the facts in the matter when I returned later.

When we finally met at Simla, it was Kathryn who encouraged Father to be gentle with me and begged him to let me stay on with them at Simla. Later I accompanied them on the long journey down to Lucknow. I had never met anyone quite like Kathryn Skye. No one I had ever known was so pleasant and cheerful, yet so firm. She actually looked very English, her hair a pale golden color and her eyes quite blue. We grew to love one another, and in due time, Father relaxed his military bearing and let me into his heart.

That, I believe, proved to be the hardest yet happiest year of my life. Kathryn would not permit me to enter the school in Lucknow, but she insisted on tutoring me in mathematics and science. I owe any success I may have achieved in physics and science to her.

My step-mother must have been truly clairvoyant. She had 'the sight' and a way of looking into the future that I have never seen since. She described many of the discoveries for which I was recognized later. How could I have admitted what I knew about science came from my own mother's teachings? Yet, it is true. She inspired me to reach out beyond myself...to reach into the future and to grasp it fully.

My father loved her dearly. I suppose I have never known any two people in my entire lifetime who could be as happy, as angry, or as sad as those two. They loved as passionately as I have ever seen a couple love since. When I returned to India after I was graduated from Addiscombe, not a trace of either of them could I find anywhere...no memorial on the house where they lived...no graves...nothing.

I went to see Captain Charles Bradley who had come through the siege unscathed while all around him others were dying, and he told me this: 'Your father was riding beside me one moment, waving his sword, and in the next instant, while I looked away. he had simply disappeared. There were no shots near us, nothing to explain what had happened. His mount stood on the spot where he disappeared. His sword lay on the ground. I thought, at first, that he had dashed away to see if Kathryn had made it to safety at The Registry, but neither of them made it to that place.'

I learned from others that earlier that same day Father had been forced to attack his own Sepoy bearer, Azziz. He could not believe that his own men would turn on him, and that had been his one and only flaw in judgment. Even Azziz joined the ranks of the mutineers. I was grieved to hear of it, for I remembered the nights we played cribbage together when Father and Kathryn went to the club or to parties on the post.

I searched for word of what happened to Kathryn and my father for months. Finally, I had to admit that Charles Bradley had been right all along when he said, 'Those two were so much in love, they were simply spirited away together I suppose. Wherever they are, they are together.'

Then I began to search for the grave of my Aunt Edith Skye. I found it just as Mistress Bradley told me I would. I also went to the archives and found the marriage of my father and Kathryn LouiseWilson. When I saw their names written in their own hands, my eyes filled with tears, for I knew I would never set eyes upon their faces again.

And so it was that I began my years of service in India. I was always at sixes and sevens inside myself until I returned to India when I went back to England on leave or on special duty. Even today, I imagine I can hear the Muslim call to prayer and can shut my eyes and smell the pleasant, mingled fragrances of spices and marigolds and cow dung burning."

Kitty returned to the marriage of Colin's father to Kathryn Louise Wilson. Her eyes had glazed over the name while she was reading as though it meant nothing. Kathryn Louise Wilson.

The name meant nothing to her. Kathryn. . . Katy. . . Kitty. They were the same. Wilson? Colin never knew her full name. His eyes must have shifted to the line above Farrell in the Marriage Register. . . or possibly to the line below. That was it!

Kitty shut the book and returned slowly to the house. Overhead the clouds gathered, but she felt the warmth of Colin's words within her. It didn't matter any longer if Olivia or Luke or Dr. Goddard or Shannon Eaton believed a word she had said. She knew she had married Christian Skye, and she meant to search for him until she found him. Somewhere he still lived, and one day she would find him. The sadness inside her welled up and spilled out in her tears. Christian! Christian! Christian! Who was Kathryn Louise Wilson?

An emptiness filled her.

When she reached the house, Shannon was in tears. "Where have you been, Kitty? President Bush is threatening to push the Iraqi's out of Kuwait by force. Saddam Hussein is threatening chemical warfare if he does go to war against him. The whole world had gone mad...Hussein is the madman setting the fuse.

Kitty laid the book on the dining room table and tried to comfort Shannon. She took her in her arms and let her cry.

"Maybe just the threat of war will change Saddam's mind." Kitty spoke hollow words.

"He has missiles that can carry deadly chemicals all the way into Arabia. Remember how he killed his own people...the Curds? Surely you haven't forgotten the pictures of women and children." Shannon turned her tear-stained face to her.

"Do you want to go into town?"

Kitty knew the effect of sharing one's worries with others. Shannon would want to be with her friends, the wives of other soldiers.

"Do you mind?"

"Of course, not. Stay as long as you need to share your doubts and fears with the others. Take my car. I won't be needing it, and if I do, I'll call upon the Harpers for a ride into town."

"I won't stay long. Just need to talk to Linda and Patti. . . to see how they're holding up. Chemical warfare! It's unthinkable."

When Kitty heard the Mustang pull out of the driveway, she went to the telephone and called Olivia.

"Olivia, do you have a few minutes to talk?" she asked.

"I'd have given anything to have you here today," Olivia began. "Ted was on a rampage, and Luke is up to his ears in the Morgan case. Are you sure you won't reconsider and come back to work."

"No, Olivia. The book arrived."

"The book What book?"

"The book I advertised for. It's in mint condition...has the most gorgeous cover...a lovely lotus blossom and gold embossing. Colin knew how I loved the lotus blossom. And Olivia, he went back to India, just as I thought he would."

"What are you saying?"

"My Colin...he wrote about us...about Christian and me!"

"No! I don't believe it."

"And you must see it. Do you want me to make copies for you? I can fax them to you the first time I go into Manhattan or up to Fort Riley."

"What are you trying to tell me? Are you saying that Colin Skye. . .?"

"I'm telling you that Colin Skye wrote *I Remember* and published it in 1910. He writes all the things I remember."

She said nothing more.

"Are you still there, Olivia."

"I'm not quite sure. I had the strangest feeling just then. . . almost an out of body experience. Kitty. . ."

"Yes, Olivia?"

"I'm sorry, kid," Olivia told her. "I thought you had cracked up. You'd better fax that book to me. I'm still not believing what you told me is true. Have you talked to Dr. Goddard about this?"

"No. Do you think I should?"

"There's no way it could have happened. What did that kid write?"

"He was a grown man...over fifty . .when he wrote in 1910. He wasn't a kid any longer, but he recalled all the things I told you about us...about Christian and me. . . and more."

"More? Do you mean there was more that you didn't tell us about?"

"Much more, but it doesn't matter. Colin didn't understand about us either."

"And his mother had died?"

"Aye. Christian wasn't his father. She met someone coming out to India, but Colin couldn't know this. He went to India to see his mother's grave and to meet his father."

"Kitty you're falling back into that speech pattern again. You'd better see Dr. Goddard, and fax me the book at once."

"It's alright, Olivia. Don't you see, Christian didn't die."

CHAPTER TWENTY-FIVE

The next months were filled with anxiety for Shannon Eaton, and Kitty shared her worst moments. When Scud missiles flew into Saudi Arabia and Israel...when everyone knew Iraq would send chemicals that could destroy entire armies into their midst...when Desert Storm was finally carried onto the deserts of Iraq, they watched with horror when Saddam Hussien declared that the "mother of all battles" was about to commence. Then it was all over. Desert Storm ended without the great losses which had been predicted. The thousands of plastic body bags were not needed.

. "It is over, at last" Shannon told Kitty. "I do believe I feel like going to church for the first time in years. Will you go with me, Kitty?"

"You silly goose. What do you think I've been praying for? Of course. I'd like to give thanks for the end of this war myself." She put down the morning paper. "The Big Red One will be returning to Fort Riley soon, Shannon. I'm going to miss you."

"We'll keep in touch. I'll move back to the base I suppose. It's been so long since I've seen that man that I won't know how to act. I can hardly remember what he looked like."

"Two will get you one that you'll learn quickly." Kitty laughed.

"I've been meaning to ask you something, Kitty."

From Shannon's tone of voice, Kitty knew it was something serious. "Fire ahead, Nurse Nancy."

"It's about *I Remember*."

"And what about it?" Kitty felt herself growing testy for no reason she could identify. Olivia had read Colin's account of their lives in India before the mutiny. At first she had believed what Kitty had told her, and then to preserve her sanity, Kitty believed, she had reversed her thinking altogether. Luke didn't like the sound of it, and made no bones of telling her so. That left Dr. Goddard and Shannon. She dared not bring the book to the attention of either of them. She knew what had happened to her could not be explained except in a supernatural manner no one could believe. Besides, having the book beside her bed was comforting to her, and she dared not face rejection again.

"I went to your room to turn off the light when you went into town to get a paper one day last winter. I found the book on the table beside your bed. I read what Colin Skye wrote about Christian Skye and Kathryn... about Kathryn Wilson. Why didn't you tell me?"

"I didn't think you would believe me. Livy didn't, even when I faxed her the pages that told about our being together back in 1856. Luke was angry. I just couldn't bear to tell you, knowing your reaction to his book may have brought on more of the same."

"I see." Shannon was clearly hurt.

"Maybe I just wanted to keep my thoughts of Colin to myself...such a personal thing...and then. . ."

"And then there was the statement of Captain Charles Bradley. Do you really think you'll find him again, Kitty?"

"I don't know."

"Tell me the truth. You do, don't you? Somewhere in that screwy head of yours, you think that you will one day just walk into a room and whammooree! There is Christian Skye, as big as life. It doesn't happen like that. You can't hope for it."

"You would have me marry Luke Filbey?"

"I like him. He's handsome, charming, full of fun...and he loves you."

"And I feel nothing...nothing I felt for Christian Skye. It isn't fair...I searched for him all my life. We had little more than a year of total happiness with only one or two bang-up quarrels. And the making up after that was wonderful!"

"You're a hopeless romantic, Kitty. Are you certain you didn't dream the whole thing? Maybe you found Colin's book and . . ."

"No. No, Shannon. I know what happened. I lived it...rode that pony down the Grand Trunk Road to Lucknow...over four hundred miles. Colin rode ahead of me all the way. Did you read that part?"

"Yeah. I read every word of it, and I'm with Livy and Luke."

"That's why I didn't tell you when the book came."

The Persian Gulf War was over, but The Big Red One still had work to do in the Middle East. It was a tremendous task to bring all the men and weapons of war home once more. Weeks passed. Then Shannon received the telephone call for which she had waited so long. Robert Eaton was coming home.

Kitty heard Shannon scream, "It's Robert! He's on his way home!"

She felt drained inside, like a bucket that has been emptied of water. "That's wonderful news, Shannon."

"Oh, I've so much to do...have to get my hair trimmed ...see that the house is ready...take the tire on the truck to town to get it repaired... everything all at once. I thought I'd be prepared for this, but Kitty...I'm falling apart."

"When?"

"They're in the states already. . . will be in at four this afternoon. Oh, my! I can't even remember what he looks like."

Shannon's hands were shaking, and she raced from one room to another, picking up the magazines on the dining room table, rearranging the pictures on the piano, plumping the pillows on the sofa, and doing the things that didn't need to be done.

"It's ten now. You have six hours, Shannon. Simmer down. What do you say we do your laundry first of all, then you can pack your clothes? I'll take the tire into town to get it repaired and twist Chuck's arm so he'll come out and put it back on the truck. Now, let's see. You'll need time to bathe and get pretty. Do you want me to trim your hair before you wash it?"

"Just the frizzy ends that need to come off. You must come with me."

"To meet Robert? Not on your life. He hasn't the slightest bit of interest in seeing me."

"I'm coming unglued. You've got to come with me. I couldn't drive into Fort Riley right now to save myself."

So Shannon washed and dried her clothes while Kitty had the tire fixed. Chuck had no one at the service station who could come out to put the tire on the truck, so Kitty decided she would give it a try. Together she and Shannon tried to jack the truck up, but at last it was two-thirty and Shannon had not bathed or washed her hair.

"Forget the truck. I'll take you into Fort Riley. You and Robert can come out and pick up the truck later."

At three o'clock Kitty was still packing for Shannon while she dressed and tried to do something with her hair.

At the last minute, Kitty took a sponge bath in the kitchen, dashed up to her room to throw on her blue denims and ran the brush through her hair.

"How do I look?" Shannon asked.

"Like a harried housewife, of course. We have about three minutes to spare. I have your bags in my car, and if I drive like the law was after me, we'll make it."

"I'm so nervous I can't even spit."

"You'll get over that. How do you think Robert feels? Besides, I've never seen you look so good."

They jumped into the car and roared away. When they reached the blacktop, Shannon cried, "Can't you drive any faster?"

"I'm doing seventy. Do you want to end up dead?"

The parking lot at the base was packed with cars, and Kitty had to search for a place to park. "I'll let you out here at the gate, and then see if I can find a spot to park the Mustang. It looks like a terrific crowd of people here already. You should be carrying a red umbrella so he can find you."

"What would I do without you, Kitty. Do I look alright?"

"Beautiful!"

"Thanks." Shannon twisted her handkerchief and waited for Kitty to pull up before the gate.

Kitty did not hurry back to the crowd. She knew many of the women who were meeting their husbands returning from Desert Storm, but she also realized that it was a private affair for families, one in which she had no role to play except to see that Shannon and Robert Eaton had a ride back to their house on the base. She walked slowly along the street, hearing the roar of the planes landing. She saw the first of the veterans of The Big Red One coming across the tarmac toward their waiting families, but she did not see Shannon. She heard the cries of joy as husband and fathers rejoined their loved ones who had prayed so hard for their safe return, but she could not share their joy.

She looked for Shannon's red hair in the crowd. For a girl so tall, she was hard to find. Then she saw her and went to her side.

Shannon grabbed her hand and held it tightly. Suddenly she let out a loud cry and dashed away. Robert Eaton saw her coming and dropped his bags. She was in his arms, and he was telling her not to cry. Kitty turned and walked away. Shannon and Robert would find her when they were ready to go.

It was all wrong. There should be banners flying, men on horseback sitting erect in their saddles, bugles playing. The men looked tired and so young. They were handling their own gear. Where was Christian?

Through her tears, she saw an officer carrying two large duffle bags coming toward her. He stopped and stared at her. He was a tall man. His eyes were of no special color, but there was something about him that was vaguely familiar.

Warm currents coursed through her, but she could not stop the flow of tears.

A young woman wearing a bright red jacket flew out of the crowd and into his arms. Her dark brown hair blew across her face in the eternal wind of Kansas. Kitty saw the man take her into his arms, and laughing together, the young woman picked up one of the officer's bags and they walked away arm and arm through the gate.

She brushed aside her tears

A young family of four stopped in front of her to embrace again, the children crying out, "Daddy! Daddy!"

An emptiness crept inside Kitty. I should not have come here today. I knew it would be like this...the loneliness I cannot bear falling over me again. The knowing that I will wander endlessly, searching for the one who can complete my life and make me whole once again . . searching for Christian. Oh, Christian, where are you?

Shannon spied her, but she did not see them until she heard Shannon's voice. "Kitty! Kitty! Over here!"

She forced herself to smile a welcome and made her way through the crowd to them.

"I want you to meet my husband. Robert this is Kitty."

Robert Eaton was tall and dark...lean and deeply tanned. He shook hands with Kitty and his grasp was firm.

"I feel that I know you already." His voice was nice.

"Here's the game plan, Kitty. We'll drop off our bags at the house, then we'll go out to your place and Robert will put the tire on the truck."

"There's no hurry about the truck. If it is inconvenient, just take me to the farm and kick me out. You can drive the Mustang for as long as you need to. I only came along, remember, so that you wouldn't wreck the car and end up in the hospital the minute Robert gets home."

"Would you mind if we don't get the tire on right away? I'll pick up a few clothes and come out later for the rest of my things."

"I'll call Chuck to bring out a decent jack. He can put the tire on in nothing flat. If I need to go anywhere I can drive the truck. By the way, I had to park a mile away. Wait for me here, and I'll bring the car around."

When she watched Shannon and Robert drive away in her car, she sighed and entered the house. She poured herself a Coke, then went to her room to remove her clothes. She kicked off her shoes. She put on an old pair of jeans and a sweat shirt and settled back with her drink. She remembered the officer whose eyes met hers. She let her mind wander, seeking out the corners where he might have been known to her. High School? College? She knew few people in the military.

Although she saw nothing in his eyes that she recognized, they held hers for what seemed an infinity. Even through her tears, she had felt them upon hers. Then the slim, young woman had flung herself into his arms, and laughing together they had walked through the gate without noticing that she stood there alone.

She put on her sneakers and left the house. The air was crisp and cool, but the wind was dying. The need to be alone became so strong that she had come to the hillside overlooking the valley below before she knew she had come so far. Still, she couldn't take her eyes off the lovely countryside her father and mother had loved.

She felt her tears falling once more. Twice in one day is too much! Still they came in giant floods of them, and when she finally entered the house where her parents had lived for over thirty-five years the emptiness was still there

I must get on with my life. Tomorrow I will go into town and see if there is a dog at the pound which needs a home. Then I'll go to the sale barn next Tuesday and buy my first cattle. I can do it. I can put the past behind me if I try.

The telephone rang, and she said, "Hello, Kitty speaking.."

"Kitty. I saw the news on television. The Big Red One has returned to Fort Riley and Shannon's husband has come home. I'm coming out to see you this week end. I have a week's vacation." Luke's voice sounded warm and familiar.

"Good. You can help me pick out my pooch and go to the cattle auction with me." She was glad to be telling him her plans.

"You're not trying to make a farmer out of me, are you?"

"No, it's just on the agenda for the coming week." Her heart cried out, I need you, Luke. I need you desperately!

"Then I need to bring my denims."

"By all means. This is a working farm from now on. I may even learn how to cook."

She heard him laughing. And then he said, "That'll be the day. I'll take you out to eat. We'll go to that steak house in Manhattan again. I don't know why we can't get good steaks in New York."

"It's because the feed lots of Kansas feed the cattle something besides hay. Our cattle are fattened on corn and silage."

"Well, I'll be. You never cease to amaze me. I'm looking forward to seeing you again. Maybe you've changed your mind."

"Not unless you decide to become a farmer. I can't see that."

"Don't tempt me, Kitty. You're still a good-looking gal. Oh, here I go again. I'll see you Saturday."

"Good-night, Luke."

"Oh, by the way. Did I tell you Anne and Ryan will be with me?"

"You forgot to mention that bit of information, but it will be fine with me."

"I have them for the summer while Lisa goes to Europe with her mother...a sort of graduation present."

"How old are they now?" Kitty couldn't imagine Luke with his children. He never brought them around in all the time she had known him before.

"Anne is ten and Ryan is fifteen."

"Do they like the country?"

"I didn't ask."

"Oh, great. I'll bet they'll expect an ice-skating rink and big screen movies." Kitty laughed. "What they'll get is cows and baby chickens and miles of bluestem with maybe a rattlesnake thrown in for excitement."

"We'll see you this week-end. Good-night, Baby."

"Good-night, Luke."

She felt warm and loved for the first time in a long while. She then realized she was as much to blame as he when he called it quits. I had no time for him, even when we lived together. I lived in my own little world, intent on my work, wanting my space. There may be a life for us yet. Maybe I just never saw it before.

CHAPTER TWENTY-SIX

She met Luke and his children at the airport on Saturday at noon. "How was your flight?" she asked.

"The usual. That layover in Topeka gets longer every time I come out here." Luke kissed her cheek and then introduced her to his children. "Ryan and Anne, this is Kitty."

Ryan held out a limp hand to her. Anne appeared cautious.

"I'm parked in a no parking zone. We'd better get your luggage off the carousel and head out of here. Is anyone hungry?"

"We've been eating since we left New York City, but Ryan eats non-stop. I could use a cold drink myself."

"Let's go then. Everyone ready?"

Neither child had spoken.

"Do you like to ride?" she asked Ryan.

"Horses?"

"I have a farm. Thought you might enjoy riding."

"Do you have stables on your farm?" Anne looked at her with big, brown innocent eyes.

"Well, not exactly stables, but there are stanchions for two horses in the barn."

"Cool!"

"Do you have your dog yet, Kitty?" Luke looked over Anne's head and winked.

"As a matter of fact, I thought we'd go to the pound after we eat. I don't know much about dogs. My old Blackie died when I was in college. I thought the children might help me choose a nice dog that will bark when someone drives up to my house. Maybe one that will help me with the cattle."

"What do you have in mind?"

"I'd like a blue heeler, one good with cattle, but I'd be surprised to find anything but a mixed breed at the pound."

They ate steaks, tender broiled over charcoal as only Kansans know how to do them...served with plump baked potatoes and a crisp green salad.

"We'll have enough steak left over for supper," Kitty said when she had only eaten half of her steak and potatoes. "Do you want a doggie bag, Anne?"

"I'm stuffed."

"Looks like your father and Ryan are going to polish theirs off. Wonder what they're going to eat tonight?" She laughed and Anne sat prim and straight on the circular corner seat.

"You will have something for your doggie," Luke laughed. "Guess this is why I come to Kansas. Everything tastes better."

She noticed Ryan watching her and wondered what Luke's son was thinking. Neither of the children looked like Luke, she decided.

"Alright, kids," Luke announced. "Let's go pick out Kitty's watchdog."

Kitty rose and when she did so, her eyes met those of the officer she saw the day The Big Red One returned from Desert Storm. She saw the small lines around his eyes when they flashed recognition, the deep tan on his face and arms, and the way his short hair curled in spite of the close cut. She looked away and found that Luke and the children were waiting for her to move ahead of them.

"Someone you know?" Luke asked sarcastically.

"Probably someone from high school days."

"I keep forgetting that you were raised in this country." Luke reached in his billfold for a tip to leave on the table, then paid for their steaks and followed Kitty into the bright sunlight.

"We forgot our doggie bags!" Anne cried.

"So we did! Would you like to run back and get them for us?"

She saw the shyness in Anne's face, and Luke said, "I'll bring the car around. You kids come with me, and Kitty will get the bags."

When Kitty returned to their table, she picked up the bags and turned to leave the restaurant. The man she had seen as she was leaving, rose from the table where he had been studying his menu and said, "Haven't we met somewhere before?"

"That is one of the oldest lines in history."

"I could have sworn. . ." His voice rumbled from deep inside himself, and Kitty looked at him with what she knew was a stunned expression on her face.

"Have you ever been to India...Major?"

"Alexander Collins. No, I have never been to India. And you are?"

"Kitty Farrell." She was not sure if she had spoken or not.

"Sorry, Mrs. Farrell. Must not keep you...your family...waiting."

"Aye ...forgot the doggie bags...starve without them. . ."

She raced from the restaurant, her heart pounding. It was the voice... the sound of his voice...his eyes upon mine...must not think of it. He has a wife...a beautiful young wife. That voice! I know it from somewhere.

"Over here, Kitty," Luke yelled at her. "Is something wrong?"

She ignored his question when she climbed into her Mustang and began to give instructions. while she waved her hands. "The dog pound is at the edge of town. Take a right when you pull out of the parking lot and follow the street until you reach the first stop light. Then make a left and it will take us out of town."

"Dog, here we come. Are they expecting us?" He put on his sun glasses and began to maneuver the car out of the crowded parking lot.

"I called yesterday. People on the base are disposing of their pets, making room for their men home from the war or moving on. I'm not certain which."

He was a big dog with feet as large as the palm of her hands, and Anne saw him first.

"Kitty, over here. He's a lovely dog. Look! He knows me already. Do you want to pet him?"

The big, yellow dog with soulful, dark eyes thumped his tail on the floor and appeared desperate to leave the pound. Someone had scrawled his name in a childish hand on a piece of paper and had attached it to his cage. "Major" the paper read. "Take good care of me and I will love you forever."

In a split second it was decided. Major would go home with them. Kitty did not ask if the dog would bark when strangers drove into her parking lot or if he would be good with cattle. It did not matter. One did not choose a dog with any criteria in mind when the time came to take him home. He looks at you. You look at him, and suddenly you both know. He is yours forever.

"He's a monster. Are you sure you can afford to feed him?" It was Luke bringing everything into focus, as usual.

So they left the pound with Major sitting between the children in the back seat.

"I do believe that monster is grinning at us," Luke said when they left the town behind them. "Look at him sitting back there like he owns the back seat."

Anne laughed and hugged Major. "He likes us already."

Ryan said, "He needs a bath."

"You'd need a bath, too, if you'd been shut up in that smelly cage. He'll go swimming in the pond when we get him home. Outdoor dogs seldom smell bad."

"Will he run away?" Anne asked.

"Not if we show him where he's to eat and sleep. And with you there, he'll make himself at home in no time at all. Look, he knows we're talking about him!"

When they reached the farmhouse, Kitty began to give instructions about where each one was to sleep. "Luke has his room downstairs, Ryan you will take the bedroom on the right at the head of the stairs, and Anne will sleep with me in the queen-sized bed on the left."

"Smooth move, Kitty." Luke grunted over Anne's head. She knew he had not planned on sleeping in the small hired man's bed again. The mattress was hard, and the bed was too short.

She smiled sweetly and said, "As soon as you are all comfortable in farm clothes, we'll take Major out to the pond and let him cool off."

While she and Anne undressed and pulled on jeans, Anne asked in a small voice, "Are you going to marry my daddy?"

"We are old friends, very old friends. Old friends seldom marry."

She had moved her emerald to her right hand and wore her wedding ring on her left hand. "Besides, I'm still married to someone else as far as I know."

"Where is your husband? Does he live here?"

"I'm not certain where he is. Are you ready to go?"

While she watched the children throw rocks into the pond and Major swim out to get sticks Luke threw into the water for him to retrieve, Kitty remembered Major Collins. Alexander Collins, and she tried to remember where or when she had known him. She knew his voice, so full and deep.

The week passed quickly. On Monday they went sailing on Tuttle Creek Lake. On Tuesday they went to the cattle sale at the auction barn outside Junction City and brought home a cow and a calf to put in the barn lot. Major was waiting on the porch when they got home and rushed to meet them. When the truck brought the cow and calf home, Major barked and rushed into the front yard pretending to be a ferocious watch dog.

"Good dog," Kitty called. "It's alright."

Major quit barking, gave one more bark at the truck and then settled back on the porch.

On Wednesday the children played with the baby chickens which were beginning to get their wings and rode horses while Kitty and Luke took books and went to the pond with Major.

"I've been thinking," Luke began and laid his book aside. "I know you're never going to return to New York. You have that dog and a cow and chickens running around all over the place. What would I do here?"

"Sit beneath the banyan tree and play checkers with the old men of the town, I guess."

"There you go, again. Sometimes I think you're still in India. Can't you just stay here?" His voice sounded irritable.

"I try, then it all comes back so strong I can't resist. Do you really mind?"

"There's someone standing between us. Every time I try to get close to you, I feel that I can reach out and touch him."

"I do get lonely...would like ...oh,well. It's no use. I'm half here, half there...living it all over again."

"I read Colin Skye's book again. For the first time since you returned, I began to wonder what happened to Kitty. Surely you were not Kathryn he wrote about. Besides that you are different. Don't ask me to understand."

"I know it happened to me, and I don't understand. Don't expect miracles, Luke."

"You've changed. You're still as smart and as beautiful as you always were, but I can't put my finger on what is different about you. Sometimes I think of you as an old, old woman. Does that make sense?"

"Aye, that it does. And I can't help it. I know I'm different...cannot tell how, but I feel it in my bones."

On Thursday they visited the county fair, ate cotton candy, rode the Ferris wheel and played Bingo at the VFW stand. They wandered about staring at exhibits and wound up watching the judging of the livestock. In the afternoon they went to the horse race at the stadium. Kitty was elated when the horse she chose won.

That night while Anne rode the ponies on the merry go round, and while the music of the calliope played, Kitty turned to Luke and said, "There's a concert tomorrow night in Manhattan. Would you like to go?" Her eyes shone and her face flushed.

"You know what I'd like more than anything?"

"What is it, Luke?" She asked with the innocence of a young girl.

"Forget it."

The children rode horses while Kitty and Luke prepared the barbecue Friday afternoon. They all dressed up and attended the concert on Friday night.

When they returned home, Anne stumbled up to her room, and Ryan yawned and fell into her father's easy chair.

"Better go up to bed, son. You're too big for me to carry if you fall asleep there."

Ryan wandered up the stairs.

"It's almost midnight. Guess I should join the kiddos." Kitty told him.

"Come here, Kitty." Luke held out his arms to her.

She joined him. He smelled clean. It was the expensive shaving lotion he used...not strong and powerful but masculine and faintly musky.

"Oh, Kitty...Kitty. . ." he cried hoarsely.

She pulled away at the sound of his voice. "This is all wrong," she told him.

"Don't do this to me, Kitty."

"I can't help it," she cried. "I can't help it."

He released her and stood beside her helplessly. "We're leaving early in the morning. Can you take us into town?"

"Yes, Luke. I'm so sorry."

"It's Christian Skye, isn't it?"

"Yes, and everything that keeps pulling me back to him. I'm sorry. I wish I could let myself love you, but you know how it is...I'm here...then I'm there. It would never work out for us. Sometimes I feel him so close I can reach out and touch him, then I realize I have lost him, and the most awful desolation falls over me."

He reached out and touched her in the darkness and said, "I wish I could help you, but I am no good at this either."

"Find someone to love you, Luke." She gave his hand a squeeze."

"It's no use. When I made a fool out of myself and walked out on you, it was the worst day of my life. I don't know how you could even stand to look at me again."

"We're friends...very old friends. You didn't believe a word that I told you, but you've stood by me anyway. I do love you, Luke."

"Do you need more time?"

"No. I have had all the time in the world, and nothing has changed actually. I still wake up in the night crying."

"I didn't know. You poor kid. I'm still your friend. Your very best friend."

"Thanks, Luke."

"Better go to bed. I'm going to have a Coke and join Major for awhile."

"Do you mind if I join you?" She knew she couldn't sleep. Luke meant more to her than he did when they lived together and searched throughout New England for the priceless antiques that filled their Federal style apartment.

He ruffled her hair and said, "No. I like your company."

"And you will look in on me now and then?" Their affair had ended long ago, yet she knew he meant the world to her.

"Yes, when I can bear to see your face without wanting to marry you."

"And how long will that take?" she asked softly.

"I really don't know. I'm not getting any younger you know."

Chapter Twenty- seven

*P*erhaps Luke and I can make it.

Then she felt the tension that had gripped her when he held her in his arms, and she knew instinctively that it wouldn't work out for them.

"You'll be alright," she told him.

They were parting once more, and Luke had been upset that morning when they left. By the time they reached the airport, he had mellowed out and smiled down at her. "The farm suits you. I never knew when we were together what kept you going. You were so intense all the time. . . couldn't sit still...always in motion. You're a different person now."

"In what way?" she asked.

"You're quieter, more relaxed, enjoying your freedom from the fast lane. I do envy you." He took her hand in his and looked out across the tarmac.

"Here comes our plane in, Dad!" Ryan yelled. "Do you have our boarding passes?"

Anne came to Kitty and gave her a hug. "Good-bye. Take good care of Major and Dusty and Midnight and Rooster and the hens and the Tootsie and her baby calf."

Kitty hugged her and shook hands with Ryan.

"Thanks for letting us come to visit you. I had a really good time. I didn't think I would, but the farm is a great place for a vacation."

"Why, thank you, Ryan. You must come again some time. We didn't even find time to go to the basement to see my father's trains."

"Model trains?"

"Yes. I haven't been down there myself. So many memories."

"Next time?"

"I promise."

Then they were standing in line, waiting to board the plane that would take them back to the city. When they turned to wave one final good-bye to her, Kitty felt a sense of relief. They were good kids. Luke was a good friend, but they were not her life, no more than Livy or her children were her life.

When she backed her Mustang out of the parking lot, she felt the thump, thump, thump of a tire going flat.

She got out of her car and lifted the trunk, wondering where the jack and spare tire were hiding.

An army truck swung up beside her, and a young man got out and asked, "Having trouble?"

"Somewhat."

"I'll put your spare on for you." He turned off the motor on the truck and hopped out. "You'd better get that tire fixed as soon as possible though. You probably picked up a nail," he said while he took out the tools and the spare tire. Five minutes later, he had the tire on and put the flat in the trunk.

When he slammed the trunk shut, a jeep drew up, and she heard a deep rumbling voice ask, "Is everything under control?"

"Just a flat tire, sir. She's on her way."

Kitty stepped around to the driver's side of the car, and the driver of the jeep said, "Good morning, Mrs. Farrell. Do you need any help?"

"I think everything is fine now." She turned to the young soldier who had changed her tire and asked what she owed him.

"Nothing, M'am. Glad to help you." He hopped into his truck and roared away.

Major Collins did not make a move to leave. He said, "I'll be glad to see that you get to the service station to get it fixed, Mrs. Farrell."

"It's Miss Farrell...Kitty." She smiled at him, and then said, "I have a service station near my farm where I can get it fixed. Thank you anyway."

She opened her car door and started to get inside, but something drew her eyes back to those of Alexander Collins.

"Are you sure we have never met, Kitty? I feel that I know you from somewhere.".

"Have you ever lived in New York City?" she asked him.

"No."

"Thank you for offering to help me," she said and got in to drive away. Alexander Collins pulled away with a wave of his hand.

Major was waiting for her when she got home and came bounding out to meet her. "Good boy!" she said and rubbed his back. "You're going to miss those kids, but we'll get along just fine, just the two of us. How about a walk out to the pond?"

She didn't miss Luke or the children, in fact she enjoyed the solitude of living on the farm. Occasionally she walked down the road in the evenings to visit the Morgans whose ranch stretched for several thousand acres to the east of her farm. They raised Angus cattle and had lived in the Flint Hills for as long as she could remember. Their daughter Linda had graduated high school in Kitty's class. She had moved away, but Eunice Morgan knew Kitty's parents, and she loved to hear her talk about the garage sales and auctions she and Louise Farrell attended.

Kitty, not knowing if she was Kitty Skye or Kitty Farrell, picked up her life and attempted to find a reason for living. There was the dog, Major. He was at her heels constantly and had proved to be good with the cattle she added to the cow and calf she had bought when Luke and the children were with her. She often rode out on her horses, first on Midnight and then on Dusty, to check the fences and to watch the cattle graze near the pond. The simplicity of country living slipped into her, but in spite of everything, she knew something was missing from her life. She knew she could not return to Christian Skye, but her longing for him returned again and again.

When she felt lonely, she rode Midnight out on the high prairie to check the fences once again. The bluestem changed continually, becoming an ephemeral landscape which at any particular moment would never appear the same again. She knew which flowers would bloom next. First the buttercups and then the daisies. For the remainder of the summer they came on one after another in an ever changing panorama of color, waving gently in the everlasting winds. Now fall was coming on, and the tall bluestem reached its rusty spikes into the sky. A field of sunflowers with a brilliant sky filled with gold-tipped clouds in the background caused her to catch her breath. Then she heard it. The sound of geese calling to one another as they flapped their wings into the wind, and she was reminded of a time in India when the ducks and geese returned in the fall of the year.

After she returned to her house late in the afternoon one rainy day, she hung her slicker on a hook in the kitchen and put on sweats and house slippers and went upstairs to her room to read once again Colin Skye's *I Remember*.

Seeing Christian Skye's name on the pages of the book was comforting. Knowing that Colin searched for them without success troubled her though. She was aware of her fate, but she wondered time and time again what had happened to Christian Skye. Edith Skye was buried at Lucknow in a corner of the churchyard. Colin's mother, Emma, was also buried in India, but Colin found nothing at Lucknow or Lahore or anywhere else up and down the Grand Trunk Line where he searched that would tell him where his father had been buried. It had troubled him greatly, and he wrote about it throughout the book.

Colin sensed what had happened to the woman he called "Kathryn;" however, with the coming of the Sepoy Mutiny, he could not know what to expect. He had come to realize it had hastened his departure so he would return to England safely. When Captain Bradley could not tell him what happened to Kathryn, Kitty knew in the deep recesses of her being that she had vanished as quickly as she had come to Lucknow in the beginning.

Kathryn, too, had never been able to account for the fact that she could look into the future and tell Colin about events which would happen in the future

Colin wrote about it. "She told Father about the mutiny even before it began. Wherever she is, I know she did not die at Lucknow when the Sepoys came over the wall."

The telephone rang in the kitchen and Kitty sprang from her bed and raced downstairs to answer.

"Hello, Kitty Farrell here."

"Kitty, it's Shannon. We need a fourth for bridge. Are you interested?"

"Noooo. . ." she told her. "I have too much to do."

"Are you all right?"

"Sure. I'm fine."

"Alex asked about you."

"Alex?"

"Major Collins. He said you had met."

"What did you tell him about me? You didn't tell him about . . .?

"Good heavens, no. He seems to think that he knows you, though."

"I can't think of any reason why he would keep asking that question. I have spoken with him exactly twice for no longer than a second or two, and each time he said the same thing." Kitty was suddenly annoyed, but she didn't know why.

"He's interesting and wants to know you."

"Well, if you see him on a regular basis, tell him I am not interested in furthering the 'Don't I know you from somewhere?' bit."

"He's really very nice."

"What are you telling me that for? I don't want to meet married men. Period."

"Alex...married? What on earth are you talking about? He's the most eligible bachelor I know."

"He has a sweetie, then. She met him when he got home from Desert Storm."

"Beautiful, dark-haired, slim, long-legged gal?" Shannon giggled.

"And young."

"You silly goose. That was his daughter Alexandria."

Kitty couldn't think of anything to say. Finally, she stammered, "Alexandria...his daughter?"

Shannon waited for her to say something else. "You still there, Kitty?"

"Yeah, I'm still here." Her voice sounded faraway even to her own ears.

"What do you say? I can fix you up with him."

"No!" She shouted. "No! I don't want to be fixed up with anyone."

"Is it alright if I come out to see you this evening. Robert is playing poker and I don't have anything to do. That is actually what I called for in the first place."

Kitty knew what she was thinking. Kitty has gone off the deep end again. She isn't acting right

"Do that. I'll grill some hamburgers and slice some dill pickles and onions." She tried to keep her voice from sounding like she was talking into a barrel.

When Shannon swung into the driveway, Kitty was actually glad to see her.

"Quiet Major! It's just Shannon."

Major quit barking, but before he left it alone, he let out one weak howl and returned to the porch.

While they were grilling the hamburger, Shannon told her about life at the fort and brought her up to date on what was happening in the lives of the women Kitty had met.

"Did I tell you that Luke and his children came out and stayed for an entire week.

"I know."

"How did you know that?"

"It seems Major Alexander Collins saw you at a restaurant in Junction City...figured you were married with a family."

"And you told him I wasn't married. You're getting to be quite the little matchmaker, Girl. I didn't know that was one of your talents."

"Don't be angry. I didn't tell him anything else except that you had once been a successful lawyer."

"And what else?"

"Oh, nothing much."

"I know your nothing much. So you told him about why you came out to stay with me, how I thought I had lived during the 1850's in India...returned when the mutiny began. I'll just bet he thinks I'm really talented...zipping in and out of time. There's not many of us who can do that, you know?"

"Kitty, don't be angry. I only told him that you had been married and that you had lost him. It's no more than happened to him."

"Don't tell me about him. I don't want to know."

"All right. All right, be that way. Now, tell me about Luke's visit. Bet he's ready to quit the law firm and move to Kansas. Did he. . .?"

"Yes, but I said 'No'."

"Oh!" For once Shannon was too stunned to speak.

"The children were quite nice about coming to see me. Ryan didn't want to come out here. He's at an awkward age, but Anne and I hit it off wonderfully well after we got Major. She slept with me in the big queen-sized bed upstairs. Luke slept in the hired man's room."

"Whew! I'm relieved to hear that bit of information."

"I knew you would want to know," Kitty laughed and Shannon burst out laughing with her and said, "I've missed your silly mixed up life. I wonder what ever happened to Colin's sons."

"I haven't the slightest idea, and don't you dare suggest that I begin searching for them. Do you realize that they would be older than my great grandparents and are long gone from this earth?"

"Let me see, if Colin had sons and they had sons and they had sons, they'd be about our ages or older."

"Don't you dare get started on that. I don't want to know them."

"Oh, all right. I know how absorbed you get in that sort of thing. Forget I mentioned it. By the way, I've begun a new exercise program at the club. Want to join me a couple of days a week?"

"I might."

"Tuesday night alright?"

"Yeah. I need to get some of the kinks out of my system. It's not too difficult for an old lady who sits around is it?"

"I hope not. Maybe we can just sit and wiggle our toes at first. Come by and pick me up, say five o'clock."

"Sounds like fun."

They sat on the porch and talked until the sun slid down behind the Flint Hills and the whippoorwills began to call to one another.

"It's so peaceful and quiet out here. I miss it." Shannon said.

"I thought it would be lonely living alone, but I keep busy...first one thing and then another."

"I've got to get back. Don't try to live in the past too much, Kitty. Put Colin's book away."

"What makes you say that?"

"I know you, Kitty. Have you been back to see Dr. Goddard recently?"

"Last week," she admitted.

"And?"

"And he tells me I'm progressing."

"Like thunder you are. You turn Luke away and don't want to meet anyone else. You're living in the past and you know it. Staying in the 1800's is not progressing, Honey. You've got to live in the here and now. We're heading for the year 2,000 and you haven't even discovered the twentieth century yet."

Kitty sighed. She knew Shannon was telling it like it was.

"It is so difficult...so difficult to forget

"But, Kitty, you must put Christian Skye out of your life and get on with it."

"I suppose you are right, Shannon. By the way, I've been looking for a manuscript I had been working on. Did you ever see it?"

"A manuscript? I don't think so.

"It was a novel my mother had started and I worked on it . . .put a lot of myself into it. Guess I'll find it one of these days. Don't worry about it, I'm too busy with dog and cows and chickens anyway."

CHAPTER TWENTY- EIGHT

$\mathcal{K}$itty found herself looking forward to the work-out session at the club with Shannon. She had gone into Junction City to purchase a new outfit in brilliant green. When she pulled up to Shannon's small house on the base, she honked the horn and waited for her to join her.

"So how is the world treating you?" Shannon asked her when she threw her bag in the back seat and settled down beside her.

"Great!"

"I hope so, for Alex is determined to see you again."

"No!" Kitty protested quickly.

"We're joining Robert and Alex for dinner after we shower." Shannon continued, ignoring Kitty's answer. "It will do you good to meet new people. Doctor's orders, so don't argue with me."

"You've talked with Dr. Goddard. I hope you're not on my payroll again. I can't afford both of you."

Shannon laughed, but she said no more. Kitty knew Shannon had won round one, and she was uneasy about it.

The brilliant green work-out suit was an instant hit. Shannon still wore parts of two different suits, the blue part which was baggy and the black was almost gray from repeated washing.

Kitty knew she was out of shape. After she finished working on the bars, she said, "I can't handle any more today. I'll sit this one out and then shower and try to do something with my hair. I wish you had told me I had a dinner date, and I'd have worn something outstanding."

"Robert thinks you're one of the best looking women he ever met. I'm not about to have you outshine me in that department with something you just happened to pick up in New York City. Remember, my girl. I've seen the clothes you never wear."

She kept working out with her weights, and Kitty went to the showers. She blow-dried her hair and put on fresh make up, using mascara and eye shadow sparingly, knowing the mascara ran when she cried.

Her hand shook and the mascara left a dark smudge under her left eye. Meeting Alex for dinner after their workout was something she had not expected. What else had Shannon told him? Was Dr. Goddard in on the scheme? Is this what he meant when he told her to find new interests?

She washed her hands and switched her emerald and wedding rings, putting the emerald back on her left hand.

Shannon showered and joined Kitty in the small powder room.

"As soon as I dry my hair, we'll head out to the officers' club."

When she had finished she looked at Kitty and asked, "Nervous?"

"Of course not. Should I be? Are jeans accepted at the club?"

"On Tuesday nights anything goes. Besides, I've never seen anyone wear jeans and shirts the way you do. That shirt with all the little do-dads on it is stunning. Where did you find it?"

"Just a little thing I bought on Fifth Avenue," Kitty laughed.

They parked outside the club and Shannon looked at Kitty and smiled a crooked smile. "Well, you may not be nervous, but I sure am."

"You needn't be. You told me Alex was nice. What more is there to say?"

"I must need a tranquilizer!"

Kitty felt the giggles coming over her and began tittering. "Oh, my! He'll think I'm a complete fool. Cut it out, Shannon. I can't stop this."

"For goodness sakes, don't. . . !"

"Stop it! We can't go in there in hysterics."

"I don't see Robert's car. They're not here yet. Let's have a soda and relax."

The suggestion cleared the air. "Good idea, but do we dare on an empty stomach. I'm famished."

"We'll wait for them in the lobby then."

They entered the waiting room and sat on hard benches. The hostess asked them whose party they were with.

When they told her, she said, "The gentlemen have a table. Would you care to join them?"

"Thank you. We will. Is that alright with you, Kitty?"

"Aye. 'Twill be fine with me."

"Oh, good gracious," Shannon groaned. "Don't start slipping back on me now."

Kitty shook her head and came into the present. "I haven't done that for a long time. I'm sorry."

Robert and Alex stood when Kitty and Shannon joined them. Robert kissed Shannon's cheek, and Alex stood quietly, looking into Kitty's eyes.

"Well, now, what are we going to have, Kitty?" Robert asked her.

"Water, please," Kitty said.

"You're looking lovely tonight," Alex told her. "I'm glad you could join me for dinner."

"Thank you." She felt something inside herself responding to his voice. When her water arrived, she held up her glass and said, "To your health."

"And to yours." He looked into her eyes over the rim of his glass.

They forgot Shannon and Robert existed.

"I have been wanting to meet you since I stepped off the plane and saw you standing there on the tarmac all alone. You were crying. Were you expecting someone?"

"Oh, no. 'Twas the loneliness of it that crept in again."

"I thought you were married," he told her.

"Luke? He is an old, old friend. We were once...well, it is all over, but I knew you certainly had a wife when you arrived. Shannon tells me she is your daughter."

He chuckled, deep and familiar, and she felt herself reeling back in time.

"Alright, Alex, try to pull yourself together so we can order. I'm starved." Shannon was speaking over their heads.

"You aren't in uniform," Kitty said.

His eyes danced mischievously. "Had to dress down, Shannon told me, for this important date. Did Shannon tell you about me?

"Not much."

"Well, there isn't much to tell." He chuckled and shrugged. "Just an old army man."

When they were seated and had ordered, Alex turned to her and asked, "How long were you married?"

His question took her by surprise, and when she did not answer immediately, he put his hand over hers and said, "I'm sorry. I should've known better than to ask that question."

She felt the tiny shock race through her at his touch. "It's quite alright. And you?"

"Diane and I were married eight years. She was killed in a one car automobile accident on the freeway twelve years ago. . . couldn't get her to go to counseling."

"Alcoholism?"

"And drugs...the things that destroy army wives. I was in Nam when it happened." He downed his Coke quickly.

"I'm sorry." It seemed an inadequate thing to say, but it said everything she was feeling. "And what of your daughter?"

"She's in college at the University of Kansas. I haven't decided if she's going to become a rocket scientist, a journalist, or a first-class tramp."

Kitty laughed.

"I love the sound of your laughter. It's as though I've heard it before. Perhaps it was when the sirens called to the men returning from the Trojan War. Do you have children?" He spoke in a familiar tone, and she wondered if she had ever heard it before.

"No." She started to say something witty but her voice got a funny little catch in it and her eyes misted.

"I'm sorry." Alex reached for her hand.

"Earth calling Kitty! Kansas calling Alex! Supper is coming and Robert and I have run out of things to say to each other."

"Edith Skye once told me that it was polite to say something to the dinner partner on my right and then turn to the person on my left. I've forgotten my manners completely. Where did you find that marvelous new wagon, Robert?"

"Do you like it?"

"It's really nice.."

"Twenty-five thousand buckaroos, and 'It's nice.'."

They ate their salads in silence, but Kitty noticed that Alex was watching her when their dinners were set before them. A thick, juicy steak filled her plate and an enormous baked potato sat beside it on a separate plate. She turned to Alex and said, "What a feast! And I'm really hungry. I don't think I remembered to eat lunch at all."

"Did Shannon tell you I was taking you out to eat tonight?"

"She sprang it on me when we reached the exercise club. I was quite surprised, to tell the truth."

Kitty turned to Shannon and said, "This is much better than the hamburger we ate last week at my house."

"Well, at least we had nice thick onions to go with it. We were perfectly sinful with the onions," she told Robert.

Alex was smiling, and Kitty saw that his eyes crinkled at the corners when he smiled.

The waitress brought their iced tea drinks they had ordered, and Robert said, "Let's drink to The Big Red One and the lovely ladies we found when we returned home."

"Here! Here!" Kitty said. She set her glass on the table.

Shannon looked at her anxiously. She thinks I'm going over the brink again. Strange, I'm feeling all warm and bubbly inside.

Robert sliced off a bite of steak and sighed. "There's no steak like a Kansas T-bone. How about it, Honey?"

Shannon agreed and then added, "Just the thing to give us all a coronary. I can't remember how many years ago I ate this much."

"I'm afraid I'm making a terrible first impression. I feel like a Roman... gorging until I can't get out of my chair and drinking iced tea into oblivion. Do you suppose we ought to try to drink coffee so soon after eating all this?" Kitty said.

"I know just the place to wear off the meal," Alex told them. "Let's go to the Penguin Room. I hear it's the 'in' place to go."

Robert left a substantial tip and Alex picked up the tab for the meals. Kitty felt his hand under her arm when they went to Robert's new station wagon parked behind the restaurant in the parking lot.

Haven't felt like this in months! Careful, Kitty! He's a large man, but so gentle and kind...and his voice is deep and melodious...reminding me of...Must not think of Christian tonight! I'll begin to get weepy and cry all over the place! Shannon would never forgive me.

"Remember, Robert, nothing strong to drink," Shannon said. "I can't remember being this high on anything but iced tea for a long time."

Kitty heard her tinkling laughter. "I hope I don't embarrass you by doing something truly outlandish."

"I'll try to keep you under control," Alex laughed.

"You have a delightful laugh," she told him.

They pulled up before the clubhouse where officers and their ladies gathered to dance and talk and play games. Kitty and Shannon had gone there to play Bingo when the infantry was in the Middle East during the Persian Gulf War. Now it was filled with men in uniform and casual dress.

Robert let them out at the front door and parked the wagon. They waited for him in the lobby and Kitty felt herself leaning into Alexander Collins. He put his arm around her and drew her to him and smiled down at her.

"Looks like everyone at Riley is here tonight," Robert observed when he joined them. "Do you suppose we can find a table?"

"Follow us," Alex said and took Kitty's arm and propelled her through the crowded room. "I see a nice secluded table behind the shrubbery. Will it do?"

"No choice!"

"Well, guess the shrubbery will hide us well enough if we get out of hand, Alex," Shannon told him.

"I see you're in fine form tonight, Mrs. Eaton."

They seated themselves and Kitty ordered tomato juice. "After all, I do have to drive home tonight," she told them.

"Rats!" Alex laughed.

Shannon laughed. "Think again, Major Collins. You're dealing with one of the fairest of them all."

"Let's dance, Kitty. This woman is unbearable."

Robert and Shannon began dancing, and Kitty paused before she stepped into the arms of Major Collins. "Is something wrong?" he asked her.

"I haven't danced since..."

"We don't have to dance if you'd rather not."

"I'd love to dance with you, Alex. I don't know what came over me."

She slid into his arms. He held her as she knew he would. Her heart raced and she felt warm currents sweeping through her.

"I know I've held you like this before. Do you know who you are, Kitty Farrell? Why have I been searching for a way to meet you since the first day I saw you. Must have been the tears!"

The way he spoke startled her. Was it the way he ran his words together, the deep rumbling sound of his voice, or what he said. If she shut her eyes, she could have sworn she had been listening to Christian Skye's voice, but the man was not Christian. It was true, he was a handsome man. His eyes danced and he had actively sought her out. Still...he was not Christian.

He began to sing along with the music, "It seems like we have laughed before and loved before, but can't remember where or when."

At midnight Kitty glanced at her new watch and said, "Well, the ball is almost over and Cinderella had better find her coach before it turns into a pumpkin. It has been a very nice evening. Thank you, Shannon. Thank you, Robert. And thank you, Alex."

Robert laughed. "And I was having such a good time!"

Kitty knew he was amused.

"All good times have to come to an end," Shannon laughed.

"Well, in that case let's see if that little red mustang is still where we left it. I could see you home safely, at least," Alex proposed.

"And spoil a perfectly wonderful evening!" Kitty told him.

When they pulled up alongside her car parked at the restaurant, Alex whispered to her, "May I see you tomorrow night?"

She heard herself saying, "I'm flying back to New York to visit a friend early tomorrow morning. Perhaps...when I get back. Good night, and thank you."

When she stepped onto her front porch, she heard the telephone ringing.

"Hello," she said. "Kitty Farrell here."

"All right what is this all about?"

"What are you talking about, Shannon?"

"About flying to New York? I told him you're not in the least bit interested in Luke. Now, I hear you're going back East. What is wrong with you, Kitty?"

"Simmer down," Kitty told her. "I felt a sudden urge to see Livy. I'm not certain what is happening and ...and. . ."

"And what?"

"I can't bear to be dumped by Alex or anyone else." She felt a catch in her throat and said, "Bye, Shannon. Better get some sleep."

CHAPTER TWENTY-NINE

"I thought you'd never leave that farm of yours, Kitty," Olivia told her when she put Kitty's bag in the back seat of her Oldsmobile. "Now, tell me what brings you to New York. Are you ready to go to work?"

"No, not at all. I just had to get away for a few days." She fastened her seat belt and leaned back, glad to be hearing Olivia's voice again.

"Does Luke know you're in town?" She started her car and put her cigarette in the ash tray.

"How is he? I haven't talked to him since he and the kids were at my place."

"You haven't called him?"

"Should I?"

"I suppose not." She pulled into the traffic and took a long drag on her cigarette.

"And how are Skip and the kids?" Kitty asked.

"Ornery as ever. They'll drive you crazy."

"I'm already a basket case. You know that."

"What does Dr. Goddard say?"

"I should meet new people...find new interests."

"Harry West is still single. We'll go to a show. Skip likes him."

"Fine. I haven't seen a good show in ages."

"Maybe you'd like to go to a really good concert."

"I'd love it. I'm buying the tickets!"

"Absolutely not. It's my idea and I'm buying. Skip and Harry will take us out to eat. It's been ages since we've done anything together. Sure wish I had time to go shopping, but Ted and I are working on a case that won't let go."

"Afraid your visit to Kansas wasn't all that exciting. Sorry I put you through so much."

"I've been reading Colin Skye's book again. You did not go to India, Kitty. I'm convinced of it. The book is a recent print...too new...someone wanting to make a fast buck put it out to get your money. The guy who wrote it got enough facts to make it sound reasonable. I'll have to admit, he did a fine job of it."

"Forget about it, Livy. I'm trying to put it behind me. If something happened no one can explain logically, it surely didn't happen at all. The further I get from it, the less certain I am it ever happened." She knew her voice didn't sound convincing enough to prove to Olivia Stewart that she was moving on with her life.

"You can ignore the things Colin Skye supposedly wrote in that book... the very things you told me about before you paid a small fortune for someone in England to come up with that book with the lotus blossom on the cover. Everything rings like a fake. It just did not happen. Besides the lady's name he wrote about was not Kitty. It was Kathryn--clear and simple as that."

"Well, even if it did happen to me, you'll have to admit 1857 was a long time ago. Now, tell me about Harry...what did you say his name was... White?"

"West. Harry West. He's single...terribly handsome...every woman's dream...kind...funny...sophisticated...rich."

"With a whole harem of women." Kitty knew the type.

"No one in particular."

"Oh, there must be something wrong with him."

"Kitty, you do come up with the strangest things. He was married once, maybe twice...has four children...all grown and successful. He'll tell you about them."

Kitty never wanted to talk about Harry West. "There is absolutely no place on earth like New York City, the smell of diesel fumes...the asphalt coming up to hit you in the face...the traffic jams...the currents that smack you in the wind tunnels between buildings. I must ride the ferry like a tourist this time. Do you know I never did that in all the time I lived here?"

The dinner was a success. The concert at Carnegie Hall a knock-out, performance. Harry West was exactly as Livy had said. He told her about his children and his work, and wonders of all, Kitty liked him and couldn't say why.

Livy was right. Harry was a dream! He was sophisticated and had more class than any man she had ever met. He was a wonderful conversationalist and a good listener. She found herself telling him more than she ever intended to tell anyone again. He took her for a ride on the Staten Island Ferry, and she threw popcorn to the sea gulls. They met Olivia for lunch at Michael's and Luke joined them there.

"You're looking fine, Kitty," Luke told her.

"And you, too, Luke. How are the children?" She felt relaxed talking to Luke again about the children. She was shocked to see him looking old, however.

"They're with their mother and making terrific grades in school. Guess they take after their father," he said with a short, unconvincing laugh.

"Tell Anne, Lucille turned out to be another rooster. I named him Lucky."

"And don't tell me Major has pups."

"He still thinks he owns the place. The Morgans and Major are keeping an eye on the farm while I'm gone. He may not let them get out of the car."

When Olivia finished her coffee, she said, "Well, some people have the life of Riley, but Luke and I have to go back to work. Will I see you at dinnertime?"

"I'm taking Kitty out. We're seeing a show. Would you and Skip like to join us?" Harry West asked Olivia.

"Don't count on it. This old body is going to fall into a tub and relax with my briefs after I grab a sandwich and head for the big chair in the living room."

"Luke?"

"I'm working late. Have to be in court tomorrow. Have fun, Kitty." He looked at her wistfully for a moment, drank the last of his coffee, then rose to accompany Olivia back to Butler, Cameron, and Filbey.

Harry West drove into the country, and they spent the afternoon browsing through antique shops. Kitty bought a Dresden figurine to take home and a Majolica pitcher in the butterfly and fan pattern to give to Olivia. They ate at an expensive restaurant and then saw a show.

"You're pretty nice, Harry. Olivia has been telling me about you for years."

"I didn't think I'd like you, either," he confessed, "but you're an all right gal."

"Thank you, and you haven't so much as held my hand!"

Harry laughed, "Olivia warned me to be on my best behavior."

Kitty laughed. Olivia was right. Harry was fun to be with. Obviously, he had money. That was it! Always the money thing. That is why he was so cagey and why so many women were interested in him. She hadn't thought of it before.

They danced later, and Kitty discovered he wore an aftershave lotion she liked.

When they said good-night, Kitty told him, "I'm leaving tomorrow. Thanks again for putting up with me."

He kissed her lightly. "May I come out to Kansas and let you show me around?"

"Call me some time. I have a silly schedule."

Skip dropped her off at Kennedy the next morning so she could catch an early flight to KC International. By noon she had picked up her car and had headed out onto the Interstate.

She turned around and pulled into a station to use the pay phone in the parking lot.

"Shannon?"

"Yeah, who were you expecting, the Princess of Wales?"

"Are you busy?"

"Yes, but come in and tell me about your big fling." Shannon's voice sounded flat.

Kitty knew something was wrong the moment she reached Shannon's house. Her old pick-up truck was backed up to the front door, and boxes were piled in the back.

"Shannon!" she called. "What in the world are you doing?"

"The play's over. The fat lady has sung, the luscious blonde is moving in, and this old, string bean of a redhead is moving out. It happens all the time in this crazy business." Her voice sounded coarse and hard. She threw a box of cleaning supplies into the back of the truck.

"Oh, my! What happened?"

"Robert simply walked in last night and said, 'It's not working out for us, Kid. I want out'. So here I go back to Dallas, dragging my old truck full of junk behind me. The other woman wins." Shannon shoved her stereo toward the truck angrily.

"Here let me help you with that," Kitty told her.

They put her stereo into the back of the truck and wrapped it in plastic. The wind whipped the lid off a box, and Shannon began to cry.

Kitty put her arms around her there in the back of her pick-up truck and said, "Go ahead and cry. I've shed enough tears on your shoulder to float a battleship. Let's get your things loaded and go out to the farm. Dallas can wait."

"I've been trying to call you, but I didn't know if you were back or not. . ." she sobbed.

They climbed out of the truck, packed her under clothes in her luggage, and emptied her dresser drawers into boxes.

"Let me put the things on hangers in the Mustang. We'll pack better later."

"I've just been throwing things in. I didn't want to be here another minute longer."

"Is this everything?" Kitty asked.

"I think so...the furniture is his." She took one last look around the small house and opened cabinet doors to be certain she had not left as much as a box of salt. Satisfied, she called out. "Let's get out of here."

Kitty put her teakettle on the stove in order to make instant chocolate and over their chocolate, Shannon said, "I'm beginning to come to grips with this already. Do you realize that Robert and I have been married almost two years, and we hardly know each other. It was a mistake in the beginning. We should have given ourselves time to know one other, but in the end, I suppose it would have been the same. How long did you know Christian before you married?"

"Less than a week. We knew the moment we met." Kitty felt her heart racing at the thought.

"Maybe that's what was wrong. I was never certain...and now I know."

They talked until late in the night about Robert Eaton and what

Shannon would do next. Never once did Shannon ask about Luke Filbey or Olivia Stewart. Finally, they fell into their beds.

From across the hall, Kitty heard Shannon call to her, "How was New York?"

"Like it always is, the most miserable place on earth this time of the year, and winter hasn't even begun yet."

"How was Luke?"

"Harry and I had lunch with Luke and Olivia? He's fine."

"Harry? Who's Harry? You never told me about him."

"Olivia's been trying to match me up with him for years. Harry West."

Shannon got out of her bed and went to Kitty's doorway. "And?" She hugged her arms around herself in the cold upstairs bedroom.

"And...we went out...saw a show...ate at really fancy restaurants...drove into the country...went to a concert."

"And?"

"And, nothing."

"Do you like him?"

"Of course, he's very nice. Nice to look at...rich...everything a woman could want."

"And. . .?"

"Absolutely nothing. I told you he was very nice. Olivia was right. He is every woman's ideal man. She was scared to death I'd do something silly like fall in love with him. She has read and re-read Colin's story...searching for flaws in my story or whoever wrote *I Remember.*

"She did what?" Shannon was still standing in the doorway..

"Well, it's like this. Don't stand there shivering in the cold. Crawl in here with me and get warm. I'm not the least bit sleepy and we still haven't finished talking."

"Alex called."

"What did he want?" Kitty felt herself stiffen. "I went to New York to get away. Why does he persist upon coming into my life?"

"Wanted to know what happened. He wanted to know if he said or did something wrong . He wondered why you turned him down flat and took off in such a hurry."

"What did you tell him?"

While Shannon began explaining Alexander Collins to her, Kitty grew warm and drowsy. Alex asked about me...wanted to know what he did wrong. He'll never call me again.

Shannon suddenly realized she was talking and Kitty was snoring softly. She pulled the blanket closer and went to sleep.

The next morning Kitty smelled the coffee brewing and reached for her robe.

"Just like old times when I first got home. You always were an early riser...had the coffee made before I knew it was morning. You're spoiling me again."

"I might as well get used to getting up early and moving about. I'll have to go back to work as soon as I get to Dallas." She poured a cup of coffee for Kitty and handed it to her.

"Do you know anyone there?" Kitty took the coffee and tipped the cup.

"My brother and his wife live there. They'll put me up until I find a place to live."

"Doesn't this just beat all!" Kitty spat it out.

"I'm sure glad you rescued me when you did. I thought about just coming out and spending the night here, but I thought again and wanted to get as far away as I could...never wanted to hear his name again."

"I know. You're mad. And it hurts, too. Life shouldn't be like this."

"I suspected something was wrong the minute he got home. Nothing seemed right with us."

"Where did he meet Miss Right?" Kitty looked at Shannon over the brim of her cup.

"She was with him all through Desert Storm."

"While you were faithful and waited for him to return.," Kitty groaned.

"Kitty, why did you run away? Oh, I know you're afraid of being hurt again, but you went to New York and went out with this Harry who-ever-he-was and thought he was wonderful. I thought you and Alex...he thought...what I mean to say is. You're right for each other. Robert and I both saw it. Is it Christian Skye?"

"I suppose so. I can't get him out of my mind, Shannon. It's driving me crazy to think about him. I feel guilty about returning. I want him and don't have any idea how to reach him. It's making a basket case out of me. Something in Alex reminded me of Christian...his voice...the way he looks at me...even the scent of him...masculine and faintly musky. I can't bear to be with him, knowing there's something strong and powerful about him I can't resist. It was the same with Christian, but he fell in love with me, too."

"I knew it! You've fallen in love with Alexander Collins!"

CHAPTER THIRTY

Shannon had been gone for almost a week, and Kitty struggled with her emotions.

"You've fallen in love with Alexander Collins!" Shannon had told her.

She fought against Shannon's revelation, trying to put down the emotions Alex evoked in her. Yet, the man had triggered thoughts in her she had not dared to admit.

She paced restlessly, rode out onto the prairie and spent hours alone thinking about Christian. When she returned to her house, she took his scarf in her arms and held it close to her, feeling the love they had shared seep into her once more. Slowly, she unrolled the scarf and saw what had been an attempt to embroider his initials. The scarf had never been finished. She had never given that scarf to Christian. Why did she have an unfinished scarf? No initials. No fringe. It wasn't the scarf she had taken from the hands of Azziz after all.

Dr. Goddard cannot know...cannot tell him.

Then her thoughts returned to Alexander Collins, and she felt something inside her churning. She remembered his warmth and his touch. She thought of the ways he was like Christian and became confused. Christian! Alex! Christian! It had to be the military. That was it!

She remembered the name Christian called her and cried out, "Ranee! Maharanee! My queen! My sweet queen!" No one was there to hear, nor had anyone ever known how he expressed his love for her...not Colin...not Azziz...not Charles Bradley.

Sometime during the second week after she returned to Kansas, she put in a call to Major Alexander Collins.

"I'm sorry," she heard the girl at the switchboard answer. "Major

Collins is in conference just now. He'll be free at one o'clock. May I ask who is calling?"

"I'll call back later. Does he go out to lunch at one?" She felt her voice faltering.

"He'll be in his office all afternoon as far as I know."

"Thank you."

She could not decide whether to wear one of her wool suits or to wear jeans. She put on jeans and remembered the only time she had gone out with him she had worn jeans, so she took them off and put on her pantyhose and a slip. Shannon was right. She had clothes she never wore.

When she left the farm, she was wearing a pale pink cashmere sweater and a wool skirt to match. She had put on jewelry, but then took it off, opting for her rings and the new watch she bought when she returned.

It was one-fifteen when she pulled up in front of the administration building where Shannon had told her she would find Alex.

She entered the building, and found his name on the directory. A soldier in uniform asked to see her identification, and she pulled out her driver's license.

"I would like to see Major Alexander Collins."

He dialed a number and asked her name.

Kitty thought of saying, "Cleopatra," but she knew the military did not think kindly of such nonsense. "Mrs. Christian Skye," she told him without thinking.

Oh! What did I say? It's too late to tell him otherwise.

The soldier repeated her name then said, "Step this way please."

Kitty was reminded at once of visiting Christian Skye in his office at Lucknow, and a strange sensation swept over her. She followed the young man to the elevator where he pushed the button for the third floor.

The elevator stopped on the third floor, and the soldier, his back ramrod stiff, stepped out and indicated that she was to step to the right.

He knocked at a door, and she heard Alex say, "Come in."

The sergeant saluted crisply and said, "Mrs. Christian Skye to see you, sir."

Alex saluted and said, "You may go, Sergeant Richards."

Kitty heard the door shut behind him and all of a sudden, she thought she would faint.

Alex stood and told her, "I didn't know if I would ever see you again, Mrs. Skye. Do you always look so stunning when you come into town?"

"May I sit down?"

"Of course," he said and pulled a chair out for her. "Kitty, what are you doing here?"

"I thought...I thought...we might. . .I seem to have picked up a bug in New York. The room is swimming around and around. I'm sorry."

He dashed into a little room off his office and brought her a glass of water. She drank it gratefully and said, "I'm better. Thank you. I hope I'm not keeping you from your work."

"Just paper work...nothing special. Are you sure you're all right now? Have you had lunch?"

"Not yet. I was in town and thought. . ." She felt her tears springing into her eyes.

She stood up and he sprang to her side. "Kitty, I wanted to call you. I was afraid you didn't want to see me again."

"Oh, no, Alex. It wasn't like that at all." A sob escaped her throat.

"Can't stand to see you crying."

It was then she realized that tears streamed down her cheeks. "I don't know what has come over me, so silly to be standing here crying."

He took her in his arms, and she knew how it would be. His lips sought hers, and she knew his kiss and felt herself melting inside.

"Kitty, Kitty! Kitty! What have you done to me! I've never felt like this before!"

"I never knew it would be like this," she told him.

"I've been half out of my mind, thinking about you...wondering why you suddenly went off to New York."

"I was afraid?"

"Afraid, Kitty?"

He drew her close to him. "Don't ever be afraid, Kitty. It must have something to do with the tears. No, it isn't that. What has happened?"

Kitty shut her eyes and said, "Don't say that, Alex. There are some things you must know."

"Let's get out of here. We'll go out to your farm. All right?" He ran the back of his hand down her cheek softly.

"We'll drive my car."

He locked his door and went to the front desk downstairs where he said, "I'll be out of my office for the remainder of the day."

He turned to Kitty and said, "I could use some food. How about a hamburger and some fries?" A smile played about his mouth.

"Sounds good to me. Shannon would tell us about the coronary, but I think I can risk it."

When they reached the driveway at the farm, Major bounded up to the Mustang.

"My watchdog," she told him with a shaky little laugh.

Kitty ran her hand over Major's coat and said, "Maybe you'd like a drink. I don't have much except sodas,.."

"Whatever you have will be fine, Kitty." He followed her into the house and watched her quietly while she poured their drinks over ice with hands that shook.

"And now," he said, "what is it that you have to tell me?"

"I've been under psychiatric care since it happened." She didn't know how to tell him what had happened, but she knew there could never be anything between the two of them until she had said it all. "Perhaps, you should talk to Dr. Goddard. Didn't Shannon tell you about it? Sometimes I'm just plain looney."

"Shannon spoke about a paranormal experience of some kind, but she didn't tell me about it. What happened, Kitty?"

He sat across the table from her, looking into her eyes, and holding her hand. Kitty wanted to slip into his arms and forget the entire business, but she knew she had to go on with it, in spite of everything. "Shannon came to stay with me when I returned...afraid I'd go over the edge."

"Returned from where? Where had you been?" He encouraged her to continue talking with a squeeze of his hand upon hers.

"I had been in India...during the days of the Raj...at the time of the Sepoy Mutiny?"

He showed no surprise. "That was in...in. . ."

"In 1857." She watched his face for something that would tell her she could continue telling him about it. When she saw that he was not horrified by what she had said, she continued, "I don't know how it could have occurred, but I am sure it happened the way I remember it."

"Go, on, Kitty." He leaned back sipping his drink. His eyes reached into hers and gave her the strength to go on.

"Luke Filbey had walked out on me several weeks earlier."

She felt him bristle at Luke Filbey's name, but when he said nothing, she continued. "I was hurt but not because I loved him. I felt a need for someone...someone I had lost and could not find. Do you understand that?"

"Yes. I think most of us have searched for someone to fill the void in our lives."

She told him what she could remember about her arrival in India and drew a deep breath before she said, "And then I found Christian Skye. I knew him at once...how his touch would feel, how he would smell, how his voice would sound...everything. We were married less than a week later."

"Go on, Kitty."

"We were meant for each other, the pieces of our lives fit perfectly...the soul split in two ...it ended during the mutiny."

"What happened next?."

"After I returned, Luke Filbey searched for the records. He could find nothing in the regimental histories. That is, he found nothing until he found the recollections of Sir Colin Skye. He had the book sent directly to me. Then I knew. I knew I had gone to India...had married Christian Skye there. My son wrote in 1910...over forty years before I was born."

"Your son?"

"Not my birth son...nor Christian's either for that matter, although Colin believed he was Christian's son. I know this isn't making sense to you at all, Alex, but you must know why you can't think seriously about me... such a jumble of things going around and around in my head. Sometimes I'm not at all certain if I'll ever be sane again."

"Where is Sir Colin Skye's book? Would you mind if I read it for myself? This is very important to me."

His voice was so tender and kind, Kitty went upstairs and brought *I Remember* down and handed it to Alex.

"A lotus blossom," Alex observed as he studied the cover intently.

"Do you know them?"

"Oh yes, quite well."

"This is his first book, the one that really matters. Sit here. The light is good. I'll fix coffee."

She brought steaming coffee, and Alex reached for the cup without looking up from the book. She curled up in her mother's chair while Alex read on and on.

Kitty watched his face, but she couldn't tell what he was thinking while he read. She dozed off and when she awoke he was almost finished with the book.

When he finished reading, he laid the book on the table, and said, "This is powerful stuff, Kitty. I hope you know that."

"Of course, but no one actually believes a word of it."

"Once when I was overseas, I fell asleep in the hotel where I was staying in Saigon. It was in a perfectly safe area, but I awoke to the sound of shattering glass. I looked outside my window but there was nothing happening there. Then I began to ask about, but no one else had heard the sound. I finally had the entire hotel staff checking for falling glass, so convinced was I that broken glass had awakened me from my sleep. No glass had been broken. The next day, I received a telegram. My father had been killed in an automobile accident the day before. All the windows of his car were shattered. Strange things happen, Kitty. I have seen things that no one would believe, yet when my ex-wife died in another accident a year after my father died, I never knew of it until they sent me word. It's the ties that are strongest which transcend time and place. My father and I were closer than anyone else I knew. Strange how it happened. What do you think brought you back?"

"Perhaps it was not so strange, after all." Kitty's hands shook, and he came to her and pulled her into his arms.

"I'd like to know more about it," he spoke softly.

"Perhaps it was nothing. I returned to Kansas...wandering like a crazy woman along a country road...looking for my car and a novel which I had been writing for my mother."

"You poor kid." His voice rumbled deep from inside his chest.

"So, now you know."

"Put on your jeans and a warm coat. I'd like to see your farm."

"Alex, it's almost dark."

"Don't tell me you're afraid of the dark. Nothing will harm us."

"Well, at least I'm not that dingy. If it were daylight we could saddle up the horses."

"I'd just like to walk out over the prairie, feel the wind in my face, think about this for awhile, and watch the sun disappear completely in the West."

"It's a nice farm. Not too large, just the size my parents wanted."

She put on her jeans, a sweatshirt, and a warm jacket and joined him in the kitchen. He smiled and tucked her hand in the crook of his arm, and they walked out past the barn where the light came on as they passed. They continued walking through the dry prairie grasses until they came to the bluff where the ravine spilled down into the valley. The last of the sunlight in the West began to fade away.

Alex drew her into his arms without speaking. He kissed her and she felt her life coming full circle again.

"Come back to the house with me, Kitty. I have something to tell you," he said.

They didn't rush back to the warm kitchen, and she felt that he was forming the words in his mind as they walked slowly through the night air.

Now it is coming. He is going to tell me why I can mean nothing more than a friend to him.

He's trying to frame the speech so it won't hurt me. It's like this when someone falls in love and the other wants out. I must think of something clever to say to him. I must not let him know how much I care.

I'm as nutty as a fruitcake...don't know my own mind since ...no, that is no good. He knows I'm as batty as they come. How could he read Colin's book and not know that?

I could never love another...still legally married to Captain Skye...his widow...his wife, you know.

I'm still wearing the wedding ring.

There was something in you that reminded me of Christian when we met, perhaps the uniform. Alexander Collins is not Christian Skye...this couldn't be happening to me.

Your voice...Oh, dear God, help me! What am I to say?

Thank you for understanding, Alex. Get out of my life!

She knew before he spoke what he was going to say, and still she had not prepared her speech.

When they reached the kitchen, he took off her coat and hung it on the peg by the back door. Kitty drew him to the kitchen table where her mother and father often sat to talk. She heated the coffee and poured one last cup for Alexander.

"What is it, Alex? Do you want to go back to town now?"

Dear God, this is pure agony. He has said nothing since he read the book.

When he began, his voice dropped quite low. "Sometimes it happens in the life of a man and a woman."

He said nothing more and she asked, "When what happens, Alex?"

"I've always known something was missing in my life. Although I married the girl I had dated in college, our lives never meshed. I blamed it on the military. We knew each other well enough, but two years into the marriage, we both became aware it had been a mistake. We didn't quarrel, .but there was no joy. We seldom found anything to laugh about or to quarrel about. Our relationship existed...nothing more. We were neither happy nor unhappy. I had a job to do and I did it."

"Viet Nam?"

"Yes, it destroyed what little was left of our marriage. From time to time I felt the loneliness creeping into me after it was all over. Alexandria was growing up and I was not with her. I thought if I could only be there with her, the emptiness would leave. I went home when Diane died, but I couldn't stay, and Alexis went to her grandmother's to live."

"She is a beautiful girl."

"Sure she is, but...Oh, well. What am I to call you? Are you Mrs. Skye or Miss Farrell?"

"What do you say, Alex? You have read Sir Colin Skye's book."

"The man who wrote that book died years ago...years before you were born."

"That is true. Olivia believes someone wrote it recently for the money."

"And you, Kitty?"

He paused and his voice cracked when he asked her, "Are you certain about all of this? Don't lead me on, if you're not."

"I can't begin to explain, but I'm sure of this. Somewhere, in another lifetime, I think it was, I lost Christian Skye."

"What if. . . ." His voice rumbled deep from somewhere deep within himself.

Don't be foolish, Kitty Farrell. The man is stunned and I am imagining that there is something in his voice and military bearing. Let it go. He isn't Christian Skye. It is my nutty imagination running wild again. I should never have let him read the book. It means nothing to him.

"It's growing late, Alex, and I am very tired. Let's call it a day. I'll take you back to town."

"It has been quite a day, Mrs. Skye."

"Indeed, it has." She reached for her coat, and he rose to help her.

Whatever had passed between them had vanished. They rode in silence back to Ft. Riley. She stopped at his door, and Alex told her good night and walked away.

CHAPTER THIRTY-ONE

When Kitty pulled out onto the highway, she felt her tears dripping from her chin before she was aware of the fact that she was crying. She knew for the first time that she needed help. She had been in denial too long. She made an appointment with Dr. Goddard the next day.

What shall I tell Dr. Goddard? Shall I tell him the truth, that I want to be released from Colin's book which has an incredible hold on me... want to move on with my life...want to live in the here and now. The book is Colin's story...Colin's and mine. No one believes it but Kitty Skye Kitty Skye and a woman Colin called Kathryn. Kathryn? Kathryn? Kathryn? Suppose there was once a woman whose identity she herself took? What could have caused such an event that became reality? Was it Kathryn in her mother's time travel story about India that she herself had become? Had something happened to her when she began to share in the story of Kathryn's marriage to Christian Sky? Had she embellished the love story? No, it was just another wild idea like so many others she had. She could not tell Dr. Goddard, but she promised him she would live in the here and now.

Upon Dr. Goddard's advice, Kitty threw herself into the work on the farm. With the help of a neighbor's son, she painted her house, the barn, the gates, and the other outbuildings. She sold her parent's old, dilapidated furniture at an auction and had begun to purchase antique furniture for her home.

It had been while she was preparing for the auction Kitty found her old watch. . . the one she was wearing when she went to India, the watch she had given to Colin at Christmas time. She had decided to dispose of her mother's costume jewelry at the auction, and in a drawer in what had been her mother's dresser she found the watch among other jewelry she was selling. How did it get there? She recognized it as the watch she was wearing when she went to India? Did she actually give the watch to Colin? If that incident didn't happen, what else might not have happened?

Suddenly, she knew. She had not given the fine, old watch to Colin after all? She called Olivia.

"Livy? I must talk to you."

"Is something wrong, Kitty?"

"I must know. Was I wearing the watch I always wore when they found me along the country road in Kansas."

"Why yes, Kitty. I put it away in a dresser drawer with some of your mother's jewelry. Why do you ask."

"Just wanted to know. And how are the children?"

She re-decorated her country home in a frenzy of activity and when winter fell over the land, she settled down in her new surroundings and began to survey her life. It was then she found the courage to go the basement for the first time since the death of her father. She turned on all of the lights, and went slowly to the transformer that set the trains in motion. Here was her father's world, the world Richard Farrell had created and shared with her for many hours when she was a child. She dared to enter, at last.

"You're an attorney," Dr. Goddard had told her when she saw him on her first visit.

The Lionel engine rounded a corner and whistled.

"Was," she had corrected him.

The train raced on through a tunnel.

"And a good one, I was told."

The Wabash cars rushed by, the Santa Fe freight cars her father had loved followed, and the Southern Pacific loaded with goods from the Southlands pulled to a stop to be unloaded at a terminal.

On and on the cars flew by, stopping now and then at the depot with the shingles she had cut from wood for his Christmas gift. Racing on and on.

She knew then what she had to do, but she chose not to return to

New York City. Instead, she rented an empty building in Junction City and began renovating it to suit her needs. After she had hung expensive wallpaper and had purchased furnishings for the waiting room and office, she went to a greenhouse outside of town where she chose potted plants and accessories. A month later she hung her shiny, new shingle outside the door. Her first client was a woman whose husband had died leaving her totally unprepared for managing her affairs. When the widow left her office, Kitty handed her a card which read, "Kathleen L. Farrell, Attorney at Law."

"You are my first client in Junction, Mrs. Weinstein. There will be no charge for my services on this visit. Please see me if you have further questions."

She called Olivia. "I am now an attorney with my own office, Livy. I'm actually making progress.

"That's fine, Kitty, but,"

"But what, Livy? Is something wrong?"

"I'm not certain about it. I found time, at last, to look over your manuscript, the one your mother wrote and the one you almost finished."

"I'm glad you found it. I've looked everywhere for it." Her voice sounded uneasy for some reason.

"I'm coming out just as soon as this case I'm on is over. We need to see Dr. Goddard to learn if there is something we don't know about."

"What are you saying?"

Olivia changed the subject. "How is the weather in Kansas in February?"

"Sometimes farmers can sow oats and sometimes there is a foot of snow on the ground. Why do you ask?

"I'll take my chances. We need to go to Topeka."

Olivia arrived five days later. "The weather is fine, Kitty. Are the farmers sowing their oats?"

"Tell me, Livy, what brings you to Kansas at this time of year?" Kitty asked.

"Something about your mother's book. Dr. Goddard wanted to see both of us. We have an appointment at ten tomorrow morning."

They heard a small knock on the door where they waited.

"Come in," Olivia Steward answered.

Dr. Goddard carried her file along with a stack of papers Olivia had faxed to him. "Good morning, Ladies. Fine weather for February."

Olivia said, "Kitty promised I would not find two feet of snow on the ground."

After the small talk had ended, Dr. Goddard looked at Kitty and asked, "When did your mother first ask you to finish her novel, Kitty?"

"I spent time with her during her last days. We talked about India and her book. It was during one of our discussions that she asked me to finish her book."

"Had you read the novel before then?"

"Oh, yes."

"Then you knew it well. Tell me, Kitty, had you given the characters serious thoughts?"

"Somewhat when I was younger, but I hadn't read the manuscript Mom gave me for a number of years. Is this something important?"

"Perhaps. When did you begin to edit and make changes in the story?"

"Mamma asked me to give the characters some life. She knew her stories about their lives at Lucknow lacked something. . . more than just facts she had gathered for her novel."

"Did you begin at once?"

"I thought about it, but I went back to New York to pick up my life there after her death."

"Were you troubled then?"

"Perhaps, but then Daddy died suddenly. I wasn't prepared for his death."

"I understand. Tell me, Kitty, are you an avid reader?"

"I have always loved to read."

"Was there a novel which impressed you more than any other?"

"I suppose it had to be Dostoevsky's *Crime and Punishment*. So many incredible details I felt I had committed the crime myself before I was half-way through the book."

"A common experience. Do you often see movies?"

"I never found the time or the money to pursue Hollywood very often."

"Actors study their lines until they come to believe in them. An actress who memorized her role as a housewife during the Great Depression believed she was an authority on that time. Another played the role of a young woman who sent her husband off to war during World War II, and she became that person. It happens frequently."

"And yet they had no idea how little they really knew about those events."

"You wrote about India and Christian Skye during the Sepoy revolt, and it became real to you."

Olivia broke in at that point, "If I may interrupt, Doctor, I noticed something happened shortly after her mother's death. Kitty began to spend a great deal of time writing. I had no idea what was happening but she began to change."

"Was it your mother's book?"

"I guess it was something like that. I wasn't aware. . ."

"And as you became more and more immersed into the story, it became you?"

"What are you saying, Dr. Goddard?"

"Did your parents have a close relationship?"

"Oh, yes."

"And as you wrote on and on about Christian Skye and Kitty Farrell, that relationship became real to you and satisfied a need which you had never before been able to fill."

"Yes. Yes. Yes."

"When the thunderstorm rolled in, the big guns in your novel were going off. Do you see what happened?

When Dr. Goddard folded his papers and wished Kitty well, she turned to Olivia and asked, "How did you suspect, Livy?"

"It was all there in the manuscript, just like you told me."

In March she was the prosecuting attorney for the State of Kansas in a case of child abuse when she saw him sitting in the courtroom. His eyes met hers, and she caught her breath in mid-sentence.

Alexander Collins!

He smiled and she continued to present the case against the defendant.

He met her as she was leaving the Court House.

"Kitty, you were great!"

"Thank you. It was an open and shut case." Her voice sounded cautious.

"How about lunch?"

"I know a place where we can actually hear each other when we talk."

"Excellent."

"Do you mind walking?" she asked him.

"Not at all."

He tucked her hand inside his arm and said, "Lead on, Miss Farrell." He grinned when he emphasized the word "Miss."

"Do you mind climbing stairs?"

He laughed a deep, rumbling roar and her heart began to race.

After the waitress brought their water and menus, Alex reached across the table and took her hand. "You look wonderful, Kitty."

"Thank you, Alex."

Why did he keep staring at her?

"I've missed you...wanted to call you, but. . ."

"I understand. It was the book. You couldn't handle Colin's book."

"I don't think you do understand."

"It's all right. You couldn't permit yourself to date a married woman... couldn't accept Mrs. Christian Skye. Dr. Goddard explained that to me and helped me go on with my life. In addition to that, you must have thought I was a real nut case...ready for the looney bin."

"I've been thinking about you...saw your name on the brass and black plaque outside your office...quite impressive...knew Kathleen was Kitty Farrell...wanted to see you."

"I don't charge for friendly visits."

"Kitty. Don't just sit there looking at me that way."

He released Kitty's hand, lifted his glass and drank from it.

"It was the book."

"Yes. I couldn't sleep for weeks until...."

"Until when, Alexander."

"Until Olivia told me about a manuscript she inadvertently took home with her."

"I don't understand."

"The novel with your mother's name on the cover page along with yours, Kitty."

"Oh, yes. My mother's novel. . . my novel about India?"

"She finally found time to read the manuscript and called me. When she told me about it, we both knew why your life had fallen apart after you lost both of your parents. You had scratched through the name of Kathryn and changed it to Kitty Farrell throughout the time travel novel. Olivia saw the changes you made and faxed a copy to Dr. Goddard. She had no idea what it meant until you both went to see Dr. Goddard."

"By then I was beginning to see it for myself."

"Dr. Goddard explained it to you, Olivia told me. Your mother had the facts of army life and the history of things happening in India during the 1850's correct. When you began to complete her story, you embellished it with a love story. At that point Christian Skye entered your life, and in your desperate need, he became real to you. Do you remember when Dr. Goddard asked you if you could recommend a good novel for him to read?"

"It never occurred to me why he asked."

"Things like this often happen during times of extreme trauma."

"Dr. Goddard told me my case was not at all uncommon."

"It happens frequently in the Army. Young men go off to war. They experience terrible times under unbearable stress, Kitty. They come home with PTSD. In your longing, you became immersed in your mother's novel which became your own life. In your desperate need, you fell in love with Christian Skye who married Kathryn Wilson, and then you embellished and enlarged upon the story. You became his wife."

"It all became so real to me. India! Captain Christian Skye. All the things I knew about when we spent a year in India. All of the situations I created."

"It was bound to happen."

"I found the unfinished red satin scarf I thought I had given to Christian Skye! Then there was the watch I gave to Colin in a dresser drawer with my mother's costume jewelry! I began to wonder how it could have happened?'

"Did it ever occur to you that you had never actually married Christian Skye in the 1850's?"

"I never really suspected until I found that unfinished scarf, the watch, and other things that didn't make sense. It was then I found myself wondering if I had created the love I found with Christian Skye."

"It was probably inevitable, my dear."

"Then I realized that there was still something missing...something incomplete in my life."

"And have you found the part that is missing?"

"I thought had, but I was so afraid."

"Afraid, Kitty?"

"Afraid to believe when things began to make sense to me."

"I've been half daft ever since you came into my life...couldn't get you off my mind...haven't been able to sleep." He told her.

"Couldn't forget Christian Skye?"

"That's about it." His voice had fallen to a hoarse whisper.

"Would it make any difference to you if I told you that I had fallen in love with you, Alexander?" She reached for his hand.

"Why are we sitting here?"

On the stairs leading down to the street, he pulled Kitty into his arms, she on the step above him, and he kissed her. They had completely forgotten to order a meal.

Someone below them coughed and said, "Excuse me."

"Sorry," Alexander said and Kitty laughed lightly.

"Tell me again, Kitty. Is it true?" Alexander asked.

"Absolutely!"

"This isn't the time or place to propose to you, Kitty, but I must know that you will marry me."

"There is a quaint little farm with a lovely view overlooking a valley. It would be a perfect place to give you my answer."

"Do you want a ring? There ought to be a ring?"

"The ring is not important."

When they reached the highest point on her land overlooking the valley below where cottonwoods stretched toward the sky and a pair of crows circled above them, he asked her, "When did it happen? When did you know it was love, Kitty?"

"A tired man returning from the war in Kuwait looked into my eyes, and I knew at once. I had begun to suspect India and my marriage to Christian Skye had been the result of my own creation, but I became so frightened that you weren't real and wouldn't care for me, I ran from you without knowing why. Oh, Alexander! Isn't God wonderful!"

ABOUT THE AUTHOR

In the late 1970's I went to India for eight weeks of study and extensive travel with twenty high school teachers in the Nebraska Asia Studies Group under a Fulbright Fellowship. We met the President, Prime Minister, and many important people while we learned about the history and the people of the country.. We were told we would want to write a book about India, but it would be impossible. I agreed. When we returned to our classes in the fall, I attended a writer's group in Kansas City and learned about the time travel novels. It was then I wanted to tell the story about the Sepoy revolt against the English army in India during the 1850's. THE LOTUS BLOSSOM was the result.

Printed in the United States
By Bookmasters